Under a
Lucky Star

**Center Point
Large Print**

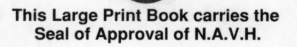

**This Large Print Book carries the
Seal of Approval of N.A.V.H.**

Under a Lucky Star

Diane Farr

Center Point Publishing
Thorndike, Maine

This Center Point Large Print edition
is published in the year 2005 by arrangement with
NAL Signet, a member of Penguin Group (USA) Inc.

The text of this Large Print edition is unabridged. In other
aspects, this book may vary from the original edition. Printed in
Thailand. Set in 16-point Times New Roman type.

ISBN 1-58547-557-2

Library of Congress Cataloging-in-Publication Data

Farr, Diane.
    Under a lucky star / Diane Farr.--Center Point large print ed.
        p. cm.
    ISBN 1-58547-557-2 (lib. bdg. : alk. paper)
        1. Large type books. 2. London (England)--Fiction. 3. Nobility--Fiction. I. Title.

PS3556.A7325U527 2005
813'.6--dc22

                                                                        2004019217

*This book is gratefully dedicated to
SUSAN ELAINE GOLLING,
without whose generosity it could not
have been written.*

Chapter One

May 1803

The Divine Sophronia was the toast of London. Her astonishing voice had ignited a fever of admiration among the *ton*. The fever failed, however, to infect Derek Whittaker. It wasn't that her singing didn't move him. It moved him, all right and tight. But it tended to move him toward the door.

The famous soprano waddled purposefully toward the footlights. An aria was plainly imminent. An expectant hush fell upon the audience. Several spectators near Derek actually leaned forward, mouths agape, in a kind of delirium of pleasure.

Derek decided he had had enough. He was positioned, as usual, at the back wall of Lord Stokesdown's box. No one would notice if he simply disappeared. During the orchestra's introductory flourish, he slipped neatly through the curtain behind him and escaped.

There were advantages, he reflected, to being a lowly secretary. He shared many of the amenities enjoyed by the aristocracy—witness his presence at the opera tonight, for example—but he labored under none of the tedious social obligations. He was free to form his own opinions because, frankly, nobody cared what they were. No one's eyes were upon him. No one observed his comings and goings. Provided he returned at the interval, when Lord Stokesdown or one of his guests might want him, it didn't matter whether he listened politely to Sophronia's caterwauling or spent the evening playing mumblety-peg in the cloak-room.

Derek hovered at the fringes of every society event, invisible as a ghost. And, come to think of it, just about as penniless. What Lord Stokesdown paid him amounted to something less than he might make as a butler or a valet. But a Whittaker, of course, could not take a post as a butler or a valet—a rule that made little sense to Derek, but which he accepted with the same cheerful shrug he accorded most rules.

What can't be cured must be endured, as his old nurse used to say. And besides, he liked Lord Stokes-down. He was busy, he was useful, and he enjoyed it when duty demanded his attendance at balls and dinners and plays. He did not resent the fact that he, Derek Whittaker, was never invited to the festivities. Often it was better to be a ghost than a guest.

He wandered down the softly lit passage, enjoying the solitude. The opera sounded faintly through the curtained openings in the wall beside him and echoed with pleasant spookiness against the high, arched ceiling. A bit of distance muffled the shrillness of Sophronia's voice and added a peculiarly haunting quality to the orchestra. He rather liked it.

An usher stood at the head of the stairs. He had been slouching against the railing, listening to the music, but Derek's arrival caused the young chap to snap to attention. Derek hid a grin. It was the evening clothes, of course. He had been mistaken for a gentleman of the *ton*. He was a bit vain about his togs—and why not? Were it not for the inconvenient birth of brother Hector, he would be, in fact, a man of substance.

He approached the usher, addressing him in a conspiratorial whisper. "I say, how much time have I got before the interval?"

"Quite a bit of time, sir."

"Anyone mind if I have a look about?" He jerked his chin, indicating an arched doorway where the well-lit passage dwindled into shadow.

The usher looked vaguely surprised. "No, sir. I shouldn't think anyone would mind."

"Good lad," said Derek approvingly. "Thanks."

With a friendly nod, Derek headed out of the light and into the shadows. He could still hear the opera in the distance, but he was completely alone. His skin prickled with pleasurable anticipation.

There was something indefinably exciting about exploring places where he had no business being. He was a little ashamed of this peculiar hobby, but it had held an irresistible allure for him since childhood. One of the many advantages of his ghostlike existence was that he could, and frequently did, slip his chain and wander about strange places unescorted.

The theater proved, to his keen delight, to be a vast rabbit warren of a place. Wherever he roamed, lamplight gleamed here and there to show him the way. It seemed a shocking waste of oil. There wasn't another soul in sight.

The narrow passage he was exploring suddenly turned a corner, and he found himself in a small, dusty room. He supposed he must be nearly to the stage area by now. Across from him, a flight of wooden stairs led up and out. At the foot of these stairs yet another lamp hung from the ceiling on a chain, feebly illuminating what appeared to be a collection of disused props stacked haphazardly about. Derek wandered from item to item, examining them with mild interest. He was idly studying the crude decorations adorning a muslin screen when a sudden tingle of awareness caused him to turn.

There came a soft footfall on the stairs to his right, and the faint slither of silk. His eyebrows climbed with surprise when a girl came into view, clutching the rickety banister as she descended. She was, oddly, all alone. When he looked at her she flinched, then froze in place. Her eyes dilated as she stared, motionless, at Derek.

Derek felt his jaw start to drop. With an effort, he reanchored it, keeping himself from gaping at her. She could have been any age between sixteen and twenty . . . and she was the loveliest sight he had ever beheld. Her beauty was unbelievable. Almost otherworldly. He had always been partial to blondes, but this girl took blondness to an entirely new level. Her fair hair captured and reflected whatever light was available, shimmering like moonlight on water even in the dim glow cast by the overhead lamp.

It was difficult to discern her station in life, for the cut and style of her simple, white gown were very much de rigueur for a young lady of breeding—but the material of which it was fashioned was scandalously revealing. The thin silk clung to every line and curve of her slender form. It was hard to tell whether she was a lady of quality or a lightskirt.

She was so astonishingly beautiful that for a heartbeat or two he could notice nothing else about her. Then he saw that her eyes were stark with fear.

"Help," she whispered. She stumbled down the stairs toward him. "Help me."

Every chivalrous instinct Derek had ever had rushed immediately to the fore. He moved toward her at once. "Of course," he heard himself say. "Anything in my power."

The girl reached for him in the way a child reaches for protection, and he caught her in much the same spirit. It seemed perfectly natural to take her hands in his, then place one arm around her to comfort her. For an instant she sagged gratefully against him. He could not help noticing how perfectly she fit in his embrace. But she was trembling with terror; he couldn't help noticing that, either.

"Hide me," she whispered.

At almost the same instant, Derek heard a door close somewhere above their heads, and footsteps, firmer than the girl's, heading toward the stairs down which she had come. The sharp intake of her breath confirmed that this, whoever the individual might be, was the source of her terror. Quick as thought, Derek pulled the girl into the shadowed stairwell. She clung to him, sending a surge of fierce protectiveness through him.

No harm will come to this girl, he silently vowed.

He didn't care who she was. Duchess or beggarmaid, princess or prostitute, if she needed him to slay dragons or walk on hot coals, so be it. He'd slay the dragons while walking on the coals, if that was the only way to keep her safe.

The footsteps on the floor above their heads halted, apparently at the top of the stairs. A dry, masculine voice spoke.

"Cynthia."

The single word managed to convey both command and menace. The tone was redolent of hostility but overlaid with silky amusement. At its sound, the girl seemed to stop breathing.

The man would surely come down if he were not stopped. Derek laid a finger to his lips, warning Cynthia to keep still, then let go of her and emerged alone from beneath the stairs.

"Oh, hallo," he said, trying to sound affable and mildly puzzled. He peered inquiringly up at the figure standing at the top of the stairs. "Didn't see you," he remarked in an explanatory tone. "You looking for me?"

There was a perceptible pause before the gentleman answered. "No," he said. His voice was hard but civil enough. "I beg your pardon."

Derek gave him an airy wave. "Not at all, not at all. Haven't disturbed me a whit." Still aping the amiable vapidity of a young man about town, and trying to convey the impression that he had, perhaps, imbibed too much wine, he wandered a bit unsteadily toward a suit of armor made from paperboard. "Just having a look round, you know. Fascinating, all this scenery and whatnot."

The man at the top of the stairs did not move. He seemed to be studying Derek with careful suspicion, weighing whether to challenge him or move on. Derek stole another glance at the chap. By moving toward the suit of armor, he had positioned himself where the light was no longer in his eyes, and he could get a good look at the fellow.

He knew the man at once, and had to return his gaze to the wall to avoid displaying his start of recognition. Sir James Filey. Damnation! How had a girl like Cynthia fallen into Filey's hands? The fellow was notorious. Gamester, rakehell, lecher—a thoroughly ugly customer. And besides that, he was old enough to be her father. Older, by Jove!

Was it possible that Filey *was* her father? There had been a note of authority, unmistakable and implacable, in that dry, sneering voice—

"I wonder if I might trespass upon your courtesy for a moment." Filey's voice was very cold.

Outwardly relaxed but inwardly alert, Derek turned politely back toward the stairs. "Eh?" he said, swaying slightly.

Filey did not bother to hide his contempt. The sneer on his face deepened. "I'm looking for a fair-haired chit in a white gown."

Well. Whatever Filey's interest in Cynthia, it clearly was not paternal. Hiding his disgust, Derek gave Filey a lopsided grin. "Hah! Aren't we all?" He winked drunkenly.

Impatience sharpened Filey's voice. "Have you seen such a female pass by here, a few moments hence?"

"No, dash it." Derek infused his voice with wistful regret. "Is she pretty?"

"Excessively pretty," snapped Filey.

"Really? By George! I'll help you look for her." He began to stagger eagerly up the stairs.

"No, thank you. That won't be necessary." Filey actually threw out a hand as if warding him off.

Derek paused, one hand on the banister. He pasted an injured look on his features. "No need to take that tone, dear chap. Only offering my assistance, you know."

"I require none, however. I prefer to hunt alone." Filey's lip curled. "I wish you a pleasant evening."

He sketched a bow and was gone, his footfalls beating an angry retreat. Derek waited until the footsteps receded into silence, then gave a grim chuckle. "That dragon was too easily slain," he remarked. The vapid drawl had vanished from his voice. He sauntered back down the stairs. "What a pity that no fisticuffs were called for! It would have been a pleasure to plant that rogue a facer."

A faint voice sounded from the stairwell. "Oh, on the contrary! I am glad no blows were exchanged."

Cynthia emerged into the light. Her attempt at a light tone was pathetically brave; now that Filey was gone, she was shaking with reaction. Derek saw that she was clenching her jaw to keep her teeth from chattering, and his heart went out to her. All humor fled from Derek's features. It was impossible to make light

14

of the situation, confronted with Cynthia's distress.

"I sent him away through a silly ruse," said Derek quietly. "I would have served you better, perhaps, had I faced the villain down."

Cynthia's eyes, celestial blue, lifted to his. Derek felt his breath catch in his throat. A thrill went through him like an electric shock, as if her eyes held divine power.

"You were splendid," she whispered. There was something dazed and wondering in her face, as if the words had been pulled out of her against her will. A sudden stillness seemed to descend upon her. And her trembling simply . . . stopped.

How beautiful she was. But there must be something else, some added element beyond physical beauty, attracting him. Nobody was this beautiful. Nobody could possibly be as beautiful as this girl seemed to him. Crazy thoughts jumbled in his brain, snatches of Shakespeare mixed with heart-pounding emotion— and somewhere above it, a detached portion of his mind was noting with calm, scientific interest, *So this is what it's like . . . love at first sight.* He had read of the phenomenon but assumed it was merely a poetic convention. Such things never happened in real life. Real people did not, could not, fall in love with total strangers.

Except that, apparently, they could and did.

They stared at each other, motionless under the flaring lamp. *Oh, she doth teach the torches to burn bright.* Madness, madness. Knowledge and intimacy, clear truth somehow born in intuition, flashed and pulsed in the air between them. How could such things be? And then, without a word, Derek opened his arms.

It was a crazy thing to do; what did he expect? No decent female would accept such an invitation. But, marvel of marvels, Cynthia walked into his embrace as if she belonged there.

In the grip of magic, reality steps aside. The normal laws of earthly existence, including the rules set forth for human behavior, simply do not apply. Whatever was happening here, it was larger, more important, more compelling, than any code of conduct. For another fraction of a second, Derek drowned in those blue, blue eyes, now so close to his own. Then he surrendered to the inevitable. He bent his head and kissed her.

She melted into his arms with perfect trust, lifting her lips to meet his. *Sweet.* Her mouth was soft and warm. Yielding. He explored it with a kind of reverence, cherishing its every curve and hollow. One did not plunder a miracle. A man could not allow petty, greedy lust to intrude upon the holy. Derek closed his eyes as if in prayer, savoring the gift of kissing Cynthia.

When he lifted his head again, her eyelids seemed to flutter open at the same moment his did. As one, they took a breath. As one, they moved slightly apart, the better to stare at each other.

Derek raised one hand and touched her cheek, placing his finger lightly along her perfect jawline. He shook his head slowly, in baffled awe. "I hope," he

16

said hoarsely, "that you do not expect an apology."

The corners of her mouth curved in a tiny smile. "No," she admitted. "In fact, I think . . . I think it might grieve me, if you expressed . . . regret." Her cheeks were turning a delicate shade of pink.

"Regret? Never," said Derek fervently. "I couldn't."

She dropped her eyes, apparently suffering a belated attack of shyness. Another moment, he realized, and she would recall the outrageousness of their situation. She would remember the rules of polite behavior and be horrified by her inexplicable lapse. And the moment after that, she would withdraw from him. He could not let that moment arrive.

"Come and sit down," he urged her softly. "You have had a harrowing experience. You should rest for a time and collect yourself." He led her to the stairs and spread his handkerchief on one of the steps to protect the fragile silk of her gown. Attempting to lighten the moment, he shot her a sheepish grin. "The gentlemanly thing, of course, would be to give you my coat. But men's fashions being what they are today, I'm afraid that's impossible."

She looked a startled inquiry. His grin widened. "Can't extricate myself without assistance," he explained. "Takes two strong men, a shoehorn, a crowbar, and a bucket of grease to get me out of this coat."

Her laugh was as clear and sweet as he'd hoped it would be. "Never mind," she told him, seating herself gracefully on the handkerchief. "What a pity that we can't cut you loose. I did bring scissors with me this evening, but I'm afraid I left them in my reticule."

He caught himself staring again. Her movements were so fluid that she made sitting on the handkerchief-draped stair seem natural and elegant. She was seated almost directly beneath the lamp. Her hair scattered light like an angel's halo, and the silk of her gown seemed poured over her, a gloss of milky white shimmering on her warm skin. A man couldn't help but notice. It was highly distracting, to say the least. He had to clear his throat before he could speak.

"Where is your reticule? Shall I fetch it for you?"

"No, thank you." A shadow crossed her features. "I must have left it behind when we—when I left the box."

Derek was not so lost in admiration that he missed the shiver that ran through her. The very thought of what had happened to her earlier returned the fear to her eyes. This could not stand; he must do something to take her fear away.

He sat beside her, frowning. "Cynthia," he said quietly, and took her hand in his. "What happened tonight? Tell me."

Color flooded her cheeks. She averted her gaze. "I'm ashamed," she whispered. "It was . . . he was . . . horrid."

"You speak of Filey." It was not a question. The scoundrel must have . . . He couldn't let his mind finish the sentence. Anger rippled through him. "Blast! I should have knocked the rascal down while I had the chance."

Cynthia glanced back at him apprehensively. "You sound angry."

"Of course I am angry! I should have known, the instant I saw you were afraid of him—" Derek's teeth clenched. "What did that villain do to you?" he exclaimed. Then his arm tightened around her. "Never mind," he growled. "If you tell me, I may have to kill him."

She looked startled. He managed a strained smile. "I'm joking," he explained.

A tiny smile curved her lips again. She tilted her chin, studying him. "I don't think you are," she remarked at last. "Not entirely." Her smile sweetened. "You joke, but there is something of the knight-errant about you."

A short laugh escaped him. "I lack the shining armor, of course. Perhaps I should borrow that suit of paperboard over there before I hunt Filey down."

Her color deepened. She dropped her eyes. "In truth, you know, he did not do anything so very . . . that is, he did not . . ." Her voice trailed off and she gave a strange, choked laugh. "He did nothing more than you did."

Surprise and chagrin jarred him, paralyzing him for a moment. He had to bite his tongue to keep from swearing. It was not as bad as it might have been, but still—Filey had kissed her! The swine had dared to *kiss* her! It mattered not a whit that the man had done nothing more than he himself had done. Had Filey walked into the room at that moment, Derek would have lunged for the dastard's throat.

Cynthia looked back up at him. She must have seen the mortifying emotions chasing themselves across

19

his face, for she smiled with what seemed a wisdom beyond her years. "You are thinking that Sir James had no right," she said softly. "No right to touch me."

"Yes." Derek's voice sounded half strangled. "Sorry! I know it sounds absurd, coming from me. Can't help it."

Amusement crinkled the corners of her eyes. "But it doesn't sound absurd at all. I agree with you. He had no right to touch me. And he certainly had no right to kiss me."

"Cynthia, you shame me." He cradled her face in his hands. Her cheeks were soft as a baby's. His heart swelled with a remorse so keen it was almost sorrow. "I had no right to kiss you, either." He opened his mouth to apologize, but she forestalled him by laying one finger gently against his lips.

"Yes, you did." Her whisper was barely audible. "You had every right."

Remorse faded, forgotten. Awe took its place. It was suddenly hard to breathe. He shook his head slowly. "How can that be?"

Her eyes were blue as the morning sky. "I don't know." Confusion clouded them briefly, and then cleared. She smiled at him. "I don't know," she repeated, but the trouble had vanished from her face. "Some things one can't explain. They are simply true."

So of course he kissed her again.

And again.

Eventually he was forced to come up for air. He moved immediately to sweep her back into another kiss, but Cynthia pulled away from him, gasping to catch her breath.

"I . . . I can't . . . Oh, what time is it?" She sat up, seeming dazed. "What am I *doing?*"

"Kissing me," he said thickly. Whatever else she had on her agenda, it couldn't possibly be more important. He reached for her again, but she held him off.

Her face was rosy from his kisses. She looked delightful, but she pressed her hands to her cheeks as if trying to cool them. "Merciful heavens. I have never in my life—that is—I mean—oh, this is madness! I don't even know you."

But on this point, Derek was very sure. "You know me." He smiled, besotted, and tucked a strand of her spun-sunlight hair back into her coiffure. "Never doubt that, Cynthia."

She gave a shaky little laugh, seeming to agree with him against her better judgment. "Perhaps you are right. What's in a name?" she said lightly. With an inward start, he recognized the words. She was not only quoting Shakespeare; she was quoting the same play that— "And yet," she continued, breaking into his jumbled thoughts, "I would like to know it."

He took a deep breath. "Of course you would. What a dunderhead I am." He raked his hair back off his forehead and tried to gather his wits. "My name is Whittaker," he told her. "Derek Whittaker. At your service, I need hardly add."

Cynthia's smile bloomed again. "Derek Whittaker," she repeated. He thought his name had never sounded so well. "And I am Cynthia Fitzwilliam." She seemed to expect the name to mean something to him, but he couldn't place it. After a tiny pause, she added, "My father is the Earl of Ballymere, you know."

No, he hadn't known. Derek's heart sank. This was *not* good news. Ballymere was obviously an Irish title, but Irish or not, an earl's daughter was above his touch. Ridiculous, that that would matter so much to him. He barely knew this girl. Was he already planning to court her?

Well, yes. He was. No doubt about it.

Her smile faded. She regarded him gravely. "I must go back." He felt her anxiety suddenly return. Tension ran through her slim body, although her face betrayed none of it. "Sir James will have returned to the box by now."

He stared down at her in amazement. "Sir James? Never tell me you came here tonight in Filey's company!"

Cynthia closed her eyes in an expression of pain. "Yes, I did," she whispered. Then she placed her palms over her face, sagging with misery. "Oh, what will you think of me?"

Derek placed his arm around her and drew her close. He said nothing. What could he say? Attending the opera with a bachelor, let alone such a one as Filey, was not the sort of thing a respectable young female would do. Had she not already told him she was an earl's daughter, and had he not already fallen more than halfway in love with her, Derek would have doubted her virtue.

Cynthia was shaking again, and seemed inclined to

burrow into his warmth for comfort. "I did not come here alone with him," she said into his shoulder. "It's not as bad as that. My mother is here as well."

Relief flooded him. "Then I shall restore you to your mother," he said firmly. "Not to Filey."

"You don't understand." She gave a mournful little sigh. "But how could you? I haven't told you all." She sat up and faced him, her expression woebegone. "My mother and I are here tonight as Sir James's guests. He is . . . he is her favorite of all my suitors. I see you find that incredible, but it's true. She was so pleased when he invited us." Another shiver went through her. "She will be very angry with me."

Derek frowned. "For going off alone with him?"

Cynthia shook her head. "No. For running away from him." Distress was in every line of her tense, quivering body. "But I couldn't help it," she whispered. She gazed helplessly up into Derek's eyes. "He wasn't you."

Emotion closed over Derek's heart like a fist and squeezed. He felt his chest tighten. Their eyes had locked again, and again he felt the undeniable tug of their connection.

But a question had evidently occurred to Cynthia. Her delicate brows knit in puzzlement. "Derek, how do you know Sir James? For it is obvious that you do."

He gave a short laugh. "All the world knows Sir James Filey."

Her puzzlement seemed to deepen. "But he did not know you."

"Oh, there's nothing odd in that. Nobody knows

23

me." He grinned, then felt his grin slip a bit. For the first time, his anonymous state struck Derek as a handicap. Whoever this girl was—and she had mentioned "suitors," plural—she was unlikely to bestow her affections on a nobody. Miss Fitzwilliam was plainly somebody.

My father is the Earl of Ballymere, you know. Hell and the devil confound it. She wasn't Miss Fitzwilliam. Earl's daughters bore a title. She was Lady Cynthia. A small thing, perhaps, but it seemed to place her even further out of reach. Damn, damn, damn.

She must have seen the shadow cross his face. "What's amiss?" she whispered. Anxiety filled her eyes.

He was trying to form an answer when a strange roaring suddenly swelled in the air around them, echoing faintly in the halls above. Derek was so lost to his surroundings that, for a fraction of a second, he failed to recognize it. Then it hit him: It was applause! Off in the forgotten world where his duties awaited him, the interval had arrived. If he did not hasten back to Lord Stokesdown's box, his absence would be noticed.

"Good God!" he exclaimed. He leaped to his feet, pulling Cynthia peremptorily up with him.

"What—what—" she stammered.

"Sorry! I lost track of time. It's the interval, dear girl. Everyone will be leaving their boxes and milling about."

"Oh, heavens." She paled. "What will we do?"

"Join them, I think, and pretend we've been milling about, too." Still, for a moment he cupped her face in his hands, loath to let her go. "I cannot stay with you," he said reluctantly. "I wish I could. Cynthia, what do you want of me? Shall I take you back to your mother? Or is there somewhere else you might go? I will gladly escort you to a friend, an aunt—"

"No. There is no one. No one who is here tonight, at any rate." She gave him a shaky smile. "You may take me back. After all, I must face my mother and Sir James again sometime."

He could not argue with her. What she said was logical, and besides, there wasn't time. He escorted her up the stairs and quickly to the edge of the common areas, where people were, indeed, milling about. But he hung back at the edge of the light, pulling her slightly toward him. "You will see me again," he said in a low tone.

She tilted her chin to look up at him. Her eyes were luminous, filled with longing. And, strangely, sadness.

"I hope so," she whispered. Then, before he could stop her, she slid from his grasp and melted into the crowd.

Chapter Two

Hyde Park, unlike the *haut ton*'s elegant ballrooms, did not require an invitation—even during the fashionable hour. For the next three days, Derek Whittaker arrived in the famous gardens promptly at five o'clock, dressed to the nines and neat as wax, and joined the army of exquisites parading up and down. The park was so crowded at this time of year with like-minded gentlemen that Derek had no trouble hooking up with cronies bent upon encountering their latest inamoratas. In company with this one or that, pretending to converse while surreptitiously scanning the crowd, Derek spent several frustrating afternoons patrolling the most frequented areas of the park . . . to no avail.

On the fourth day, he hired a hack. The expenditure was more than he could comfortably afford, but the advantages of being on horseback were immediately apparent. Not only could he scour the park more thoroughly; he could view the throng from a height that enabled him to see farther and better. He trotted along the Serpentine, then doubled back to the more crowded areas of the park. Halfway down Rotten Row, his efforts were crowned with success. He saw Cynthia.

She was seated in an open barouche, facing him. The barouche's progress toward where Derek rode was impeded by the crush of other vehicles, a circumstance for which Derek was thankful. The slowness of its approach gave him a bit of time to recover his composure. On seeing her, his heart had given such a bound that the horse, sensing his sudden tension, danced and fretted beneath him.

She was a vision. Sunlight filtered through the plane trees and struck the edge of her parasol, illuminating the lace as it fluttered high above her face. Her face was slightly averted as she listened to her companion's conversation, but she looked up when Derek's eyes fell on her, as if she felt his gaze. As their eyes met, he felt again the shock of recognition and the irresistible pull of attraction between them. There was something beyond her beauty that drew him to this particular girl. He felt it as surely as he felt the sunshine on his face.

He urged his mount forward, smiling eagerly. He was actually lifting his hand to his hat brim, preparing to bow, when he realized that Cynthia was not acknowledging him. She had glanced away, back to her companion.

Confused, Derek hung back. It was the lady's prerogative, of course, to recognize their acquaintance or not. But surely, surely his Cynthia did not intend to give him the cut direct. They had not been formally introduced, but—

Well, of course! Ignoring him was a mark of her good breeding, nothing more. They needed an introduction.

He spied an opening. The middle-aged lady sitting beside Cynthia he had never seen before in his life, but he recognized the portly chap sitting across from them. What the deuce was the fellow's name? Henderson. Something Henderson. He had attended a political dinner at Lord Stokesdown's residence a few weeks ago.

It was a feeble excuse to approach the carriage, but desperate men take desperate measures. Derek approached, tipping his hat to Something Henderson.

"Henderson!" he exclaimed, with every indication of pleasure. "How are you, sir? Fine weather we're having."

"Eh?" Henderson blinked doubtfully at him. "Ah. Yes, indeed. Very pleasant." It was painfully obvious that he had no idea who Derek was. "How d'ye do?"

"Very well, thank you, sir." Derek turned to include the women in his easy smile. "Ladies." He touched the brim of his hat in a polite salute, being careful to do no more than glance at Cynthia. Then he turned back to give poor Henderson a clue. "You may be interested to hear, sir, that Lord Stokesdown means to give an address next week. On the taxation dilemma, I believe."

Light seemed to dawn. The association with Lord Stokesdown had obviously brought Derek's face into focus for him. "Is that so? Well, well. In the Upper House, I suppose?"

"Just so, sir." He thought he had better change the subject before Henderson realized that Derek's face, although vaguely recalled from the Stokesdown dinner, had not been among those actually at table with him. He directed his most charming smile to the middle-aged woman sitting with Cynthia. "But we mustn't bore the ladies with political talk."

He had always had a way with older women. She visibly unbent, permitting herself to smile at Derek. "Not at all, young man. I don't believe we've met," she remarked, arching a brow in polite inquiry.

Derek silently blessed the woman. To save the unfortunate Henderson from further embarrassment, he lifted his hat and bowed. "Derek Whittaker, madam, at your service."

"Very pleased to meet you. I am Maria Henderson, as you have no doubt surmised. I see that you are acquainted with my husband, but have you met Lady Cynthia? Cynthia, my dear, allow me to present Derek Whittaker. Mr. Whittaker, Lady Cynthia Fitzwilliam."

Derek bowed very low. "I am honored."

Cynthia lifted limpid blue eyes to his and murmured something polite. Her poise was remarkable, but he noticed that her cheeks were pinker than they had been two minutes ago. She lowered her gaze modestly to her lap, but a tiny quirk of mischief trembled at the corner of her mouth. It stayed, although she steadfastly regarded her gloves while Derek fell into easy conversation with chatty Mrs. Henderson.

He dared not overstay his welcome. He and Cynthia had been officially introduced; that was enough for today. After a few more pleasantries, he bowed and bade farewell. As he gathered the reins and prepared to ride off, however, Cynthia threw him a bone. She looked up again, actually daring to meet his eyes, and uttered two sentences.

"It was a pleasure to make your acquaintance, Mr. Whittaker," she said. Her expression was perfectly neutral, and there was no hint of warmth in her voice. He had to admire her show of indifference. "I daresay we shall meet again at the embassy ball."

Mrs. Henderson laughed. "Oh, all the world and his brother will be there."

Derek, naturally, knew nothing about the embassy

29

ball. But he instantly resolved to attend it, by hook or by crook. He managed a bland smile, expressed a conventional hope that Cynthia's prediction would prove true, and with a last bow—nicely aimed at the air precisely in the middle of the carriage, rather than to any one person in it—rode away.

He lost little time in returning the hack and striding purposefully back to Lord Stokesdown's town house, where he tossed his hat on a table, shut himself in the library, and dug briskly through a stack of discarded invitations. If "all the world and his brother" were expected at this ball, Derek had no doubt that Lord Stokesdown had been included in their number. Ten minutes later, he emerged from the library triumphant with a square, white card in his hand.

The embassy ball would be held three nights hence, and the embassy in question was that of the Austrians. All that remained was for Derek to convince his employer that the ball would be worth attending . . . for political reasons. This would doubtless be a stretch, but political reasons were the only considerations likely to weigh with his lordship— which is why Derek's duties took him to many excellent dinners and occasional theatrical excursions, but few balls. An embassy ball was even less likely than most to appeal to Derek's employer, since his tastes ran to domestic policy rather than foreign affairs. Still, Derek did not despair. Lord Stokesdown had come to rely on Derek's judgment regarding which invitations to accept and which to decline, so if Derek recommended that he attend this particular ball, his lordship might agree without a murmur.

The more difficult hurdle would be to convince Lord Stokesdown that his secretary's presence at the ball would prove useful. Derek decided, after nervously weighing and discarding several arguments, that he would cross that bridge when he came to it.

As it turned out, however, no convoluted arguments were required. When Derek casually suggested that Lord Stokesdown appear at the embassy ball, secretary in tow, a strange little pause ensued. Then his lordship gave a sudden bark of laughter. "Hah!" he exclaimed, clapping his startled employee on the back. "You've met a girl."

Derek felt himself flush to the roots of his hair.

Lord Stokesdown waved this off. "No, no, my boy, no need to color up. I'd be glad to see you creditably established."

"Oh, as to that—I—I, sir, I have only just met her."

"Pooh! Who cares for that? You must be well and truly smitten, to try cajoling me into attending some rubbishy ball just to catch a glimpse of her." Another crack of laughter escaped him. "I'll go, never fear! If only to watch you trying to wheedle your way into the *ton*. Should be most entertaining. If you expect to encounter this chit at the embassy, she must be well connected. Eh? Excellent! A very good thing for you."

"Well, sir—I'm afraid, sir—that is, I think she might be a bit—well—" Derek took a deep breath and faced his employer squarely. "I'm afraid you'll think she's above my touch, sir."

The friendly twinkle in Lord Stokesdown's eyes

31

dimmed a bit. "You don't say. Who is she?"

Derek wished he hadn't been quite so candid. It was one thing to be aboveboard with one's employer but quite another to bandy Cynthia's name about. "She's—" He swallowed hard. "It's my understanding that she is Lord Ballymere's daughter, sir."

"Ballymere." Lord Stokesdown's smile faded. He stroked his chin, apparently troubled. "Ballymere. Well, it's an Irish title, of course. And there's nothing wrong with your breeding, dear boy. If your family's estate hadn't been left in that havey-cavey way, I'd call it a respectable match. Not brilliant, of course. But respectable."

"Yes, sir," said Derek woodenly. "Thank you, sir. But my family's estate *has* been left in a havey-cavey way. I shan't inherit. My brother's holding the reins." He smiled wryly. "And he and his wife are already setting up their nursery."

"Ah. Expecting, are they?" Lord Stokesdown looked properly sympathetic. "I hadn't heard."

"And there's one other small obstacle to courting Ballymere's daughter." Since he was baring his soul, Derek supposed he might as well bare it all. "She's a beauty."

Lord Stokesdown's look of sympathy deepened. "Dear me. A beauty. Well, well. Her family's likely to be ambitious, then. High expectations and all that."

"Yes, sir."

"Well, lad, I wouldn't get my hopes up," said his lordship bluntly. "But you're a good-looking boy, and you've a pleasant way about you. Engaging manners and so forth. Never know but what the girl may lose her heart to you, eh? And Ballymere may have modern notions, for all we know. Ready to let the daughter choose, rather than marry at his bidding."

"Yes, sir. That is my hope."

Lord Stokesdown seemed ready to turn the subject, but then he paused, an arrested expression seizing his features. "Ballymere," he muttered again. "Good God. Never tell me—" He halted in midsentence and bent a piercing look upon his secretary. "I hope you haven't formed a *tendre* for Cynthia Fitzwilliam. If you have, heaven help you."

A frisson of alarm ran through Derek. "How so, sir?"

"Then you *have?*" Lord Stokesdown gave a queer sort of groan. "Devil take the boy! He's fallen for the Frost Fair." He shook his head mournfully. "You'll never win her, lad. She's the coldest wench in England." He must have seen the affronted astonishment crossing Derek's face, for he hastily added, "If the reports are true, that is. I'm not acquainted with her."

"Well, I am, my lord," said Derek stiffly. "A little. Did you say something about a 'Frost Fair'? What is that supposed to mean, if you please?"

Lord Stokesdown coughed. "You haven't heard that? Well. No wonder. It's a pity you haven't, for it might have given you warning." His expression was not unkind, but his brows were knitted with concern. "Don't know who started it, my boy, but that's what everyone calls her."

Derek began to feel genuinely angry. "I should like

33

to know why anyone would call her that, my lord. It seems unjust."

"Well, well, don't poker up. The wags always bestow nicknames on the latest beauties, you know. Sometimes they stick, and sometimes they don't." He studied Derek, the concern in his sharp eyes deepening. "This one stuck," he added gruffly. "So I warn you, Derek. The sobriquet may sound silly to you—most of 'em are silly—but it would not have caught fire had it not seemed apt to a great many people."

An explanation suddenly occurred to Derek. Relief shot through him. "Perhaps the nickname refers to her appearance," he suggested. "Her coloring is extremely fair."

"Well, I daresay that's part of it. For your sake, I will hope it's the largest part," said his lordship, still frowning. "But that's not what one hears. I'll go to this absurd ball, and I'll take you with me. But I'll be candid with you, lad—I'm hoping you meet someone who will chase the Frost Fair from your thoughts. I'm a busy man, and I can't afford to have my secretary driven into a decline."

Derek laughed out loud. "No fear of that, sir. Is that her reputation? That she drives healthy young men into declines?"

Lord Stokesdown did not join Derek's laughter. "It is," he said grimly. "So guard your heart, boy. Now, what about that letter to Sheringham? Do I sign it or not?" And he briskly returned to business.

Derek dressed for the embassy ball with greater care

than he had ever dressed for anything, feeling grateful that the prevailing mode did not require men to deck themselves with jewels, fancy buckles, expensive laces, or fabrics threaded with gold. Fifteen years ago, a secretary could never have afforded this masquerade. Tonight, however, Derek looked every inch the gentleman and would be dressed as gorgeously as any man present; beautifully cut broadcloth and clean linen were the order of the day. A waistcoat turned out in a modest but elegant brocade was as far as he need go to flaunt his supposed social standing.

He stared hard at the mirror when he was done, then gave a wry nod. "It will do," he muttered.

He looked prosperous enough to pass as Lord Stokesdown's son . . . to those who did not know his lordship's family. Was that cheating? He hardly knew. After all, he didn't intend to *lie* about his prospects. The Polite World was full of purse-pinched gentlemen, many of whom had little more than Derek had. "All policy's fair in love and war," he reminded his reflection sternly, then picked up his hat.

The first ordeal, throughout which Lord Stokesdown grumbled under his breath, involved standing in a long line to pay their respects to the ambassador and a string of other dignitaries. When a gorgeously wigged and liveried person bawled, "The Earl of Stokesdown! Mr. Whittaker!" Derek stepped forth and bowed as if to the manor born. As far as he could tell, no one cared or questioned who the young man at Lord Stokesdown's elbow might be. Lord Stokesdown had seen fit to bring him; that was apparently enough. Amazing.

The rooms were very crowded. It was just such a gathering as Derek would have relished—had he been privileged to observe it rather than participate. As it was, enjoyment was not first among his emotions. Nerves on the stretch, he prowled along the edges of the ballroom, surveying the crowd. His Cynthia was nowhere to be seen among the shifting knots of smiling strangers.

The orchestra was tuning up, barely audible above the din of chatter. The ball would soon begin. Derek hovered at a discreet distance from the entrance to the room and kept a weather eye on the doorway.

She soon appeared on the raised threshold, as he knew she must. Derek felt his breath hitch. She was dressed similarly to a dozen other girls in the room, but somehow the effect was entirely different on Cynthia. The other females looked well enough, draped like so many Greek statues . . . but Cynthia was Aphrodite in the flesh. Her head held regally high, her white shoulders sloping elegantly, the light seeming to ripple along the crown of her flaxen hair, she wore the clinging gauze with graceful confidence. She came in with a group of others who clustered round her, but Derek could not have said who they were; he had eyes only for Cynthia.

Again, she seemed to immediately feel his gaze touch her. Her lovely head swiveled, and her blue eyes went unerringly to his. This, Derek thought groggily, must be what the ancients meant when they spoke of Cupid's arrows. He felt the point slam home in a flash, fairly rocking him back on his heels. Super-aware of her, he saw the quick rise and fall of her breath—but once, and once only. She immediately mastered whatever emotion had shaken her. Her eyes slid away from Derek as she returned her attention, with a visible effort, to her companions. And then, arm in arm with another lady, she drifted down into the ballroom and away from him.

What the deuce— This was carrying discretion a little too far.

Piqued, Derek started to muscle his way through the crowd toward her. He soon found himself at the rear of a jostling line of men, genially elbowing one another out of the way as they jockeyed for position near the two ladies. There was a great deal of laughter and good-natured ribbing taking place, but Derek wasn't feeling particularly good-natured. He hung back, struggling to quell the outrage he felt at having to wait his turn.

The chap next to him gave him a friendly nudge. "I say, which d'you fancy? The Incomparable Isobel or the Frost Fair?"

Derek stared at him. "Sorry?"

"Which d'you fancy?" the young man repeated patiently. "I don't care which of 'em I dance with. Don't mind claiming the Frost Fair if it's the Incomparable you like, or vice versa. By the time we get near enough to speak, most of their dances will be spoken for, y'know. So if you do fancy one above the other—"

Something like horror tied Derek's tongue for a moment. But surely, he reminded himself, Cynthia would save him a dance. She all but *asked* him to come here tonight. He would not be here otherwise. He forced a smile. "I'll take my chances," he told the fellow next to him.

But when he stepped into the inner circle, so close to Cynthia that he imagined he could feel the heat of her body, she still did not acknowledge him. She stood like the statue she resembled, as lovely and perfect as marble—and as lifeless. Her gaze was fixed on, apparently, the opposite wall of the room. What on earth was the matter with her? The girl they called Incomparable Isobel was a lively brunette whose chatter masked Cynthia's silence—but as Derek was focused entirely on Cynthia, her silence seemed louder to him than Isobel's merry prattle.

When he could bear it no longer, he chose a moment in which everyone save himself and Cynthia was laughing and lightly touched her elbow. "Cynthia," he murmured in a low and urgent tone.

She stiffened. After a fractional pause she glanced in his direction, her eyes wide with reproof. And . . . with fear? The emotion flitted so swiftly across her features that he was not sure whether he had seen it or no. "Sir?" she said icily. She did not quite meet his eyes.

"Lady Cynthia," he amended hastily, sketching a bow. It must be gossip that she feared. Very well, he would play the game, if she wished him to. It was hard to pretend that Cynthia meant nothing to him, but she was right to guard her reputation. He gave her his most charming smile, the one he might use with any attractive acquaintance. "I seem to have reached the head of the queue at last. I hope you have managed to save me a dance."

She bestowed upon him a distant, faintly bored smile. "I'm so sorry," she said politely. Then, apparently as an afterthought, she added, "Another time, perhaps." And she turned her shoulder to him in dismissal.

Derek was stunned. Had he done something to offend her? If so, he must make amends—at once. He stepped back into her line of sight and touched her elbow again. "I beg your pardon," he said with an earnestness that he hoped was audible only to Cynthia. "But I wonder if . . . if . . ." He cudgeled his brain, trying to think of some innocuous thing to say. "I wonder if I might bring you a glass of punch?"

"Thank you, no," she said calmly.

She did not appear angry. She did not appear, actually, to be feeling anything. But her faint, slightly incredulous smile seemed to put him at an infinite distance. Before he could recover his wits and think of another gambit, a broadly grinning man in a striped waistcoat walked off with her and into the first set that was forming.

Derek stared after them, absolutely flummoxed.

The jovial chap who had addressed him earlier gave him a friendly dig in the ribs. "She frosted you, begad! Seen her do it before, a dozen times. But you walked right into it, old man." He peered more closely at Derek. His good-natured grin faded a bit. "I say, don't take it so hard. She's famous for that sort of thing, y'know. Does it to everyone."

Not to me, he wanted to say. But he said nothing. The words would be indiscreet, he told himself. The more painful thought—that the words would also be patently untrue—he shoved to the back of his mind. He would think about that later. Not now. Not in public.

He gave the friendly chap a rather strained smile. "I suppose that's why they call her the Frost Fair?"

"Oh, aye! Didn't you know? Ha! Ha! No wonder you look bewattled." He shook with laughter. "The closest you'll get to her is a dance or two, my friend. And never twice in the same night, mind! Not that you'd want to spend more than ten minutes with the chit. No one does."

"Why not?"

"Well, if it's your notion of a good time to dance with a wench who stares down her pretty nose at you and won't say more than three words together . . ." The fellow shrugged, grinning. "If she weren't such a treat for the eyes, I daresay no one would bother with her."

Derek frowned. "It can't be that much of a punishment to dance with her," he said with some asperity. "There were enough men queuing up for the chance."

"Oh, certainly! As you say. She's all the rage. One must be in the mode, you know, so one dances with the Frost Fair—when one can. And besides, she *is* a treat for the eyes." He stared hungrily after her. "And a man likes a challenge, too, o'course. She won't dance with just anyone. So it's a bit of a feather in one's cap to steer Lady Cynthia round the floor."

"I see." Derek's neckcloth suddenly felt too tight. He watched, helpless, as the leering buffoon in the striped waistcoat moved through the figures of the quadrille with Cynthia. It was ghastly to behold. The pattern of the dance brought her first to the side of one man, then to another. Every time one of them touched her hand or spoke to her, a stab of jealousy knifed through Derek.

The evening of his dreams rapidly dwindled into nightmare. He spent the next several hours propping the walls or leaning against one of the columns that lined the ballroom, moodily watching Cynthia as she floated from one partner to another. She behaved toward them all with the same cool reserve, but that struck Derek as small comfort; she behaved toward him with something less than that. As far as he could tell, she was utterly indifferent to his presence. She seemed completely unaware that his eyes followed her wherever she went. He found the latter hard to believe, but the alternative was worse: that she *was* aware of him and was deliberately ignoring him.

It was inexplicable. Why hint that he should come to the ball, if she meant to cut him dead when he did? And, more important, why cut him at all? She must have felt what he felt, that night. She *must* have. How could she turn her back on that? How could she turn her back on *him?*

Was she, perhaps, being watched? He scanned the crowd, searching for signs that a suspicious parent lurked in the background, monitoring Cynthia with sharp eyes, but he saw no one. She had arrived with what seemed to be a family party, but had then been allowed to wander off with Isobel and choose her own dance partners. That did not argue for close supervision.

Had someone told tales about him? But who would do such a thing? And why? He had led a fairly blameless existence. Women sometimes seemed to like him more than they should, perhaps, but he had never broken any hearts beyond repair. A man couldn't be on the town without encountering a willing victim or two. He had no enemies, as far as he knew. And besides, he wasn't well enough known for tales to spread, had there been anything interesting to tell.

Had she, perhaps, caused discreet inquiries to be set afoot and learned something of his background? But what? His family was not contemptible. No hereditary madness or criminal exploits, or anything of that nature. He came from perfectly respectable stock; not the aristocracy, of course, but certainly the gentry. The Whittakers had been landholders for centuries, and his branch of the family had owned the estate where he grew up, Crosby Hall, for four generations. They were the largest landholders in the neighborhood, in fact. He, himself, had nothing, but . . .

But surely his Cynthia would not be that mercenary. She would not care for riches. Not in light of what they had together, which was so much more important. He'd never felt anything like what he felt when he met her, and he'd bet a monkey that she'd never felt anything like it, either. It was, just as the cliché said, bigger than both of them.

Wasn't it?

By the end of that interminable evening, Derek was no longer sure. He was no longer sure of anything. He felt wrung out, drained dry—the natural result of several hours of emotional crucifixion. It was incredible, literally incredible, but Cynthia had not only declined to dance with him; she had, afterward, not spoken to him again. He had looked forward to this ball in a fever of anticipation, expecting an evening of secret romance, tender whispers, and stolen delights. But apart from that one piercing moment when she first entered the ballroom, Cynthia had never even *looked* at him.

He clambered into Lord Stokesdown's coach in the wee hours of the morning, numb with disappointment. His lordship gave him a sharp look as he sat across from him but said nothing until the door was closed and they were on their way. Then he leaned forward and shook Derek's knee in a friendly way.

"Eh, lad," he said gruffly. "Pluck up. You look as if you had a worse time than I did—and that's saying something."

Derek forced himself to smile. "You have every right to be annoyed with me, my lord. Thank you for your forbearance—and for the opportunity to attend the ball, which I otherwise would not have had."

"Hmpf," his lordship snorted. "I've an affection for you, Derek, as I hope you know. Otherwise I'd remind you of what I said earlier."

"That you warned me how it would be?" He gave a short, mirthless laugh. "Aye. I should have listened to you."

"Always," agreed Lord Stokesdown. His stockings gleamed white in the darkness as he crossed one leg over the other and leaned back against the squabs. "But I was thinking more of my admonition to you not to fall into a decline." His voice was very dry. "I hope you have more sense, my young friend, than to waste time in pining for the chit. I never saw a girl telegraph her intentions more plainly. Your suit is unwelcome."

Pain moved in Derek's heart. He stared woodenly out the small window carved into the coach's door. Lord Stokesdown was right. Every instinct Derek had was screaming that it could not be true—but it was. What her reasons were, he could not fathom . . . but, in the end, it mattered not a jot what her reasons were. She had cut the acquaintance. There was no more to be said. Once a lady had done that, only a churl would pursue her. A gentleman must bow out of her life and not trouble her again. Those were the rules.

"I shall endeavor to keep my chin up, sir," he said, mustering his pride. "After all, I scarcely knew her. And whatever the old wives may say, people don't die of broken hearts."

But he soon came to think that if they did, he would even now be stretched out in the plot reserved for him at Crosby Hall.

His sufferings over the next interminable days were intense . . . but silent. He owed that much to his employer. And besides, a man had to keep his self-respect. He said nothing and forced himself to appear cheerful, but his health soon began to deteriorate. The difficulty was that nothing interested him, including food. And sleep was well-nigh impossible. His mind raced over the same tired ground, night after night, grappling with unanswerable questions. Dark circles formed beneath his eyes. His skin took on an unhealthy pallor. He began to look haggard, and his clothing seemed to be growing looser.

Fortunately, before there was time for him to fall into the decline Lord Stokesdown had warned him of, an end to his grief arrived. It was printed for all to see in the pages of the *Morning Post*. Derek was at his desk, composing a letter to the Prime Minister, when Lord Stokesdown walked in, opened the newspaper to the page in question, and silently tossed it down before him.

The announcement seemed to leap off the page and shout itself inside Derek's head. He stared dumbly at it. He read it several times over. At first he did not believe what he was seeing. Then he took a deep, ragged breath, and—through an enormous force of will—believed it. Sheer, cold fury swept through him in a bracing tide, wiping away his misery.

Cynthia was engaged. And the man she had agreed to marry was Sir James Filey.

Chapter Three

March 1806

Derek reached down and gave his horse's neck a reassuring pat. "Almost there, Max," he told the big gelding. "You'll sleep in a duke's stables tonight. What d'you think of that, eh?"

Max blew softly through his enormous nostrils and nodded his head. Derek chuckled. "Right you are. I'll see that His Grace's best oats are saved for you. You deserve them, my friend."

It had been a long journey on horseback, from Crosby Hall to the estate owned by his sister's father-in-law, the Duke of Oldham. The chill had been penetrating, and there had been little in the scenery to divert him; winter's drab palette of brown, gray, and white had not yet yielded to the rainbow hues of springtime. Still, he did not regret his decision to ride Max rather than make the trip boxed into a stuffy coach. Winter had been harsh this year, and the roads were in sad shape. He had made better time riding than he would have in a coach. And time was of the essence.

His sister, Natalie, the person he loved best in the world, was about to deliver her second child. It had been a difficult pregnancy, she was far from home, and she was feeling low. That had been enough to bring Derek to her as swiftly as Max would carry him.

He had tossed her letter aside the instant he had finished reading it and taken the stairs two steps at a time in his haste to pack. Crosby Hall could muddle along without him for a few weeks. Natalie needed him.

It seemed ridiculous to have to travel so far to reach her, when she and her husband were Derek's nearest neighbors. Lord Malcolm's property, Larkspur, adjoined his land, and their houses were within easy walking distance of each other. But Natalie was not at Larkspur. She had been whisked off to the Chase family seat—again—as soon as her pregnancy had been confirmed. Malcolm's elder brother, the Marquess of Grafton, had improvidently filled his nursery with daughters, so it was incumbent upon Lord Malcolm Chase, the duke's second son, to sire a boy. Malcolm's late wife had given him only a daughter, and, so far, Natalie had done no better. But hopes were high once more, and Malcolm had dutifully brought Natalie to the ducal palace in Lancashire so that the long-awaited heir—should this child prove to be male—might be born on the estate he would one day rule.

Derek judged that he and Max had reached the last five miles of their journey. He slowed the tired animal to a walk, looking around him with interest. Watery sunshine had taken some of the damp out of the air this morning and breathed a bit of life into the drabness of bare trees and frozen earth. To his right, the distant hills of the Peak District added variety to the landscape. This country would be beautiful in another six weeks, he supposed. And his sister might be giving birth to a child who would one day be its most important resident. A strange thought, that.

"My nephew, the duke," muttered Derek, trying the notion on. The absurdity made him grin.

What strange twists his life had taken in the past couple of years. It was miracle enough to find himself master of Crosby Hall, against all odds—prosperous, independent, and an important man in his community. But also, thanks to his sister's marriage, he was closely connected to one of the most prominent families in the kingdom. The swiftness of his unexpected rise had been almost dizzying.

He rounded the bend and saw, not far ahead, a bright splash of cranberry red, brilliant against the muddy colors of winter. It was a lady's riding habit, and the lady in it was leading a lame horse.

Since the lady was heading in the same direction as Derek, her back was to him. He ran an appreciative eye over her slim form. His opinion of the duke's neighborhood rose a notch. Really, it perked a chap up, knowing that a lady who looked that good in a riding habit might be entering his orbit. And if he wasn't mistaken, that was blond hair glinting under her hat. He'd always been partial to blondes.

Then, as if feeling his eyes upon her, she turned and looked at him. For one crazy instant, the world seemed to tilt on its axis. Derek almost swore aloud from the shock of it. The lady looked exactly like Cynthia Fitzwilliam.

Damnation! The lady *was* Cynthia Fitzwilliam!

It was fortunate that he was on horseback. Max carried him calmly forward despite the sudden paralysis that seized him. But there was no time to compose himself, no time to recover from the reflexive rage coursing through him, before he pulled even with her and was forced, through common courtesy, to rein Max to a halt. He stared down at her, his jaw set. He could not bring himself to speak.

Damn her. She was as lovely as ever. A little pale, and her jaw as firmly set as his, but apparently the witch who had troubled his dreams for three years still walked the earth in human form. He had often wondered whether his fevered imagination had embellished the memory. Apparently not. She was exactly as he remembered her, from the impossible blue of her eyes to the soft curve of her lower lip. Every plane of her face was familiar. The way she held her head. The set of her shoulders. The deceptive softness of her skin, which looked like porcelain but felt like . . .

God help him.

The pretty lips parted. She spoke, in a voice that shook only slightly. "You do remember me. I wondered if you would."

"Yes," he said hoarsely. "I remember you." *Ten thousand times a day, I remember you.* What the devil was she doing here, dropped into the wilds of Lancashire like a meteor fallen from the sky?

"Thank you for stopping, Mr. Whittaker."

He hoped his smile didn't look as bitter as it felt. "I never could resist a damsel in distress."

Painful thoughts of their first meeting flashed in the air between them, like swords crossing. He could almost hear the hiss and clang of steel.

Cynthia looked away. "A noble quality." She was plainly trying to sound arch, but her voice was barely audible. She cleared her throat and looked back at him. "I would have greeted you with more dignity, but my mare has cast a shoe."

"So I see." Then the import of her words hit home. He frowned. "You were *expecting* to meet me here?"

She nodded. "I thought it only fair to . . . to forewarn you. I thought it might be strange for you to walk in and find me staying at Oldham Park."

An indescribable mix of emotions crashed over Derek like a wave. Chief among them were disbelief and horror, but rage, grief, and chagrin were discernible as well. Cynthia at Oldham Park! Fate must have a cruel sense of humor, to deal him such a blow.

His expression must have reflected some of what he felt, for after glancing at his face Cynthia dropped her gaze nervously to the ground. "I thought if you walked in and saw me—if you remembered me at all—you might say something, or . . . or do something that would betray our . . . our prior acquaintance. And I thought it would be better if . . . if you did not. So I rode out to meet you. I did not want my presence to take you by surprise."

She peeked at his face once more. Whatever she saw there caused her to look away again. She turned to stroke her mare's nose, as if unconsciously seeking comfort. "I meant it kindly," she said defensively.

When he still said nothing, her cheeks began to turn pink. She cleared her throat and tried again. "I am stopping at Oldham Park as the guest of Lady Hannah

Chase. Lord Grafton's daughter, you know. My mother thought it would be prudent to accept her invitation, at least until the roads clear. When they do, I promise you, we will be off to London for the Season. Please believe me, Mr. Whittaker, I had no idea—that is, I knew that Lord and Lady Malcolm would be there, but I did not know that you . . ." Her voice trailed off. She swallowed hard, then tried again. "When I learned that Lady Malcolm's brother was expected to visit, I never dreamed it would be you. I did not know her maiden name, or anything about her. Even when she mentioned her 'brother Derek,' I . . . I thought it was only coincidence. And then I heard them speaking of 'Mr. Whittaker' and . . ." She shook her head helplessly. "All I could do was wait until the morning you were expected, and then ride out to warn you. I was not even sure whether a warning would be necessary, but . . . but I see that it is. So I'm glad I did."

He supposed that once his anger had cooled, he would be glad as well. But he could not bring himself to thank her.

"We should not keep the horses standing," he said. His voice sounded perfectly flat. "Hand me your lead rein."

She hesitated, then did as he asked. Despite their gloves, she was careful not to touch his hand—a futile gesture, since she would have to do so in a moment. He gathered the reins in his right hand and silently held his left hand out to her. She stared at it, her expression blank.

"Take my hand and step on my foot."

Comprehension flashed across Cynthia's face and, with it, dismay. "Oh, I—I couldn't."

He smiled derisively. He had no intention of showing her any extraordinary courtesy. She didn't deserve it. "What would you like me to do, my lady? Give you my horse and gallantly walk beside you all the way to Oldham Park? No, thank you. It's been a long journey, and I'm tired."

Color flooded her lovely face. She bit her lip. "Of course. How silly of me."

She took a deep breath, then resolutely grasped his hand. As she stepped on his foot, he pulled her neatly up onto the saddle before him. Their movements seemed to synchronize naturally, rendering the difficult maneuver as smooth as if they had rehearsed it a hundred times. But the jolt of touching her again, of having her actually *in his arms,* was almost more than Derek could bear.

"Well done," he said, hiding his pain behind sarcasm. "It's hard to believe we've never even danced together."

He felt her stiffen, but she said nothing. He could not see her face. Was she blushing? He doubted it. He doubted if she had the grace to feel shame over what she had done to him. From what he knew of her, Cynthia was rarely moved to feel shame—or, indeed, much of anything.

He had made it his business, after it was too late, to learn what he could about her. It had been almost an obsession, trying to make sense of what had happened. He had thought that if he understood her, if he found that there had been compelling reasons why she had acted as she did, it would help him achieve some peace of mind. The attempt had failed. He had never made his peace with Cynthia's rejection. But he had learned to despise her, and that had answered nearly as well; by nursing his anger he had been able to set the incident aside and move on with his life. For that's all that his association with Cynthia had been: an incident. He would not ruin his life over a girl he had known for less than an hour.

He had to remind himself of that resolve frequently during the next few minutes.

Five miles to Oldham Park, he promised himself desperately. Five miles only. He hoped his calculations were wrong and it was less. Much less. At this excruciatingly slow pace, leading a lame horse, sharing a saddle with Cynthia was sheer torture. How long must he hold her like this? An hour? It might kill him.

The silence between them was louder than thunder. It was driving him mad. He had been so sure, so absolutely certain, that if he ever saw her again—which he had confidently expected he never would—he would be completely unmoved. He had worked so hard, cultivating his resentment. He had hardened his heart against her, to the point—he thought—where he was, if not completely indifferent to her, at least reliably angry. But the longer she perched on his saddlebow, soft and warm and beautiful, the more difficult it was to hate her.

He had to despise her. He would lose his mind else. He cast about, striving to find his rage again.

Finally he thought of something snide enough to say.

"Is it too late to offer my condolences for the loss of your fiancé?" he inquired with false politeness. "Apoplexy, wasn't it? I heard that he died very suddenly, and only a few weeks before the wedding. What a tragedy that must have been for you."

He felt tension ripple through her before she replied. "You, of all men, know exactly how *tragic* it was for me." Her voice was low, but he heard every word.

"On the contrary. I know nothing about it." He scarcely recognized himself, he sounded so harsh. "I know nothing about you, in fact. Why don't you tell me how it was?"

She squared her shoulders. "I accept your condolences," she said coolly. "Let's leave it there, shall we?"

Ah, that was better. Anger whipped through him like a tonic, clearing his head.

She obviously felt that she owed him no explanations. Very well; he needed none. He knew she had not suddenly, over the course of a week, moved from fearing Sir James to loving him. She had chosen Filey despite her loathing of him and had agreed to marry him for the coldest of reasons. His investigation, superficial as it had been, had easily uncovered that much.

Sir James Filey, with all his myriad flaws, had been fabulously wealthy. Cynthia had simply sold herself to the highest bidder. Derek had never had a chance of winning the Frost Fair's hand, because the Frost Fair's hand was not winnable. It could only be purchased.

In fact, the more he thought on it, the more suspicious he became of her presence at Oldham Park. Why would a mercenary mantrap like Cynthia Fitzwilliam waste her time hanging about in a house full of females? The duke's two sons were married and unavailable. He wouldn't put it past Cynthia to make a play for the elderly duke, but there would be no profit in that, either; the duchess was in excellent health for her age. Cynthia certainly had not landed on the duke's doorstep in expectation of Derek's arrival. For one thing, his visit had been unplanned; it was Natalie's letter that had brought him. For another, even now, in possession of Crosby Hall, his fortune was not large enough to tempt the likes of Cynthia Fitzwilliam.

What, then, was her game?

They finished their journey in silence. His arms ached from the effort to avoid touching her more than strictly necessary, and he'd warrant her back ached from her own efforts along that line. She had sat up, stiff as a poker, rather than rest her body against his.

When their little procession wound its way up the last of His Grace's graveled drive, a groom came running to meet them, concern and alarm in every line of his features. Derek pulled his weary horse to a halt, and the groom reached up to help Lady Cynthia alight.

"Lack-a-day, what's this, then? Did she cast a shoe? I hope you were not hurt, my lady," exclaimed the groom.

"No, of course not, Jacobs. I am perfectly well." She landed on her feet, a bit unsteadily, and straightened her hat. "Thank you." She did not turn to thank Derek. Instead, she walked toward the house without a backward look.

Derek climbed stiffly down, tossed the groom a coin, left a few instructions for Max's care and stabling, and followed where Cynthia had gone. The few items he had brought with him would be carried up to the house in good time. Meanwhile, he wanted to forget Cynthia and turn his attention where it belonged, to Natalie.

The enormous foyer was empty when Derek trudged up the steps to Oldham Park's grand entrance. Cynthia had disappeared. Just as well. He discerned the duke's butler, a dapper old gent with a kindly mien, hastening toward him down the side passage.

"Mr. Whittaker, sir! We've been expecting you all morning, but I never saw you arrive. I'm sorry to leave you hanging about in the hall."

"Not your fault, Cummings; I came by way of the stables. How are you?"

"Oh, very well, sir, thank you. Well as ever. I trust you've had a pleasant journey?" Derek supposed that his expression, whatever it was, spoke volumes. Cummings's quick eye ran over him and, before he had a chance to reply, the butler's smile widened with sympathy. "Ah, well, you needn't answer that. It's over and done with, at any rate! Might I bring you a little something in the library, sir? Or would you rather I show you to your room?"

"My room, please. I think a wash would do me as much good as a glass of brandy."

"You shall have both," Cummings promised, leading the way. "We've put you in the blue room, sir. I hope it meets with your approval. It's not as large as the suite you had when last you visited, but we've put the Ellsworths in those rooms, so it can't be helped."

"Anything will do, Cummings. I consider myself one of the family, you know."

"Indeed, sir, that you are," said Cummings warmly. "And if I may say so, sir, Lady Malcolm will be overjoyed to learn of your safe arrival. Have I your leave to take word to her directly?"

"The sooner the better. How is she, Cummings?"

The butler must have sensed Derek's anxiety. He shot him a look that was almost fatherly. "Perfectly stout, I assure you, sir. Nothing to worry about. But, if I may speak frankly? Thank you, sir." His voice dropped to a confidential whisper. "I believe she's feeling a bit low, Mr. Whittaker. It's rather a burden, you know, being surrounded by the family, and everyone so anxious for a boy."

"Aye, it would be," agreed Derek.

"Here we are, sir. The blue room."

"Thanks very much. I say, Cummings."

"Yes, sir?"

"Do I know the Ellsworths?"

Cummings looked mildly surprised. "Do you not, Mr. Whittaker? Dear me. I should have explained. They are very old friends of the family, sir. Sir Peter Ellsworth is the holder of a large estate in Derbyshire.

He and Lady Ellsworth generally visit with us for a few weeks this time of year. And a friend of Lady Hannah's, Lady Cynthia Fitzwilliam, is stopping here as well, with her mother, Lady Ballymere."

"And that is all?"

"Yes, sir. Lord Grafton and his family, Lord Malcolm and his family, the Ellsworths, Lady Ballymere and her daughter, and yourself. A small party. With Lady Malcolm in a delicate condition, it was thought best that we refrain from entertaining on a grand scale this year."

"I see. Thank you." Derek was about to dismiss the butler, but paused. What had Cummings said about the Ellsworths? *A large estate in Derbyshire.* And doubtless known to make an extended stay with the Chase family this time of year. Had he stumbled on the reason for Cynthia materializing at Oldham Park?

He looked back at Cummings. "Tell me, Cummings. Do the Ellsworths have a son with them, by any chance?"

The butler looked even more surprised. "Yes, sir. They do, indeed. Their son, John, a most amiable young man."

"Their *eldest* son, no doubt?"

"Their only child, sir. How did you know?"

Derek gave a bark of mirthless laughter. "Just a lucky guess, Cummings. Just a lucky guess."

Chapter Four

B y the time Cynthia reached her bedchamber, reaction had set in. Her hands were shaking. Her lower lip was quivering. It was only through an effort of will that she prevented tears from welling in her eyes. The shock of seeing Derek again had been greater than she had anticipated. And his contempt for her had been intense, deeper even than she had feared it would be.

It now seemed laughable that she had doubted he would remember her. Of course he remembered her. She had been a fool, telling herself how unlikely it was that he would. She had deluded herself into believing that things were different for men, that the encounter that had changed her forever had probably meant nothing to him. But it had meant something to him. Cynthia had humiliated him, and a man never forgot that.

Thank heaven she had ridden out to meet him. She had told herself that she was going to warn him, "just in case." But her attempt to intercept him, to warn him that he must brace himself to endure her company, had really been an attempt to arm herself. She did not want to see him again for the first time in a room full of other people.

Well. She had doubtless received the treatment she deserved. He obviously remembered her just as clearly as she remembered him. And he despised her, as any right-thinking man would.

The change in his demeanor was hard to bear. Recalling the ardent warmth that had lit his face when he looked at her, it was painful to see how cold and forbidding his aspect had become. He was still breathtakingly handsome, with the same heart-melting brown eyes, the same tall, athletic build, and that gorgeous hair that made a lady long to run her hands through its thick, dark waves. It hurt to think that she would never have that opportunity again. It hurt to think that he would never smile at her with his heart in his eyes, the way he had three years ago. She had thrown it all away. She had killed it.

At the time, she had honestly believed that she had no choice. If that was true then, it was just as true today. But *was* it true? She was no longer certain. At seventeen, everything had seemed so clear. But the older she grew, it seemed, the more she questioned . . . well, everything. With every year that passed, she knew less and doubted more. It was horrid, but she couldn't seem to help it.

She closed the door behind her and leaned against it, removing her hat with trembling fingers. She was exhausted. She had slept little last night. As soon as she had known, beyond doubt, that Derek Whittaker was Lady Malcolm's brother—in truth, the physical resemblance was so strong, she felt she ought to have guessed it immediately—her anxiety had been at fever-pitch. She had ridden out directly after breakfast to make sure she encountered him on the road. Her objective achieved, all she wanted now was rest.

Part of her longed to crawl back into bed and stay there for a week. But that was, of course, the most cowardly part. She would not surrender to her fear. She would get up again, go downstairs, and face Derek. Eventually. She moved numbly toward the narrow couch, unbuttoning her jacket and trying not to think.

"Cynthia, dear? Is that you?" Her mother's fretful voice sounded from the adjoining room. "Heavens, child, where have you been? I've been half mad with worry."

"I'm sorry, Mama. The mare cast a shoe," called Cynthia. "I've only just returned." She sank down on the couch and dropped her head back against the ridge of smooth mahogany that ran along its back. She closed her eyes, heaving a deep sigh. *Rest now. Think later.*

But, of course, she would not be allowed to rest after making such a sensational announcement.

"Mercy on us!" Rapid footsteps approached. "Were you thrown?"

"No, Mama." She opened her eyes. Her mother, clad in a loose dressing gown and clutching a still-wet pen, stood in the doorway that linked their bedchambers.

"Well, thank goodness for that. Put your feet up, child. I'll ring for a nice, hot bath. We can't have you falling asleep over your cards tonight. I heard you promise Mr. Ellsworth a hand of piquet. And although it's often best to let the gentleman win—"

"A bath sounds lovely," said Cynthia quickly, before her mother could go any further down that path. She softened her interruption by obediently putting her feet up. "But I'm not as tired as I would have been. I only had to walk for a short while." She took a steadying breath, bracing herself to say Derek's name without betraying any emotion. "I happened to encounter Mr. Whittaker on the road. Lady Malcolm's brother, you know."

"That was fortunate." Lady Ballymere tugged briskly on the bell rope. "So he brought you back to the house, did he? What's he like?"

Cynthia closed her eyes again, to avoid meeting her mother's keen gaze. "Young," she said vaguely. "He looks quite a bit like Lady Malcolm, in fact. Tall, like her. And he has the same dark eyes. The same smile. His hair is like hers, too."

"Oh, I don't care for curly-haired men," said Lady Ballymere a bit too quickly. "There's something distinctly feminine about curls, don't you think?"

"Yes, Mama," said Cynthia obediently, suppressing a flash of irritation. But she could not resist adding, "Although Mr. Whittaker's hair is not as curly as his sister's."

Lady Ballymere gave a rather unconvincing little laugh. "You seem to have studied him quite carefully."

Cynthia again felt the frisson of annoyance, and again suppressed it. "I saw what anyone would see."

Fortunately, a housemaid scratched on the door in answer to Lady Ballymere's summons, so her mother was occupied for a moment in ordering Cynthia's bath. By the time the door closed once more behind the maid, Cynthia had recovered her poise. It would not do, to let her mother see how close her emotions were to the surface.

Lady Ballymere hovered, irresolute, near the center of the room. "Well," she said at last, "I shall just go and finish up my letter to your father. Enjoy your bath, my love."

Cynthia managed a smile. "Thank you, Mama."

Lady Ballymere swept out of the room, but paused just beyond the doorway. "Is he handsome?"

Cynthia tried to look puzzled. "Whom do you mean?"

"Young Mr. Whittaker, of course."

She pretended to consider the matter. "Yes, I believe you would call him handsome. But you may judge for yourself tonight, Mama. I daresay he will be present at dinner."

"Pooh! As if what *I* thought made any difference." But Lady Ballymere seemed reassured; Cynthia must have convinced her that Derek had made no particular impression. She left Cynthia alone, at any rate, to bathe in peace.

It was excessively tiresome to be watched all the time, but Cynthia understood her mother's reasons. It would be catastrophic for Cynthia to fall in love. Her entire family was bound in a silent conspiracy to prevent that calamity. So far, they had been successful . . . as far as they knew. Lady Ballymere's attempts to monitor Cynthia's opinions regarding every man she encountered were annoying, but at least they were transparent. Cynthia saw the little digs and prods coming and was able, therefore, to deflect them somewhat.

She used to feel guilty about the tiny deceptions she practiced every day, pulling the wool over her mother's prying eyes. No more. The battle to maintain her privacy had loomed ever larger over the years. Her need for privacy now superseded, in her mind, her mother's right to know. And in the present circumstances—with so much to hide—she would fight fiercely to evade her mother's constant poking and probing. A girl had to have *some* secrets.

The relaxing effect of the bath enhanced her tiredness. She dried her hair before the fire, then crept between the sheets of her bed and slept dreamlessly. She woke, hours later, to her mother's gentle shaking.

"Cynthia, my love, are you ill? It's time to dress for dinner."

She sat up groggily. "As late as that? No, Mama, I am not ill." She swung her legs over the side of the bed and yawned.

Lady Ballymere regarded her worriedly. "I hope you are not contracting a cold. It's most unlike you, to sleep the day away."

"I didn't sleep last night." The unguarded words slipped past her sleep-drugged wits. Cynthia immediately regretted them.

Her mother's eyes sharpened. "Why ever not?"

"I don't know." That was almost a lie, and Cynthia was sorry for it. She amended it by saying, "It doesn't matter." Still, she could not meet her mother's eyes. She stood and wandered toward the wardrobe. "Shall I wear the yellow crepe tonight, or the blue silk?"

Matters of dress were Lady Ballymere's chief preoccupation. As Cynthia had hoped, her mother's thoughts were instantly diverted. "You wore the blue silk last Wednesday."

"I don't mean the dark blue. I mean the new one." She lifted the gown from the box where it had been packed. Tissue paper drifted to the floor. Shimmering folds of ice-blue silk cascaded over her fingers. "I've never worn it."

"No, no, my dear. That's glacé silk, not suitable for a mere family dinner—even at Oldham Park. We're saving that one. Tsk! Let me repack it; you'll crease the fabric." Lady Ballymere almost snatched the dress from her and began deftly folding it, frowning as she did so. "You must not be careless with your clothing, Cynthia. You know perfectly well how limited our resources are."

Oh, yes, she knew perfectly well.

The complaining tone in her mother's voice did not escape her, either. She knew it was considered her fault that the family's resources were limited—not that she had done anything to limit them. She was held responsible for doing nothing to *replenish* them. The fact that her betrothal to Sir James had brought ten thousand pounds into the family's coffers three years ago had not satisfied her parents. On the contrary, it had whetted their appetite for more. And no one but Cynthia saw any unfairness in blaming her for the family's straitened circumstances. True, everyone agreed that it was Lord Ballymere's enthusiasm for fast horseflesh and high living that had run them into debt. But since everyone believed that Cynthia could rectify the situation, if she only *would,* the family's resentment was aimed squarely at her.

And, lately, she had begun to aim a little of her own resentment right back at them. This phenomenon was so unsettling that Cynthia could scarcely acknowledge it, even to herself. But her resentment was quietly growing, nevertheless.

She donned the shell-pink dinner dress her mother chose, deferring, as usual, to her mother's authority. But beneath the surface, Cynthia suffered tiny stirrings of mutiny. She said nothing, of course. She just wished—silently—that she could have worn the ice blue.

She needed to feel herself the Frost Fair tonight. She needed to look the part. She looked far too inviting in baby-soft pink. It warmed her complexion and softened all the edges she worked so hard to sharpen. The flattering hue made her look lush and winsome and approachable. Tonight she needed to look—she needed to *be*—as remote and untouchable as the winter moon.

The drawing room at Oldham Park was cozy. Magnificent, but cozy. The effect was achieved through a wood fire that crackled at one end of it, and a diminution of the room's gigantic proportions through judicious placement of the furniture. When Derek arrived, a footman was just lighting the last of the tapers that brightened the seating area. The duke and duchess had settled near the fire, but both rose courteously to their feet as Derek entered.

66

"Mr. Whittaker, how lovely to see you again," murmured the duchess, extending her hand with old-fashioned charm. "Welcome to Oldham Park."

Derek bowed over her hand, expressed his appreciation at being allowed to come and keep his sister company, then turned to bow to the duke. The formality of the duke and duchess's manners maintained an illusion of distance, but Derek knew that their hospitality was sincere. Malcolm's parents cherished warm feelings for their children, and, for Malcolm and Natalie's sake, were even prepared to extend those warm feelings to Derek.

The duke invited Derek to sit. He did so, taking a place near the duchess, and she favored him with a slight smile. "How did you find your sister, Mr. Whittaker?"

"Very well, thank you, Your Grace." His eyes twinkled. "Although she doesn't seem to realize it."

The duke nodded in approval. "So I think. Nothing to worry about. She has a fine, healthy glow about her."

The duchess gave a mournful little sigh. "Ah, poor girl. To me, she seems quite worn down. But you men know nothing of what we women suffer."

"Nor do we wish to," Derek agreed. "I'm told the child kicks so hard at night that it wakes even Malcolm."

"Excellent," exclaimed the duke. "He'll be a true Chase. Strong and vigorous."

Derek almost winced. Natalie had told him, in despairing tones, that His Grace invariably used the masculine pronoun when referring to the babe. She dreaded handing the Chase family another disappointment. Pippa's birth had been bad enough. Everyone adored the toddler now, but when she had first arrived, the entire Chase family had been cast into gloom.

As if summoned by his thoughts, the drawing room door opened to admit the Honorable Philippa Chase, who ran in as fast as her short legs would carry her. Derek instantly abandoned the formality he had donned for the duke and duchess. He dropped on one knee, opened his arms, and shouted, "Pippa!"

The child ran straight at him, squealing with delight. "Unca Deck!" she crowed. He caught her, laughing, and planted a loud kiss on her plump cheek.

"Have you been a good girl?"

"Goo' girl," she asserted, nodding so emphatically that her dusky ringlets bounced.

Malcolm's older daughter, Sarah, was never far from Pippa's side. She entered the room with the dignity befitting an elder sister, scolding with mock exasperation. "Pippa, I *told* you not to run. How are you, Uncle Derek?"

"Missing my best girl. How are you, sweeting?" He scooped Pippa up in one arm and rose to give Sarah a hug with the other. Sarah considered herself too old to be petted like a baby, but Derek suspected that a girl still several months shy of her ninth birthday was young enough to need a little cosseting. She ducked her head shyly, but she did hug him back, and her cheeks went pink with pleasure.

It always tickled him to see Sarah and Pippa

together. There was no discernible likeness between the half sisters, because each favored her mother. Robust Pippa had Natalie's dark curls and enormous brown eyes, and seemed to be born to laugh. Sarah was delicate and serious, with pale hair and paler skin, and the spectacles perched on her little nose made her look wise beyond her years. But their mutual devotion was a pleasure to witness. It spoke volumes for Natalie's ability to link her little family with bonds of affection stronger than mere blood ties.

Malcolm and Natalie walked in behind Sarah, bringing up the rear. Natalie leaned heavily on Malcolm's arm. She was wearing a loose gown that made her seem huge, but Malcolm handled her as gently as if she were the daintiest object in the room. He saw to Natalie's comfort, settling her beside the duchess in the place Derek had vacated, before turning to shake hands with his brother-in-law.

"How are you, you young ruffian? Natalie tells me you rode all the way up here *ventre à terre,* you were in such a hurry to reach her. Don't you think I know how to take care of my own wife?"

Derek grinned. "I didn't want to miss the big event. Looks to me like I arrived in the nick of time."

"Oh, I do hope you are right," exclaimed Natalie fervently. "It seems to take forever."

The duke coughed. The conversation was obviously growing a little too frank, in his austere opinion, for the innocent ears of his granddaughters. "Sarah, child, come you here," he commanded, patting the stool before him. "Tell your grandpapa what you did today."

Sarah obediently left Derek's side and went to sit with her grandfather. Derek, still holding Pippa, pulled Malcolm aside.

"I've listened to Natalie all afternoon. Now I'd like to hear what you think," he said, lowering his voice so the others could not hear. "Is it true that your brother and his brood are hanging about, waiting for her to deliver the babe? Can we do anything to encourage them to leave?"

Malcolm gave a short laugh. "Well, that's blunt," he remarked.

"Sorry! I've nothing against Lord Grafton—"

Malcolm waved this off. "I know, I know. But Arthur and his lot have no business crowding round while my poor wife is trying to deliver a child. The weight of everyone's expectations is getting to be a bit much. I feel it myself."

"His Grace referred to the babe a moment ago as 'he.' "

Malcolm's lips pursed ruefully. "He does so on a regular basis. And the rest of the family has fallen into the same habit, I'm afraid."

"I say, Malcolm . . ." Derek hesitated, then plunged ahead. "They do think of Natalie as a Chase by now, don't they? What I mean is—"

"I know what you mean," Malcolm interrupted. "And yes, they do. Her acceptance here is *not* contingent upon her producing a boy."

"Well, that's all right, then," said Derek, relieved. "The thing is, you know, Natalie once feared that your family would disapprove of her. I've always been grateful that your parents seemed to accept her without a murmur—but I've wondered, and I daresay Natalie has as well, how much of that was due to . . . well . . . the circumstances of your marriage."

Malcolm grinned. "You mean the fact that I never mentioned her to my family until I had already married her?"

Derek grinned back. "Well, yes. Since you put it so frankly."

Malcolm shrugged. "If my parents felt any qualms about my choice of bride, they never expressed them. Perhaps they never felt any."

"The point is, dear chap, we'll never know," said Derek dryly. "Since you presented them with a fait accompli."

Malcolm's gaze traveled to his wife, and his expression softened. "I admit, it never crossed my mind at the time. I wanted her, and I married her. I daresay I should have dragged her up here and put her through her paces beforehand—to set her own mind at ease, if nothing else. But Natalie has a natural elegance about her, an elegance of mind as well as an air of good breeding. And if that weren't enough to win over my starchy relations, the fact that she makes me very happy—not to mention my little Sarah—was more than enough to seal the bargain. Everyone adores her, Derek, as I knew they would." He turned back to his brother-in-law, amusement crinkling the corners of his eyes. "She knows it, herself, when she's not suffering through the end of a pregnancy. Producing a child apparently turns a woman's brains to mush."

"So I've heard." Derek cocked an eyebrow at Malcolm. "It occurs to me that if you can't convince the others to depart, you might take Natalie somewhere else. Even the dower house?"

"Out of the question." Malcolm rubbed his chin, frowning. "Tempting as it sounds. My father would be furious, in his own subtle way." He straightened, animated by a new thought. "It's bad enough that the family is hanging about, but did you know we've got outsiders here as well? Ghastly. You'll meet them in a minute, I daresay. The Ellsworths. They're very old friends, but this is the wrong time to fill the house with people whom Natalie doesn't know. And then, to top it off, Lady Ballymere and her daughter landed on us—complete strangers, at least to Natalie and me— and we're stuck with them as well."

Derek had spent the better part of an hour mentally preparing for this moment, when someone would mention Cynthia. Still, he had to consciously relax his shoulders to keep his tension from showing. "That's odd," he said casually. "What brings those two here?"

Malcolm shrugged. "Apparently Lady Cynthia was invited by Hannah, God alone knows why. You'll remember Hannah, Derek. Arthur's middle daughter. The two eldest married last year and the two youngest aren't out yet, so Hannah is the young lady of the family these days. At any rate, once she invited Lady Cynthia, Lady Ballymere had to be included. And now they mean to stop here until the roads improve." His voice had gone very dry. "Since the roads are generally abysmal in England, no one can fathom how long their visit might last."

"Well, the roads *are* in bad shape at the moment," Derek admitted. "I can vouch for that. But you're right; even in the best of conditions, one never knows when a sudden downpour will render the roads impassable. What's their game?"

"Game?"

"What's their true reason for coming here? If you know."

Derek realized, too late, that his tone sounded unnaturally urgent. Malcolm looked mildly surprised. "That's a strange question. Do you think they have some ulterior motive?"

The answer was *yes,* but Derek could not say so without setting the cat amongst the pigeons. While he wrestled with how to reply, Pippa suddenly began squirming. "Down," she demanded. Derek obliged, and she scampered off to clutch at her mother's ample skirts.

The door was opening again. Derek's nerves jangled briefly, anticipating Cynthia's entrance, but subsided when Malcolm's older brother, Arthur Chase, Lord Grafton, entered with Lady Grafton. Three of their five daughters trailed in their wake. Directly behind them came several persons whom Derek did not recognize. His interest piqued, he studied them intently. These must be the Ellsworths—the hapless targets of Cynthia's greed.

Sir Peter was a genial-appearing soul. Lady Ellsworth seemed pleasant as well. The son, however, was the member of the party that irresistibly drew

Derek's eye. He was younger than Derek had thought he would be—and utterly unremarkable. Modest of height, modest of dress, he had a slightly pompous way about him that added nothing to his consequence. He wasn't ugly. He was simply . . . ordinary.

Derek felt slightly let down. He had hoped to find something spectacular about John Ellsworth. Whether he had anticipated spectacular loathsomeness, such as Filey had had, or spectacular worthiness, he hardly knew. But *something*. Nothing whatsoever stood out about Mr. Ellsworth. In fact, the chap was downright muffin-faced.

Apart from his wealth, was there anything about Mr. Ellsworth that might honestly attract a female? Especially a female of Cynthia's radiant beauty? Derek burned with unholy curiosity. As soon as he decently could, after greeting Lord Grafton and his family and making his bow to Sir Peter and Lady Ellsworth, he went to shake John Ellsworth's hand. He was determined to engage the fellow in conversation. He was a little ashamed of the impulse that drove him, but he could not resist.

Mr. Ellsworth's face was round and his hands were soft. He was so much shorter than Derek that Derek could see where, notwithstanding his youth, Mr. Ellsworth's hair was thinning at the crown of his head. Still, he seemed a harmless sort of chap. He beamed up at Derek in a vague, good-natured way upon making his acquaintance.

"Whittaker, isn't it? Ah de do? They tell me you're Lady Malcolm's brother."

"Yes, that's right."

"Well, well. Dessay she'll be glad to have a familiar face about."

"I hope so." Derek cudgeled his brain to think of something to say. "I understand you live in Derbyshire."

Mr. Ellsworth perked up. "Yes, that's right. D'you know Derbyshire?"

"No."

"Ah."

There seemed to be nothing more to say. Mr. Ellsworth hooked his thumbs in his waistcoat and rocked on his heels, humming under his breath.

"You a sporting man, Mr. Ellsworth?"

"Eh? Oh, ah, not much. I've been known to take a rod out from time to time. Bit of an angler, you know." He illustrated his words with a helpful casting motion, evidently to prevent misunderstanding.

"Is the fishing good in Derbyshire?"

"Tolerable. Tolerable." He rocked again, humming. "Don't get out as often as I would like," he added at last.

The conversation ground once more to a halt. Derek opened his mouth to try again, but the drawing room door opened and he made the mistake of glancing up.

Whatever words he had been about to say died on his lips. His brain seemed to disconnect from his body and float up to the ceiling. There his wits hovered, out of reach, while he gaped like a helpless idiot below.

Cynthia. The sight of her shot him through with actual, physical pain. It was as if Cupid's evil shadow had arrived, firing arrows dipped in poison. How could a man harden his heart against such beauty? The answer was: He couldn't. All he could do was stand his ground while the arrows hit home, one by one by one. A quiverful of anguish, aimed unerringly at Derek's bosom. He could almost hear their stinging onslaught: *Ping. Ping. Ping.*

He dragged his eyes from the vision that was Cynthia and forced himself to concentrate, however dazedly, on the woman who entered with her. This must be Lady Ballymere. She was a slim, pretty, nervous-looking woman, as high-strung and graceful as a thoroughbred mare. As she glided into the room, she gave a rather artificial-sounding laugh.

"Dear me! We always seem to be the last to arrive. I hope we have not kept you waiting, Your Grace."

"Not at all, Lady Ballymere," said the duchess placidly. "We have still several minutes before the hour strikes. Are you acquainted with everyone here, I wonder? I think you may not have met Mr. Whittaker; he has only arrived this afternoon."

Lady Ballymere turned to Derek with an overly bright smile. "No, I don't believe we have met."

The duchess extended her hand, indicating that Derek should step forward. "Pray allow me to introduce you. Lady Ballymere, this is Lady Malcolm's brother, Derek Whittaker. Mr. Whittaker, Lady Ballymere."

Derek managed a creditable bow and said the expected. "I am honored."

What a blessing social rituals were. At times of

76

crisis, they were invaluable. No need for rational thought; one simply moved and spoke as one had moved and spoken a hundred times before.

Lady Ballymere's sharp gaze flicked over Derek. Her smile, already patently false, cooled even further. "How do you do?" she said coldly.

This was so strange that Derek's befuddled wits gathered and focused. Lady Ballymere was evidently taking him in dislike. He could not imagine what he had done to offend her. Nothing whatsoever, it seemed, since he had never laid eyes on her until this moment.

It occurred to him that this must be where Cynthia had learned her manners. His lip curled in cynical amusement.

The duchess, oblivious to the hostility gathering in the air above her, gestured toward Cynthia. "Lady Cynthia, may I present Mr. Whittaker?"

Cynthia had stayed in the shadows near the door. Now she moved quietly into the light. "Thank you, Your Grace, but Mr. Whittaker and I have already met." She paused. Derek wondered whether she would acknowledge meeting him in London. Evidently she would not. She continued with, "He very kindly escorted me back to the house today, after my mare cast a shoe."

"Indeed?" The duchess looked from one to the other. Derek had no idea what, if anything, his expression conveyed; he could feel a muscle jump in his jaw as he tried to appear impassive. Cynthia gave nothing away. She stood with eyes downcast, detachedly studying the carpet. He envied her her poise.

"Well, that was highly fortunate," said Her Grace with her customary calm. "I am sorry to hear that your mount went lame. So distressing! I shall send word to the stables that they must be more careful. I'm glad you were not hurt, my dear."

"Thank you, Your Grace."

Lady Ballymere was still watching Derek through slightly narrowed eyes. "I vow, 'twas monstrous kind of you to take my daughter up in your carriage, Mr. Whittaker."

She did not sound grateful. She sounded highly suspicious. Nettled, Derek gave her an urbane smile. "'Twas even kinder than you think it was, Lady Ballymere, since I had no carriage. We had to share a horse."

He had hoped, uncharitably, that his words would annoy her. But the effect was more than he had bargained for. Lady Ballymere's eyes widened in momentary shock—and, he could have sworn, fear. She shot a look at Cynthia that he could not interpret, then turned back to him.

"I hope my daughter did not inconvenience you," she said. Her lips were stiff with disapproval.

What was the matter with her? He tried to make his smile more convincing. "Not at all." He meant to reassure her. However, he could not resist adding, "It was my horse that was inconvenienced. I was merely crowded a trifle."

Lady Ballymere plainly did not like the picture that his remark conjured. Her lips compressed into a thin

78

line. "Crowded? I see. But I suppose you could have relieved the crowding, had you elected to lead the animal."

"Certainly," Derek agreed. "That would have been easier on the horse. But not nearly as enjoyable for me."

John Ellsworth gave a muffled guffaw, and Lord Grafton's three daughters giggled. But the duke and duchess were not amused, and neither was Lady Ballymere.

Cynthia's glacial calm seemed undisturbed, but Derek was hyperaware of her. He sensed, rather than saw, the alarm that quivered through her at his jibe. She immediately intervened to break the moment, stepping languidly forward to say, with every appearance of boredom, "It was a large horse, Mama, and the distance was not great. I believe Mr. Whittaker is joking you."

"Is he? I see," said Lady Ballymere tonelessly. "Very amusing."

Chapter Five

She could feel his eyes on her. At every lull in the conversation they fell on her, willing her to look up and return his gaze. Resisting their pull took enormous concentration. She longed to meet his gaze. She wished she dared to stare right back at him. She wished he would look away, so she might have the luxury of gazing her fill of *him!* But that was unthinkable, of course. Even were it possible to sneak a glance at him undetected, she would not dare to try. She must not. Derek Whittaker was not for her.

Avoiding Derek's eyes seemed to diminish the rest of her senses. She tasted none of her dinner. She heard none of the pleasantries that flowed around her. When called upon to contribute to the conversation, she answered almost at random. By the time the covers were cleared away, her head ached with the effort to behave normally. Beneath her calm exterior, every nerve was jumping.

In addition to Derek's burning gaze, she was keenly aware of her mother watching her with accusing eyes. Cynthia felt trapped between the two of them. Derek she could avoid—she hoped—but Mama's recriminations must be dealt with. It was best to get them over with sooner rather than later. When the ladies withdrew from the table, Cynthia deliberately fell into step beside her mother, bracing herself for yet another trial.

She was not kept waiting. Lady Ballymere took her arm at once, leaning in so they would not be overheard.

"You did not tell me that Mr. Whittaker shared his saddle with you."

Cynthia shrugged, trying to appear indifferent. "Did I not? I suppose it did not strike me as important."

"It strikes *me* as important." Her tone had a definite edge to it. "You are not the blacksmith's daughter! Why did you not have a groom with you? Or a footman?"

"This is not our home, Mama. We are guests. I

thought it would be vastly inconsiderate to take a servant away from his tasks merely to suit my whim."

Her mother pounced on this. "In that case, you should have asked Mr. Ellsworth to accompany you. He is a guest as well, with nothing better to do. I'm sure he would have been happy to oblige."

"It did not occur to me to ask him," said Cynthia truthfully.

Lady Ballymere frowned in exasperation. "Cynthia, when will you learn to consult me before you act?" she exclaimed. "There are so few situations where a lady may, with perfect propriety, spend time alone with a gentleman! Had you asked Mr. Ellsworth to ride out with you, you might have furthered your acquaintance without poor Hannah following you about like a Tanthony pig."

Cynthia felt herself tense. She did not like to hear her mother speak disparagingly of her one and only friend. Cynthia had many admirers, but friends, she had found, were harder to come by.

"Mama, pray do not forget that we owe our presence here to Hannah's invitation."

"I do not forget it," said Lady Ballymere crossly. "It's just unfortunate that Lady Hannah demands so much of your attention. Attention that would be better bestowed *elsewhere*." This last was said in a significant whisper. "I merely point out that you squandered an opportunity today."

"Yes, Mama," said Cynthia listlessly. "I will try to do better."

Lady Ballymere seemed mollified by this. She

81

patted her daughter's arm and addressed her in a more affectionate tone. "The truth, I suppose, is that you simply wanted to ride alone. You have ever been thus."

This was a safer subject. Cynthia embraced it with gratitude. "I am fond of solitude," she admitted.

"I daresay your father and I have indulged you over-much." Lady Ballymere gave a regretful little sigh. "We ought to have impressed upon you that a lady does not ride about the countryside unchaperoned. It is dangerous."

A ripple of laughter escaped Cynthia. "Dangerous? I am an excellent horsewoman. Papa saw to that."

Her mother's irritated frown returned. "I do not doubt your skill, Cynthia. But I'm afraid I must question your judgment. It adds nothing to your consequence, to be seen sharing a horse with a gentleman. I cannot imagine why you consented to do so." She pulled her shawl more closely round her shoulders, giving the fringe a sharp little tug. "And, to be sure, it says little for Mr. Whittaker's judgment," she added tartly. "Taking you up before him, as if you were the veriest hoyden. Most ill-bred, upon my word! Far, far too familiar. But then, he seems a flippant, disrespectful young man. He should have given you his horse. You should have insisted upon it, my dear."

Cynthia tried not to sound as annoyed as she felt. "Mama, that is unfair. Pray remember that he was just completing an arduous journey. How could I ask him to walk?"

But here they reached the drawing room and their privacy was, perforce, at an end. Cynthia was glad of it. She entered the lighted area with relief, joining Hannah on the settee. It was a refreshment to the spirit, she thought, just to be with Hannah. Hannah was so undemanding.

Her friend gave her a shy, admiring smile. "How beautiful you look," she blurted. Hannah's complete lack of envy was one of her most endearing qualities . . . and, Cynthia often suspected, was the only thing that made their friendship possible. "Did you have that gown made up in London?"

"No. It is Irish." Cynthia smoothed the gleaming folds of taffeta across her lap. "I would not admit that to another living soul," she said teasingly.

Hannah giggled. "Your secret is safe with me. Such a lovely color! I wish I could wear that shade."

Hannah was dressed very correctly for a girl of nineteen in a modest, but elegant, Indian muslin. It was true that the white of her gown was a better choice for her than soft pink would have been. The delicate tint would have made Hannah's already pink complexion appear red as a beet.

"Your own costume is quite becoming," said Cynthia loyally.

Hannah pulled a face. "Thank you. I look plump as a pigeon in it, of course. But that can't be helped."

Cynthia was hard-pressed to think of an answer to this. Hannah *was* short and plump; there was no denying it. Fortunately, Lady Ballymere drifted over to the two friends and perched on a nearby chair, smiling archly. She interrupted them before Cynthia needed to reply.

"Lady Hannah, I am agog to know your opinion of Mr. Whittaker. You have known him for some time, have you not? A most handsome young man. Or so I think."

Cynthia felt her hackles rise again, but Hannah seemed to see nothing suspicious in Lady Ballymere's overture. "Mr. Whittaker is very handsome," she agreed innocently. "He and Lady Malcolm are often mistaken for twins. And I think my aunt Natalie a very pretty person."

"He seems agreeable as well."

"Oh, he is more than that." Hannah suddenly sat up, animated. "He is the kindest man imaginable. You know, I have always been stupidly afraid of horses—always!—and last year he taught me to ride. Just a little, but no one had been able to teach me anything before. He was so patient, and never once laughed at me. I was excessively grateful."

"Oho! Handsome *and* kind. He sounds the perfect match for some lucky young lady." Lady Ballymere shot an amused glance at Cynthia, inviting her to share the joke. "I wonder why he singled you out, Hannah, dear? What reason could there possibly be?"

Hannah looked startled. "I don't believe he singled me out, precisely."

Lady Ballymere gave an indulgent laugh. "Was he teaching other young ladies to ride? No?" She tilted her chin as if considering, then laughed again, shaking her head. "Well, I daresay you would think my view of the matter quite impertinent, so I shall not voice it."

She rose and floated off to join Lady Malcolm and the duchess by the fire, so she did not see the bright blush that suffused Hannah's face.

"I . . . I never thought of that," muttered Hannah, stiff with distress. "I *wouldn't* think of that."

"You are too modest," said Cynthia quietly. Pain moved in her heart. Was it jealousy? She refused to examine it. She would think about it later. For now, she kept her attention firmly focused on Hannah's embarrassed face. It bothered her that Hannah evidently thought so little of her own charms. "Is it such a strange thought?" she asked her gently. "That a gentleman might admire you?"

Hannah gave a tiny gasp. Her hands fisted in her lap, clutching her muslin skirts. "Admire *me?* Derek Whittaker?" She shook her head with mute vehemence. "It wasn't like that. I cannot explain, but it wasn't like that."

Cynthia was watching her friend closely. "The notion seems unwelcome to you."

"Of course it is!"

"Why?"

Hannah seemed, for a moment, to be at a loss for words. Then she found her tongue. "Because I wouldn't know what to do with it," she exclaimed, then gave a shaky laugh. "Only think how awkward it would be! I've never been admired, you know. Not in that way. And to have a gentleman like Mr. Whittaker admire me—a man who is such a favorite of the ladies, so sought after . . ." She blushed again, biting her lip. "Oh, it's preposterous! I would never catch the

85

eye of a man like that. You should see the way women look at him! And he is *family,* you know. He is Aunt Natalie's brother. There is something . . . I don't know . . . wrong about it. Or it seems so, to me."

It was silly, Cynthia scolded herself, to feel relieved. Derek's interest in other women was none of her business. Hannah's interest in Derek, had it existed, would also have been none of her business. And yet she was conscious of feeling, rightly or wrongly, that a great weight had been lifted from her mind. She was still wrestling with her wayward emotions when Hannah slipped a hand into hers.

"And besides," Hannah whispered shyly, "I am in love with someone else."

This was news. Cynthia stared at her, amazed. "You are? With whom?"

"Someone I have loved for simply *ages.*"

"You never said a word!"

"You didn't know him."

"Do I know him now?"

Hannah nodded, her eyes sparkling. She suddenly looked much prettier. "Can't you guess?"

Cynthia couldn't. Her mind went completely blank. Hannah, in love! And *not* with Derek Whittaker. The idea that any girl who was acquainted with Mr. Whittaker could somehow fall in love with someone else struck her as inconceivable. She blinked at her friend in baffled astonishment.

Hannah's face was rosy with blushes. She leaned in to Cynthia and breathed, "It's John Ellsworth, of course."

Of course? Cynthia's first reaction was incredulity. It seemed impossible that Hannah—or, indeed, anyone—could harbor a secret longing for the supremely uninteresting John Ellsworth. But Hannah had burst into a whispered explanation, as if spilling her secret had unleashed a torrent of confidences she had been longing to share.

"I've known him all my life. He is only two years older than I, so we often played together as children, and I promise you he has always been so good—so decent—just everything a man should be." Hannah was aglow with tender emotion. "I had the measles when I was eight, and he would come and read to me. Can you imagine? He never showed the least fear of catching the contagion. I was lonely and miserable, and frightfully ill, and he brought in his toy ship and showed it to me, and promised we would sail it on the fish pond when I was well. He sat with me for hours and hours, making things with his hands—he's very good at making things—and talking to me, even when I was too ill to answer properly. I never shall forget it."

"And . . . and you have loved him since you were *eight?*"

Hannah nodded, laughing. "I believe I have. Yes."

This was terrible. Hannah in love with Mr. Ellsworth! Cynthia found she had to look away, to hide her growing consternation. What could she say, to convince Hannah to look elsewhere?

"Perhaps," she suggested at last, "you simply find it easier to talk to Mr. Ellsworth than to other gentlemen. Since you have known him all your life."

"Oh, certainly," Hannah agreed. "I know I am shy, and that I ought to make an effort to overcome it, but I can't seem to help it—especially with men. Most men are very off-putting, don't you think? I never know what to say to them. But I'm completely at ease with John."

"Yes. But that is the point I meant to make." Cynthia cleared her throat delicately. "In other words . . . perhaps if you knew other gentlemen as well as you know Mr. Ellsworth, you might find them agreeable, too." Inspiration struck. "Only look at Mr. Whittaker, for example. When you gave him a chance to be kind to you, he was."

"Oh, I'm sure many men are pleasant and kind. Perhaps most are." Hannah looked thoughtful. "I don't know why it is, but somehow—out of all the kind and pleasant men in the world—one's heart seems to fix on a particular man and want no other."

Cynthia's spirits sank. She certainly could not argue with Hannah's observation; she knew it was true. How many men had danced attendance on her since she turned seventeen and was thrust into the Polite World? It was impossible to count them. And yet, out of all that horde, only one had touched her heart.

One question remained. She studied Hannah's face, trying to read every nuance in her friend's expression. "Does Mr. Ellsworth return your regard?" she asked softly.

Hannah's face fell. "I don't know," she admitted, sighing. "He has never spoken." She fidgeted with her skirt, trying to smooth the area she had twisted earlier.

"We are very young," she said hopefully. "Some girls do marry at nineteen, but John is only one-and-twenty. That's an early age for a man to choose a wife."

"Yes, that's true." Cynthia had to suppress a twinge of guilt. She and her mother had been trying to use Mr. Ellsworth's youth and inexperience to their advantage. But the very qualities that would assist a beautiful girl to trap a man into a loveless match would work against a plain girl who truly loved him.

"And I'm very sure of his friendship," Hannah added. "So, in that sense, I know I have his regard."

Cynthia hesitated. Oh, she had to spare her friend heartbreak if she could! But how to say it in a tactful way? Meanwhile, Hannah had noticed her friend's silence. She was looking puzzled, and slightly hurt.

"What is it?" Hannah whispered.

Cynthia shook her head. "Nothing. It's just that . . . I have heard that men often overlook what is under their noses. I am wondering if . . . if it would be easier, actually, for you to win the affections of someone else. A man who was *not* already your friend."

Hannah seemed about to speak, but her attention suddenly shifted to a point over Cynthia's shoulder. Cynthia turned, following the direction of Hannah's gaze. The door was opening. The men had arrived.

Cynthia felt her pulse begin to race. *Be calm,* she told herself sternly. The duke walked in first, deep in conversation with Lord Grafton and Sir Peter Ellsworth. Lord Malcolm followed, his eyes immediately seeking his wife. Cynthia felt a twinge of wistful envy at the smile they exchanged; it was so warm that one felt compelled to look away, as if intruding on something private. Malcolm headed directly for Natalie's side. Behind him, out of the shadowy passage and into the light, came Derek and Mr. Ellsworth.

She felt Hannah sit up straighter, and, out of the corner of her eye, caught her friend's welcoming smile. Poor Hannah! Now that Cynthia knew her friend's secret, Hannah's feelings for Mr. Ellsworth were painfully obvious. Cynthia thought she would rather die than be so transparent.

Still . . . there was something wonderful about Hannah's wholeheartedness.

What would it feel like, she wondered, to smile like that, with no thought of whether one's smile would be returned? What would it feel like, to wear one's heart on one's sleeve? It took *courage,* Cynthia suddenly realized. She looked again at Hannah, new respect dawning in her. Hannah, for all her shyness, was brave in ways that Cynthia was not.

It was a disturbing thought. Did she owe her legendary poise, the self-possession she prided herself on, to *cowardice?* She had to admit it was possible. It was definitely fear she felt as Derek walked through the door. In response to her fear, she assumed her customary posture of graceful impassivity—aware, for the first time, that it was a defensive gesture. It was fear that was setting her features, even now, into their habitual mask of serene reserve. Donning her Frost Fair disguise made her feel safe. Or, at least, safer.

From behind her wall of self-control she watched Derek. Inwardly she was a mass of quivering insecurities, confident of nothing. Outwardly she displayed utter composure. She knew she had perfected the pose; no one would guess the turmoil she felt, just being in the same room with him. No one would guess, from her cool, faintly bored demeanor, that she would lie awake tonight burning with heartache.

And, as fate would have it, Derek had entered with Mr. Ellsworth! Seeing them side by side, in stark contrast to each other, it was impossible to deceive herself. Hannah was right. One's heart settled on a particular man and wanted no other. Waves of despair battered Cynthia. What a colossal fool she had been, telling herself that all she required in a husband—after escaping Sir James Filey by the grace of God—was a kind heart.

She had no reasonable hope of finding happiness wed to John Ellsworth, however kind he was. It had been a mistake to pretend, even to herself, that she might. And now, in addition to the misgivings she already felt about Mama's ambitions, Cynthia must face wounding Hannah through her actions.

All in all, it had been a dreadful day.

Chapter Six

It was blessedly cold in the passage. Cynthia halted on her way back to the drawing room and pressed her exhausted forehead against the cool wallpaper.

Solitude. Thank heaven. What a wonderful thing it was to be alone, away from the flaring candles and the roomful of eyes.

The eyes in the drawing room expected her return. She could not hide from them forever. She wished it were possible to escape to her bedchamber but, unfortunately, she had already slept for several hours this afternoon. If she excused herself early, claiming to be tired, her mother would be alarmed. And she could not face another inquisition. Not tonight.

The chill silence enveloped her, soothing her. She closed her eyes and slumped against the wall, limply allowing it to hold her up. Soon it would be possible to go back. Soon. But not yet. She needed a minute's time. Just a minute to herself. Then she could face them all again and go on with the charade . . . pretending that she felt nothing, when in truth she was miserable.

It was colder than Greenland out here in the passage. Where the devil was she? She'd freeze to death in that wisp of a frock she was wearing.

Not that he cared, of course.

Right.

Derek's lip curled in bitter amusement at his own folly. He did care. It was ridiculously obvious. He didn't know how to stop caring. He had tried anger, and anger had failed him. What next? Was he doomed to pine for the heartless jade forevermore?

And there she was. He halted in his tracks, the cold air forgotten. He had come in search of Cynthia—the more fool he. Well, he had found her. Now what was he going to do about it?

And, more to the point, what was wrong with her?

She seemed to be half-swooning. Her slender form sagged against the wainscoting. Her face was pressed to the wall. The remnants of Derek's hostility melted into nothingness at the sight of her distress.

He stepped forward. He had to, though he cursed himself for it. He could no more turn away from her pain than he could stop breathing.

"Cynthia?"

She gave a startled gasp and spun to face him. She was still pressed against the wall. Now her hands moved back to clutch it, fingers splaying against the flat surface. It was an oddly vulnerable, self-protecting gesture, as if she sought reassurance that there was something solid at her back.

He understood the impulse. For him, too, the world seemed a suddenly dangerous place. A world where three years' worth of anger could crumble in an instant was a world where anything might happen. The furniture might dissolve. The floor might fall away. Solid walls might evaporate. The line between reality and fantasy had blurred, and Derek was no longer sure he was awake.

He must be dreaming; her eyes were too blue. Nobody's eyes were that blue. Only Cynthia, Cynthia in his dreams, had eyes like that. How could she be real? How could she be *here,* in this house, in this passage between the rooms, in this private place with him, alone?

But she was here. She was real. No dream could be this vivid. He could see her eyes dilating, see the tiny flutter of her pulse beating in her throat. He could sense the rush of her breath. The tremble of her lower lip, a tremble echoed at her neckline where the warm flesh beat high against the silk, betrayed the emotions she struggled to hide from him.

Oh, Cynthia. A rush of unexpected tenderness swamped him. *You cannot hide from me.*

She mustn't cry. Why did she feel like crying? He had startled her. The shock of being near him again, all unprepared, must be too much for her. He had caught her off guard, that was all.

No. That was not all. Had she forgotten? There was something about this man that crumbled her defenses. Oh, how could she have forgotten that?

Helpless, she stared at him and felt her knees go weak. All her resolve, the will to be strong, seemed to drain out of her. She might hide her secret self from all the world, but not from this man. From this man, she could hide nothing.

A sense of hopelessness washed through her. Was it possible to feel despair and exhilaration at the same time? Evidently it was. She had tried so hard to erase him from her heart! Until today, she actually believed she had succeeded. It seemed incredible to her now, that she had ever convinced herself of such a lie. And yet, had they never met again, she might have gone on believing it.

Was she glad or sorry to have the truth revealed? To know, indisputably, that she had been touched by something that people searched their entire lives to find? She was glad. And, of course, she was sorry. She

94

had never felt so glad about anything. She had never felt sorrier. Gladness and sorrow, exhilaration and misery, spilled through her in a rush of cold and hot and utter confusion.

She had told herself, over and over, that her so-called feelings for Derek had been wholly imaginary. She had come to believe that the man she longed for did not exist, that she had created him out of dreams and yearning, as young girls will, and that the man she remembered was largely a product of her own imagination. But here he was, as solid and inescapable as reality itself. She could no longer delude herself into thinking she had exaggerated that long-ago encounter. Here stood the man she remembered, in the flesh, to prove that whatever she had felt when she met him had been every bit as earth-shattering as it had seemed.

He stood so close it made her dizzy. His shirtfront gleamed in the dim light. He smelled good. Everything about him shot pleasure through her, from the strong planes of his handsome face to the expression in his eyes when he looked at her. His eyes . . . so dark, so compelling. She stared into them, her heart soaring and breaking simultaneously, and saw them fill with compassion. Tenderness.

The bitter stranger who had shared his horse with her was gone. Before her stood Derek. Her own Derek, the man she had dreamed of and longed for, despite all her efforts to forget him. Her secret love.

She seemed to glow in the semidarkness, pale and

pastel and shimmering. She was a creature of ether, fragile as gossamer, insubstantial as illusion. If he tried to touch her, would she shatter?

No matter. He was going to touch her, if the contact splintered them both. Angel or phantom, shadow or solid, he was going to touch her.

He reached for her. He had to. The impulse to reach for her was stronger than his pride. And she swayed toward him as if in a trance. They came together like magnet and steel, caught in a mutual, spontaneous pull and dragged into each other's arms as if by an irresistible force.

There was nothing gentle about this kiss. Nothing tentative. Derek saw Cynthia's features swim out of focus as she dreamily lifted her face, heard the sharp intake of his own breath, and then crushed her mouth beneath his. The instant their lips met, insanity seized them both. Years of desire denied, of emotions suppressed, burst their confines and exploded.

He plunged into the kiss, famished. And she responded, incredibly, with a hunger that outpaced his. She met him move for move, clinging to him, frantic with need. Her eagerness urged him to greater and greater madness. Spurred by his own amazement—for this was *Cynthia,* beyond all hope, beyond all imaginings, *Cynthia* in his arms—he dived into the flood of sensations and willingly drowned.

It could not last, of course. He lost all sense of time and place but knew, even through the swirling emotions pounding him, that it could not last. Eventually she tore her face away, gasping, and hid her features in the breast of his coat. She pressed her forehead against the broadcloth the way she had pressed it against the wallpaper earlier—as if hiding her face could make the world disappear.

Deep, shuddering breaths wracked her. His own chest was heaving. For a few moments, neither of them could speak or move. Then Cynthia, with what seemed a Herculean effort, pulled herself out of his arms and turned away from him. She lifted a shaking hand to her mouth, as if checking to make sure her features were still in place after that ruinous kiss.

"Cynthia," said Derek hoarsely. It was as far as he got. She lifted her hand in a sharp, urgent gesture, palm out, imploring him to be silent. Begging him to keep his distance.

He waited quietly, watching her averted face. It was obvious to him that she was trying, pathetically, to reassemble her fractured composure. She was still struggling for breath, but soon she would fight her way back to normalcy. And once she regained her poise, she would undoubtedly try to belittle what had just occurred. He could not allow that.

He stepped forward, ignoring her gesture of supplication, and placed his arm around her. She threw her head back as if in agony, sucking in a ragged gulp of air.

"That's enough," he said with quiet authority. "You have tormented yourself long enough. And me," he added.

Cynthia gave a strange little moan, shaking her head. "You don't understand," she said in the thread of a voice.

Well, that was true. He didn't.

"Come," he said gently, leading her resistless body to a settee against the wall. They sat, and she sagged against his body in defeat.

"Oh, this is terrible." She seemed to be speaking to herself; her voice was barely audible. "What shall I do?"

"Marry me, I should think."

He could have kicked himself. What an idiotic, flip thing to say. The problem was it was impossible to behave properly while his heart was singing with joy. Cynthia was in his arms, and he didn't care why or how she got there. He was drunk with happiness.

His absurd proposal had no discernible effect on Cynthia. She neither stiffened in outrage nor turned her face up for another kiss. She merely sat there, expressionless, as if she had not heard him. Then she sighed.

"We must go back," she said tonelessly.

"Not yet," said Derek firmly. "You can't ignore a chap's offer of marriage. Granted, I did it badly. But the words have been said. They require a response."

She gave him a wan little smile. "I wasn't sure I heard you properly. I—I'm not thinking very clearly."

"Nor am I." He sat up and took her by the shoulders, turning her to face him. Her expression was woebegone. He longed to wipe the unhappiness from her eyes. He cradled her cheek in his palm, his fingers gentle as they curved against her soft skin. "But I'm thinking more clearly every minute," he whispered. His throat was thick with emotion. "Cynthia, I love you."

She flinched, her eyes darkening with fear. "No."

"Yes." He was completely sure. "I don't pretend to understand it. But I love you."

"Then you must stop." She shivered, pulling away. "You must stop loving me," she repeated dully. "As I must stop loving you." She took a deep breath and faced him again, trying to smile. "It can't be that hard. We don't even know each other. Our lives have never touched. We can go our own ways and never miss each other."

He searched her eyes and saw that she was serious. His brows knitted in consternation. "That's rubbish. I know we haven't had a chance to become well acquainted. But whatever has sprung up between us is real. It can't be set aside. It can't be ignored."

"Then it must be forgotten."

"I tried for three years to forget it." He spoke with unaccustomed vehemence. "Didn't you?"

She closed her eyes against the pain. "Yes," she whispered. She sighed again, rubbing her forehead tiredly. "What a shambles I've made of my life."

Down the passage a door opened, spilling light and sound into their sanctuary. Lady Ballymere emerged, peering about like Diogenes, lamp in hand. When she saw Cynthia and Derek sitting side by side in the darkness, alarm flitted across her features. "Cynthia? Are you unwell?"

Derek rose politely. "I found her leaning against the wall a moment ago," he said. "I thought she should sit down. But I think she's better now."

"Yes," said Cynthia a bit unsteadily. "Thank you,

Mr. Whittaker." She allowed him to help her rise.

"Good heavens." Lady Ballymere's eyes darted suspiciously from Cynthia's pale face to Derek's and back again. "Good heavens," she repeated, moving forward to take her daughter's arm. "My poor darling." She touched Cynthia's forehead with the inside of her wrist, checking for fever. "I wondered earlier if you felt unwell."

"Just a touch of headache, Mama. Perhaps I should go upstairs and lie down."

"Certainly, my love. An excellent idea." Lady Ballymere pulled Cynthia gently away from Derek, then glanced over her shoulder at him. The temperature in the passage instantly seemed to drop ten degrees. "I wonder if you would make our excuses for us, Mr. Whittaker."

He bowed. "Of course. I hope Lady Cynthia feels better by morning."

"I'm sure I will be myself again," said Cynthia tonelessly.

Derek caught her hidden message. Feeling better and feeling like herself again were not necessarily the same thing. Perturbed, he watched them head for the stairs, Lady Ballymere holding the lamp high and guiding Cynthia's steps with a firm arm round her waist.

How strange. He had confessed his love and had been told that his love was returned. This should be a joyous moment. And yet his predominant mood was one of disquiet. He didn't like the way that Cynthia allowed her mother to lead her. There was something passive and listless about it. Something that he knew, instinctively, boded ill for him.

He watched Cynthia ascend the stairs, each slow step she took moving her farther and farther out of his reach. The light went with her, and Derek was left alone in a place that seemed darker and colder than before.

Chapter Seven

"Drink your chocolate, my love." Lady Ballymere, her dressing gown billowing around her, sank onto the spindle-legged chair near Cynthia's window. The morning sun streamed in behind her, bathing her daughter's bed in blinding light.

Cynthia winced, shading her eyes with one hand. "It's terribly bright this morning. Mama, would you mind—"

Lady Ballymere hesitated, tapping one nail on the arm of her chair. "Very well," she said at last. She rose and, with obvious reluctance, drew the draperies back across the window. "Although I think the sunshine might do you good."

Cynthia felt she had scored a small victory. Being forced to face her mother, pinned by harsh light while Mama sat with her own face shadowed, would have definitely put her at a disadvantage. She relaxed against her high-piled pillows and sipped obediently at the edge of the porcelain cup. "Thank you, Mama."

Lady Ballymere returned to her chair. Now that

Cynthia was no longer dazzled by the undraped window, she saw that her mother appeared unusually tense. When she spoke, her voice was taut. "I trust you are feeling well enough to face the day?"

"Yes, Mama."

"I am glad to hear it." Her fingernail tapped rhythmically against the chair arm. "You worried me yesterday."

"I am sorry, Mama. It was nothing. I was just a trifle out of sorts."

"It was not your headache alone that worried me." *Tap. Tap. Tap.* "If you are truly feeling better, I feel I must speak to you. I hesitate to voice my concerns, Cynthia. I hope I am mistaken."

Cynthia felt her pulse jump. *Here it comes.* She said nothing and kept her eyes firmly on the cup and saucer she held, refusing to alter her docile expression.

"It seems to me that Mr. Whittaker, in the brief time he has been here, has . . . Well, I hardly know how to put this. He has not taken liberties, precisely. At least, I hope he has not." Lady Ballymere paused, one eyebrow delicately raised.

She was plainly inviting Cynthia to confirm or deny this. When Cynthia said nothing, her mother's expression darkened. "Well. Be that as it may, it seems odd that within the space of a few short hours he managed, first, to take you up before him on his horse. And, second, to seclude himself with you in a darkened passage. Very odd, indeed." When Cynthia still said nothing, her voice became sharp. "I hope you will put my mind at ease, Cynthia, and tell me that these incidents were coincidental."

"They were coincidental, Mama."

"Were they harmless?"

"Yes, Mama."

"He took no liberties?"

Indeed, he had taken no liberties. Cynthia had given freely. "None, Mama."

Tap. Tap. Tap. Lady Ballymere looked far from satisfied. "I must take your word for it, of course," she said peevishly.

"Thank you, Mama."

Her meekness was not producing the desired effect. Lady Ballymere looked even more dissatisfied.

"Cynthia, I wish you would be open with me," she exclaimed, pressing her palms together for emphasis. "We have had this discussion before. I thought you understood that we cannot afford to take you to London, Season after Season, with no results. It is imperative that you marry *this year*."

"I know it, Mama."

"Very well. Then you also know that we must, we absolutely *must,* guard your reputation. You cannot allow even the *appearance* of impropriety. The slightest whisper of gossip would be fatal."

Cynthia almost choked on her chocolate. She replaced the cup carefully in the saucer, trying not to laugh aloud. "Mama, it is far too late to fret over that, surely? I have been the target of malicious gossip for years. Since I made my first curtsy, in fact."

"Pooh. The gossip you speak of is the type that arises from jealousy, pure and simple," said Lady Ballymere scornfully. "I do not regard it. A girl with your degree of beauty must always cause a sensation. That is not the sort of gossip I fear. If anything, it *adds* to a man's interest in you."

"It has been hard to endure, nevertheless," said Cynthia. Her voice was quiet but steady. "And—forgive me?—I do not agree that the gossip about me is idle talk. Nor do I think its source is jealousy. Not all of it, at any rate."

"What do you mean, child?"

"I did not understand, at first. All the whispers and the stares. I did not know what I had done to bring such censure down upon my head. But now that I have been abroad in the world a trifle, I realize how . . . how *inappropriate* some of our choices have been."

Lady Ballymere shifted restlessly in her chair. "Nonsense. Do not try to change the subject, Cynthia. We are speaking of Mr. Whittaker. I am cautioning you to keep him at a distance."

The saucer had begun to tremble in Cynthia's hand. She set it on the bedside table before the rattle of the teacup could betray her agitation. She was conscious of an impulse to speak her mind, for a change. Did she dare? Her mother had asked her to be more open. Very well. She would try a little openness and see how Mama liked it.

"I am not changing the subject," she said, trying not to sound defiant. It went against the grain, to contradict Mama. "We are speaking of the dangers of gossip. You told me I must avoid the—what did you call it?—the appearance of impropriety." She took a deep breath. "I am saying that, in my opinion, we have given the appearance of impropriety for the past three years. And especially during my first Season."

Lady Ballymere goggled at her. "What, in heaven's name, are you saying?"

She wished she could stop trembling. What she was about to say had bothered her for so long! It was high time she said it aloud. She *must* say it aloud. It was childish, it was cowardly, to feel such morbid dread of incurring her mother's displeasure.

"Mama," she said carefully, "I understand why you thought it necessary to bring me out at seventeen. I realize the exigencies of our financial situation. In hindsight, however, I think it was wrong to dress me so frequently in gauze and tiffany. I must tell you, I believe many of the gowns you had made up for me were immodest. Almost *indecent*."

Surprise held Lady Ballymere silent for a moment. She blinked once. Twice. "It was the fashion," she said at last.

"Not, I think, for very young girls."

But her mother's moment of feeling nonplussed was over. She rallied, waving a dismissive hand. "One must follow the mode. Would you have me dress you like a dowd? I think not. Trust me, love, your innocence shone through. And even in your first Season, your conduct was irreproachable."

"Oh, exemplary! My behavior was so circumspect, in fact, that I became known as the Frost Fair." Cynthia looked ironically at her mother. "You know of that nickname, do you not?"

Lady Ballymere seemed to be hiding a smile. "It came to my ears once or twice," she admitted.

"I adopted the guise early. I maintained it in part because I was still a child, and unsure of myself," said Cynthia softly. "And in part to defend myself against the impression created by my gowns."

"Pooh!" scoffed Lady Ballymere. "What a to-do about nothing. The sobriquet did you no harm. In fact, my love, I can tell you now that my choice of style for you was deliberate." She sat up, growing animated as the discussion shifted to matters of dress. "I own, I still think it was an inspired choice! The combination of your Nordic coloring, your extraordinary beauty, the revealing clothes, and your naturally off-putting manners—well! I cannot but think that we owe your success to the juxtaposition of these elements."

Cynthia stared, amazed, as her mother's eyes grew dreamy. "You are very lovely," Lady Ballymere explained, "but you have a great deal of natural reserve. Had we dressed you just as all the other young girls were dressed, you might have been overlooked. I could not take that chance." She laughed gently. "It's astonishing how much of a woman's appeal is determined by her personality. Many of the females who pass for beauties are no such thing! They merely have charm. You, my dear Cynthia, have true beauty."

"But no charm," said Cynthia woodenly. Was this what her mother thought of her?

Lady Ballymere made a little moue of disagreement. "I did not say you had *no* charm. But you lack vivacity."

"I see." She took a breath to steady herself. "So, in order to stand out from the crowd, I had to reveal as much of my body as possible."

No wonder she had attracted the notice of every rake in town. The painful truth grew clearer every moment. Her mother had dressed her like a doll and then set her out as bait for men who wanted a pretty toy.

Lady Ballymere prattled on, seeming oblivious to her daughter's growing horror. "Mind you, I could not have put you in those clothes—beautiful as you were in them—if you *were* vivacious. That would have created a very off impression. But since your demeanor was so perfect, so utterly unapproachable . . ." She shrugged lightly. "You took your rightful place among the most sought-after females in London."

Cynthia had to glance away; she could not bear it. "I certainly attracted a great deal of attention."

"That you did." Lady Ballymere sounded pleased with herself.

"Including the attention of Sir James Filey." Cynthia's hands fisted as she remembered. She forced herself to meet her mother's eyes. "I attracted his attention almost immediately."

Lady Ballymere's pleased expression faded a little. "Yes. Well. In hindsight, that might have been unfortunate, I grant you."

Cynthia covered her face with her hands. "Unfortunate. Oh, Mama. How could you?"

"I said it *might* have been unfortunate," said Lady Ballymere testily. "All's well that ends well."

"Mama, I almost married him! And it was all your

doing." She dropped her hands and stared at her mother, anguished. "I did not know what you were about, but you surely did. You *sold* me to Sir James."

Lady Ballymere stiffened. "Cynthia, really! Marriage is not slavery."

"My life would have been a living hell."

"Pooh! You exaggerate."

"You don't know." Cynthia tried, and failed, to keep her voice from shaking. "You don't know the things he did to me. The things he said. He had a . . . a penchant for extremely young girls. He told me so. And he seemed to think that my reserve, my aversion to being touched and kissed by him, was"—her voice dropped to a shamed whisper—"exciting." Tears of revulsion welled in her eyes. "The more frightened I became, the better he liked it. He—he went out of his way to frighten me, Mama. To make certain that I loathed and feared him." She shook her head in helpless horror. "I can't tell you how it was. I have no words to explain such . . . such wickedness."

Lady Ballymere looked genuinely aghast at this. "My poor darling! Is this true?"

"Of course it is true! Would I *invent* such a tale?"

Her mother wore the oddest expression, a mixture of shame and disbelief. "I cannot believe it," she said in a low tone. She seemed to be talking to herself. "Oh, I cannot believe it."

Cynthia was silent. It was obvious to her that her mother did, in fact, believe her. The words of denial were a reflex, no more.

Eventually Lady Ballymere lifted troubled eyes to

her daughter's. "Why did you not tell me at the time?"

It was Cynthia's turn to look surprised. "I tried to tell you, Mama."

Her mother almost flinched. It was true that Cynthia had tried to tell her. She must remember, as clearly as Cynthia did, the times when Cynthia would beg her to listen and she would refuse, slamming out of the room while Cynthia collapsed in tears. At any rate, Lady Ballymere seemed unable to face the memory of those days. Her restless hands clasped tightly in her lap.

"Sir James's death was a judgment on him, I daresay," she said hurriedly. "To pass so suddenly, almost as if struck by the very hand of God—well! People whispered at the time that it was a judgment on him. His reputation, I think, was . . . unsavory. I liked him less and less, the more I saw of him. But, indeed, child, I did not know the whole."

"Mama, you *should* have known." Cynthia took another deep breath, bracing herself to say what she must say. It was so hard to criticize her mother! "You should have made it your business to know. You should have inquired on my behalf. Or you should have had Papa do so. Did you not know that Sir James made an offer for one of the Laxton girls, only a few years before we met him? And that she ran away to escape him?"

"That was only a rumor," said Lady Ballymere defensively. "I thought it untrue. He paid court to her, to be sure, but she married Lord Mablethorpe directly afterward, and everyone said it was a love match—"

"But you knew the rumor?" Cynthia exclaimed.

"You had heard it? Why, oh, why, did you not investigate?"

"That will do," said Lady Ballymere sharply. "Cynthia, you forget yourself. I have always had your best interests at heart. Sir James made a very handsome, very flattering offer. His terms exceeded everything even contemplated, let alone proffered, by your other suitors. We were not in a position to turn down such a generous offer. Although," she added hastily, "you may rest assured that we would have protected you somehow, had his behavior passed the bounds of decency."

Cynthia gazed bleakly at her mother. "You would have done nothing. Once the knot was tied, you would have had no power to help me." She lowered her eyes to her lap, afraid of displaying her rising anger. "You cared more for Sir James's thirty thousand pounds than you cared for me."

"Rubbish. And, besides, he had a great deal more than thirty thousand pounds," said Lady Ballymere with asperity. "You would have been an exceedingly rich woman. Thirty thousand is merely what he agreed to pay in marriage settlements. Not, of course, that any amount of money would have compensated us, had he mistreated you. But he did not mistreat you."

"Only because he did not, after all, marry me."

"But he did not marry you," snapped Lady Ballymere. "This is a fruitless discussion. You are bemoaning a fate that did not befall you."

Cynthia gave a strangled little laugh. "That's true," she admitted. "What a pity that Sir James did not live

110

to see our wedding day. Forgive me if I cannot extend the wish *past* that date, but had he survived the ceremony you would have had your thirty thousand. And I would have been free of all your expectations."

Lady Ballymere gasped aloud. "Cynthia! I am surprised at you."

"I'm sorry, Mama." She bit her lip, as surprised by her outburst as her mother had been. It *was* unlike her, to express herself sarcastically. "I do not mean to sound ungrateful or . . . or unfilial."

"I should hope not." Lady Ballymere fidgeted with the cuff of her dressing gown. "And you must not think we are ungrateful to you, by the way," she added grudgingly. "It would have been a sacrifice, I know, for you to have married Sir James. Under the circumstances, I am glad you were spared. And although we had received only the first third of what he had promised, ten thousand pounds is still a considerable sum. Do not think us unappreciative."

"Thank you, Mama," said Cynthia hollowly.

Lady Ballymere's voice softened. "But we—all of us—must sacrifice in the name of duty, dear child. It's a hard world, I'm afraid. And hardest on females."

"Yes. I know. That is the way of the world." *But why?* She longed to ask, but knew there would be little point. Her mother would think she was complaining, and a well-brought-up female did not grumble. So she gave her mother a strained smile and kept the rest of her questions to herself.

Lady Ballymere beamed affectionately at her daughter. "I do not think it unreasonable, my love, for you to prefer a husband who will treat you well. I am glad we have found a younger, kinder man for you this time."

She meant John Ellsworth. Something like panic shot through Cynthia. She plucked at the edge of the coverlet, trying to organize her jumbled thoughts. "Mama," she said hesitantly, "would it be so very dreadful if I did not marry Mr. Ellsworth? He may not offer for me, you know."

Agitation propelled Lady Ballymere from her chair. She bounded to her feet with an agonized exclamation. "Cynthia, do not say so! Do not even *think* it. You must make more of an effort, my love." She began pacing, her dressing gown swirling around her. "Mr. Ellsworth is very young. Young men require encouragement. Your standoffishness may work very well with older men, men who have found their way in the world. Older men appreciate a challenge. But you cannot keep a man like Mr. Ellsworth at a distance and expect to win his affections."

"I do not wish to win his affections."

The statement came from her heart; it passed her lips before she realized she had said it. The words stopped her mother in her tracks. Lady Ballymere turned and stared at Cynthia, apparently thunderstruck.

Cynthia hurried into speech, afraid her courage would desert her if she delayed. "I am sorry, Mama," she said quickly, "but I think your plan will not work. Pray do not blame me! I learned last night that Hannah loves Mr. Ellsworth."

Dismay flitted across Lady Ballymere's features. "Good heavens." Her mouth worked soundlessly for a moment. "Good heavens," she repeated faintly. "Does he return her regard? I have seen no sign of it."

"I do not know. But—"

"Oh, I am sure he cannot. It is impossible. He cannot love her." She returned to her pacing, obviously thinking hard. "And you are so beautiful, my dear, and so much more experienced than Hannah in attracting men. Whatever he may feel for her at the moment, I am confident you will have no difficulty in luring him from her side. So we need not worry overmuch, even if he does feel a slight *tendre* for poor Hannah."

"Mama! You cannot expect me to deliberately steal the affections of a man whom Hannah loves! She is my friend."

Lady Ballymere halted again, rounding on Cynthia with an outraged gasp. "Indeed? And what am I to you, pray?"

Cynthia shrank back against the pillows as her mother advanced toward the bed, her eyes narrowed. "Do you place your friend higher than your parents? Higher, indeed, than your entire family?"

Cynthia felt a little dizzy. This was exactly what she had feared. She had pushed too hard and had brought down her mother's wrath upon her head. "No, Mama. Of—of course not."

"You have a *duty,* Cynthia. You are not free to follow your inclinations in this matter. Your father and I have tried very hard to defer to your wishes, as far as we could. You said you wanted a kind husband;

very well, we have found one for you. Do you think that men of substance grow on every tree? Has it been *easy* to locate a suitable partner for you? You know it has not. Unless you wish to look among the merchant class, Cynthia—something that would grieve us very much—you will not find such another as John Ellsworth. Wealthy gentlemen are exceedingly hard to find, and wealthy *young* gentlemen are even rarer. Once Mr. Ellsworth reaches town he will be surrounded by females competing for his notice. Here in this secluded spot we have the perfect opportunity to attract, and retain, his undivided attention. For heaven's sake, Cynthia! Do not squander this chance."

Cynthia hid her shaking hands beneath the coverlet. She loathed her own cowardice, but she could not seem to help it. She feared anger, all sorts of anger, in herself as well as in others. Her mother's anger was hardest of all to bear. Still, for Hannah's sake, she must make one more push.

She swallowed hard. "What of Hannah?" she asked. She did not sound defiant. She sounded miserable. "Am I to ignore her feelings entirely?"

Lady Ballymere sat on the bed, studying her daughter's face with a keen scrutiny that sent alarms ringing all through Cynthia. "I think," she said slowly, "that if you wish to do Hannah a good turn, you should direct her attention to Derek Whittaker."

She could not hide her shock. "You're joking."

"Not at all."

"But—but that will not do. You hinted at it last

night, and Hannah did not care for the idea."

Her mother smiled cynically. "She thinks she cannot attract a man of Mr. Whittaker's obvious charms. And in the ordinary course of nature, she could not. But she is, after all, the daughter of a marquess and the grand-daughter of a duke. Lady Hannah Chase may marry whomever she chooses."

Cynthia's heart was racing like a rabbit's. She forced herself to breathe evenly. "That may be, but I think she will not choose Mr. Whittaker. She thinks of him as a member of her family."

Lady Ballymere gave a dismissive snort. "Non-sense. He is her uncle's brother-in-law—not a true relation. I call it an excellent match. She is sufficiently above his station to tempt him, despite her lack of beauty. And his personal gifts are such that he could easily turn her affections from Mr. Ellsworth to him-self."

Of that much, at least, Cynthia was sure. Still, she blinked at her mother in frightened amazement. "But this is beyond anything," she blurted. "It is bad enough to set our caps for poor Mr. Ellsworth! Are we now to try our hand at matchmaking?"

Lady Ballymere shrugged lightly. "You said you wanted to consider Hannah's feelings. Really, my dear, we cannot afford to let Mr. Ellsworth slip through our fingers. The best way to cushion your friend from heartbreak, therefore, is to turn her eyes elsewhere."

Cynthia played nervously with the edge of the cov-erlet. "What if . . . what if we left Mr. Ellsworth alone and turned *our* eyes elsewhere? Since Hannah has already formed a preference. What if"—she glanced fleetingly at her mother's face, then returned her attention to the coverlet—"what if I set my cap for Mr. Whittaker instead?"

There. She could not believe she had actually said it. How had she dared? One glance at her mother's angry, incredulous face told her all she needed to know: She would never be allowed to marry a mere country gentleman. Mama was shaking her head in refusal, just as Cynthia had known she would.

"I knew it," said Lady Ballymere bitterly. "I knew Mr. Whittaker was dangerous the instant I laid eyes on him. Tall, dark, and handsome! And not a penny to bless himself with, I daresay."

"He cannot be penniless, Mama. He has an estate near Lord Malcolm's."

"Not one more word!" Lady Ballymere held up a warning finger. She was quivering with rage. "He is a nobody. Do you hear me? His sister's marriage was held to be an amazing stroke of luck. No fortune, no connections, *nothing* to recommend her. Lord Malcolm could afford to marry beneath him, but you, my darling, cannot. I will hear no more discussion on the subject."

Cynthia was properly cowed. She bit her lip and was silent. Lady Ballymere rose from the bed, shaking out the folds of her voluminous garments. "Your father and I have never beaten you, Cynthia," she said in a tight, clipped voice. "But if you continue to play the ice maiden with Mr. Ellsworth, I shall be sorely tempted. *Sorely* tempted. I want you to encourage him, and I want to see you doing it."

She swept to the door and opened it, then turned to level a penetrating stare at her daughter. "I expect to see a change in your behavior, Cynthia. Do I make myself clear?"

"Perfectly, Mama," whispered Cynthia, not daring to move.

"Good." The door clicked shut behind her.

Cynthia took a deep breath, exhaling with a shaky sigh. She was miserable, as she always was when Mama was angry with her. But there was another, newer emotion playing beneath the surface of her misery. Something hot and sharp, something that made her jaw clench and her fingers curl into fists.

Why, she was *angry!* The recognition of it brought her up short. Was it undutiful, to feel anger against one's mother? Was it a sin, to dislike being ordered about?

No matter. She did dislike it. And she was angry.

Chapter Eight

It was a good thing, Derek mused, that he enjoyed wandering about for its own sake. Another man might have worked himself into quite a temper by now, searching high and low for Cynthia and failing to find her. Derek's feathers, however, remained unruffled. The best feature of a ducal mansion, as far as he was concerned, was that the place was vast enough to offer hours of entertainment. One never seemed to come to the end of it, however far one roamed.

Cynthia had not been in any of the places where one might expect to find her. Had she been seeking him as he was seeking her, she surely would have loitered in the breakfast room, the library, or the morning room. She was not in any of these obvious places. Ergo, she was not seeking him.

This was vaguely disappointing, but understandable. Was she deliberately avoiding him? Probably. But Derek did not despair. He was confident of his ability to find her, wherever she might hide. For one thing, he was highly skilled at . . . well . . . skulking and lurking. For another, he was so drawn to her that he half-believed the best way to find her was to close his eyes and follow his feet. He seemed to carry an internal compass that forever pointed him in her direction. So he rambled unhurriedly this way and that, down the spacious, modern corridors and through the ancient, twisting passages of stone, certain that around some corner or another he would encounter Cynthia.

It was simply meant to be.

It was impossible to feel pessimistic in the clear light of morning. What might Cynthia have said, had her mother not interrupted them last night? The possibilities were tantalizing. He could not rest until he got Cynthia alone and asked her, point-blank. Whatever the obstacles fate, or Cynthia, or her family, had placed in the way of their union, he would overcome. He knew he would, because he must. He did not yet know what task lay before him, but whatever it was, he was impatient to begin it.

His wandering feet led him up a servants' staircase—admittedly an unlikely spot to search, but he could not resist its cunningly hidden doorway—and into a long, carpeted hallway. He recognized this place. Malcolm's suite of rooms was here, near the old nursery, which had been recently refitted to house and entertain Malcolm's daughters. It seemed nearly as unlikely a spot as the servants' stairs, but to his surprise he heard Cynthia's voice floating through the open nursery door. He could not make out the words, but he would know her voice anywhere. And he was even more surprised when he heard Sarah Chase reply to it. Sarah said, very clearly, "Snowdrops."

The nursery door was open. That was invitation enough. He strolled over to it with a keen sense of anticipation. Why Cynthia was in the nursery he could not imagine, but there she was, bending over a low table where his niece sat, hard at work. Sarah always took her spectacles off when she was truly hard at work. She claimed that it helped her concentrate, removing everything from her vision except what was directly in front of her. And there lay the spectacles, tidily folded at her left hand.

Neither Sarah nor Cynthia had noticed his arrival. Cynthia lightly touched the paper Sarah was working on and murmured, "I'd know them anywhere." Then, as she usually did, she seemed to sense his eyes upon her. She looked up. Derek felt a pleasurable jolt of electricity when her eyes met his, and the colors in the room immediately brightened. Remarkable.

He broke into a grin; he couldn't help it. "Good morning."

Cynthia straightened and, to his disappointment, visibly withdrew behind her curtain of reserve. "Good morning, Mr. Whittaker."

The delight on Sarah's face almost made up for Cynthia's lack of enthusiasm. "Uncle Derek! I didn't expect to see you." She reached for her spectacles as a blind person would, her hand going unerringly to the place where she had laid them.

"What's toward? Let me guess. Watercolors." He walked over to join them in studying the sheet of paper. Since the table contained several tumblers of dirty water, an open paint box, and an array of sable-tipped brushes, his guess did not require a leap of genius.

Sarah settled her spectacles firmly on her nose. "Very good," she said, giving him a cheeky little grin.

"Sauce-box." He rumpled Sarah's hair until she squealed and swatted ineffectually at his hand. "When will you learn to treat me with respect? I should upset the water on you. Teach you a lesson."

"Pooh! You never would," said Sarah confidently. She looked up at Cynthia. "His bark is worse than his bite," she explained.

"Where did you hear that phrase?" demanded Derek.

"Nowhere. I read it in a book."

"Well, that's what comes of educating females." He shook his head in mock disgust. "I warn you, don't start mouthing proverbs at me. I won't stand for it."

Sarah giggled, then looked self-conscious when she noticed Cynthia's unsmiling face. "He doesn't mean it, you know," she said anxiously.

Cynthia, seeming to recall her manners, gave Sarah a strained little smile. "Of course not."

Derek sensed that Cynthia was retreating further and that if he did not draw her into the conversation, she would find an excuse to leave the room. He winked at her, jerking his chin to indicate Sarah. "She's a little tyrant, isn't she? Don't let her rope you into admiring her watercolors."

Cynthia looked startled. Sarah cried indignantly, "I haven't *roped* her—have I, Lady Cynthia?"

"No, my dear, you certainly have not." She laid a hand protectively on Sarah's shoulder. "I enjoy looking at your work. You are extremely talented."

"She comes here every morning, Uncle Derek. She likes it here."

He rolled his eyes. "What a rapper! Why would a grown woman *like* hanging about in a nursery?"

To his secret delight, Sarah and Cynthia immediately joined forces and turned on him.

"Uncle Derek, she is a friend of mine—"

"I have always enjoyed the company of children—"

"—and I won't let you drive her away."

"—and Sarah is a particularly delightful child."

He threw up his hands in a gesture of surrender. "Very well. You needn't shout."

"We weren't shouting," said Sarah with dignity. "We were just telling you."

Cynthia had turned slightly pink. "You are joking

again," she observed, giving him a look of reproach.

He smiled at her. "Right. Sorry."

"He is always joking." Sarah gave a disdainful sniff. "It's best to pay no attention to anything he says."

"Here, now!" exclaimed Derek. "Watch what you say, brat. I'm frequently in dead earnest. Frequently," he repeated sternly when Sarah stifled another giggle. "As you'll soon discover, if you don't mend your ways."

"I'm not afraid of you." She lifted one of her wet brushes and pretended to flick water at him. Derek, roaring like an outraged bear, dashed around the corner of the table. A brief chase ensued, followed by a tussle for control of the paintbrush. Throughout, Derek was aware of Cynthia watching in amazed silence as he pinned the wriggling, laughing child to the floor, straddled her, and emerged triumphant, waving the brush like a flag.

It seemed that Cynthia did not know what to make of all this. Derek scrambled to his feet, tugged his waistcoat back into place, and reached out a hand to Sarah, who was still on the floor. Sarah took it, and he hauled her to her feet.

Cynthia looked a little anxious. "Are you all right?" she asked Sarah, moving to smooth the little girl's hair and to brush invisible dust from the back of her frock.

Sarah looked surprised. "Of course."

"It's good for her," said Derek firmly, tossing the paintbrush onto the table. "Keeps her in line."

Sarah leaned affectionately against Cynthia. "He's quite my favorite uncle, you know," she confided.

Cynthia smiled. "Does your mother not mind that he plays so roughly with you?"

"No, for he's her favorite brother as well."

Derek grinned. "That's not saying much," he admitted. "I daresay you haven't met her other brother. No? I congratulate you. Hector's a rather nasty piece of work."

Now Cynthia definitely looked shocked. Derek hastened to reassure her. "He's our half brother. I'll tell you the story one day. I wouldn't want you to think ill of us—Natalie and me—for keeping our distance from him. Once you hear the tale, you'll understand."

Cynthia still stood with one hand resting on Sarah's shoulder. "Your family is quite different from mine," she said softly.

Derek felt his ears prick up. "How so?"

She seemed to hesitate before she spoke. "It's difficult to explain, really. I suppose I would say you are much . . . freer with one another. In various ways." A slight smile disturbed her gravity. "I was never allowed to play with my brothers, for one thing. Or, needless to say, my uncles. Not that it would ever have occurred to me to try." She glanced down at Sarah, who was looking up at her with a very serious expression. Cynthia almost laughed. "Does that seem tragic to you?"

"Well," said Sarah gravely, "I haven't any brothers. But I think that if I were not allowed to play with Uncle Derek, I might be rather lonely."

"You have a sweet little sister."

"Oh, yes, quite! And I do love Pippa. But it's not the same."

"Pippa doesn't pummel her hard enough," explained Derek. "And she's too small—yet—to pin Sarah to the floor."

Cynthia looked puzzled. "But no one enjoys being pummeled and pinned to the floor."

Sarah and Derek exchanged glances. Derek shrugged. Sarah looked back at Cynthia, her expression indignant. "He would never *hurt* me."

The bewilderment on Cynthia's face made Derek chuckle. "Give over, Sarah. Lady Cynthia has never been properly pummeled. Until the day she is, she'll never understand how much fun it can be." He leaned back against the edge of Sarah's table, watching Cynthia. He tried to banish the image that had just taken strong possession of his mind: himself pinning Cynthia to the floor . . . and making sure she liked it. "Tell us about your family," he suggested. "How are they different? Are they more like the Chases than the Whittakers?"

She bit her lip. "It can't possibly interest you."

"On the contrary." He signaled Sarah to second his entreaty. She peered obligingly up at Cynthia, looking like a kindly little owl in her spectacles.

"Pray tell us, Lady Cynthia," she urged. "Are they frightfully stuffy?"

Cynthia laughed aloud at that. "Certainly not. My papa is anything but stuffy. He's quite the avid sportsman. In fact, he taught me how to ride as well as my brothers do. It was mostly *indoor* things I was not allowed to do. Sitting on the floor, for example, or kicking the legs of my chair, or speaking too loudly, or slouching. Running in the house. Taking the stairs two steps at a time. Things of that nature." Her eyes took on a faraway look as she remembered. "I was punished once for sliding on the dining room floor in my stocking feet after it had just been polished. It was great fun, as I recall. Rather like skating. But it wasn't ladylike."

Sarah opened her eyes at this. "You weren't a lady yet," she announced, firing up in defense of the child Cynthia. "And how did you play at jackstraws if you couldn't sit on the floor?"

"I played at a table."

Sarah looked skeptical. "Dull work," she remarked. "I had rather sit on the floor."

This was all highly illuminating, Derek thought. Repressed as a child, Cynthia had grown into a reserved, secretive woman. A woman who feared . . . what? Divine retribution, if she crossed some invisible line? He studied the nearly imperceptible changes in her expression as thoughts and feelings raced through her. There were hidden depths of emotion in Cynthia, as he well knew. He sensed a growing chaos there, as if long-held assumptions, carefully instilled in her by her strict upbringing, were being unexpectedly challenged, one after the other. Was he the source of her confusion? He hoped so. A little confusion never hurt anyone. In fact, it often proved a catalyst for change. And he intended to bring changes to Cynthia's life. Big changes, and soon.

"Judging by the look on your face when I gave my opinion of Hector, your family never speaks ill of one another," he remarked. "We might do well to copy that. What say you, Sarah? Shall we turn over a new leaf? Stop ragging each other?"

"We don't rag each other." Sarah frowned. "Only in jest. That's different."

"But we never mind our tongues, do we?"

"We don't need to." She settled her spectacles more firmly on her nose. "People who understand each other know the difference between a joke and a scold. And everyone needs a little of both."

Derek laughed. "Sarah, my pet, you are wise beyond your years."

"She is certainly talented beyond her years." Cynthia came to the table and bent over the delicate blooms rendered so beautifully by Sarah's hand. "These are lovely. Good enough to illustrate a gardening text."

Sarah ducked her head and beamed, expressing both shyness and pleasure. Seeing that his niece had momentarily lost her tongue, Derek chimed in. The best way to ease Sarah's self-consciousness was to say something ridiculous.

"If you *must* know," he said in a pained voice, "we're all very proud of her. I'm just doing my part to keep the brat humble. A difficult task, as I'm sure you can appreciate. I try to limit my compliments to one per week; no more. Deprivation is good for the soul."

Cynthia looked amused. "Whose soul? Yours or Sarah's?"

He feigned surprise. "Why, Sarah's, of course. My soul was whipped into shape long ago. Hers is still in the formative stage."

He loved to see the spark of laughter in Cynthia's eyes. "Who whipped your soul into shape?" she inquired. "Did you have an uncle, too?"

"No, alas, I was not so fortunate. I had to wait for life itself to teach me, and thus learned everything in the hardest possible way."

"I could wait for life," Sarah offered. "You needn't put yourself out, trying so hard to *help* me."

He placed one hand against his heart and lifted his eyes piously toward heaven. "Dear child! If you only knew the trouble you cause me. But I was never one to shirk my duty."

They both laughed at that absurdity, which pleased him. He held the chair for Sarah and she sat, removing her eyeglasses and placing them, again, at her left hand. A dreamy look came over her as her world went out of focus. She selected a brush, one of the tiniest of her set, dipped it in the water, expertly swirled it against a cake of color, and bent close to the paper. Derek knew, from long experience, that she had already entered a trance-like state, so utterly focused on what she was doing that she was oblivious to their continued presence. They would have to shake her if they wanted her attention now. He smiled. Sarah was an odd duck, but he was, actually, quite proud of her. Fond of her, too.

He glanced at Cynthia and saw that she, too, was aware of Sarah's powerful ability to shut out the world—and that knowledge of this oddity did not lessen her admiration or affection. She lifted her eyes to his and for a flash of time they smiled at each other, walls down. Then she dropped her eyes, and the unguarded moment passed.

He sought to bring it back. "I'm glad you see what we see in her," he said softly. "Not everyone does."

She seemed to know what he meant. "Has she found it difficult to make friends of her own age?"

"I think so."

"Extremely clever children are often a bit eccentric." A wistful smile curved the corners of Cynthia's mouth. "I envy her a little. I wish I had invented, when I was a child, such an excellent way to escape reality."

Sarah's absorption was so complete that they might as well have been alone. Electricity seemed to hum in the air between them. Cynthia evidently felt it, too. She folded her arms in front of her in an unconscious gesture of protection.

"Well," she said, offering him a forced little smile, "I think I shall leave Sarah to her work. Good day, Mr. Whittaker."

She was already halfway to the door, but he caught up with her in two quick strides. "May I ask where you are headed?" He kept his tone neutral, pretending it was the sort of idle inquiry she might receive from anyone. "I would be glad to escort you."

"I don't need an escort, thank you."

He gave her his most disarming grin. "I didn't say you needed it. I said I would be glad to provide it. A subtle, but important, difference." He held the door for her.

She hung back for a moment, seeming irresolute. "Thank you," she said tonelessly. "But I had rather you didn't."

"Perhaps I haven't expressed myself clearly. It would be my *pleasure* to accompany you." She had looked away, so he bent himself nearly double, catching her lowered eyes by placing his face, willy-nilly, in her line of vision. "Come now, Cynthia," he said coaxingly. "Don't make me beg. For such a little thing?" He held up his thumb and forefinger, pinching them nearly together to demonstrate how tiny the favor was that he asked of her. "I promise to do nothing alarming."

Her lips twitched. "Very well," she said resignedly. "But only because I fear you would follow me everywhere, like a duckling, if I refused."

He straightened at once. "How well you know me," he remarked in a pleased-sounding voice. She laughed, then passed through the open doorway. He felt a strong impulse to whoop in triumph but managed to suppress it.

"Where are we going?" he asked, falling into step beside her.

"Well, I had thought of walking in the garden."

"Excellent."

"But now it looks as if it might rain."

"Does it?" He smiled down at her. He could not stop smiling. "I see nothing but sunshine."

She blushed! *A hit, by thunder, a hit.*

"Mr. Whittaker." There was a slight quiver in her voice. "Pray do not smile at me so."

"I can't help it."

"You put me out of countenance."

"Impossible. You are never at a loss."

Now she looked vexed. "You are teasing me."

"Teasing you?" he exclaimed. "Nonsense. I never knew anyone with so much poise. You're famous for it. I daresay I could beam at you like the village idiot for hours on end, and you'd never turn a hair."

She covered her mouth with one hand, stifling a tiny gasp of laughter. "I beg you will not make the attempt! Pray remember, Der—Mr. Whittaker, that you promised to do nothing alarming if I allowed you to escort me."

"Oh, would that alarm you?"

"Exceedingly!"

"Then I shall refrain," he promised. "For the moment."

She looked flustered. She looked very pretty flustered, of course. They walked on while she seemed to struggle with herself. "I hope you understand," she said at last, "that I am wholly unused to this sort of thing."

"What sort of thing?"

"Teasing. And flummery. And, well, I don't know what else to call it. Blarney!"

"Ah, yes. You were reared in Ireland." He chuckled. "I've never been to Blarney."

"Well, no one would guess it," she said tartly. "You've such a gift for nonsense, I imagine the Blarney stone would kiss *you* if it could, rather than the other way about."

He cocked an eyebrow at her. "Cynthia, me darlin', I hope that's a compliment."

She choked. "It isn't. And that's the worst attempt

at a brogue I've ever heard."

He grinned. "It made you laugh, at any rate. I like to make you laugh."

Her smile was alight with it, but she shook her head. "I don't know why you make me laugh," she remarked. "It isn't the things you say, precisely. It's something in your manner."

"Right," he agreed. "What I lack in actual wit, I make up in silliness."

"Oh, dear. Is that what I said?"

"Something like it. Never mind! I don't much care if you think me a simpleton, as long as you find me amusing."

She looked scandalized. "Derek, really! No one could possibly think you a simpleton."

They had wandered down to the ground floor by now. Voices could be heard down the passage; evidently a group of some kind had gathered in the library. Cynthia headed automatically toward the hum of conversation. Derek placed a hand on her arm to stop her. She halted, the amusement vanishing from her face.

"Don't go in," he said seriously, lowering his voice so they could not be overheard. "I hunted everywhere for you this morning. After expending so much effort to find you, I intend to keep you." He tried to return to flippancy, hoping it would relax her guard. "I think I deserve it. Don't you?"

With his hand on her arm, he could feel the tremor that ran through her. "*Keep* me?" she repeated faintly. "I don't know what you mean."

"Keep you with me," he amended. "For the present." It wasn't what he had meant—not entirely—but it would do for now. He lowered his voice further. "We have much to say to each other."

The mood immediately shifted. The very air seemed to thicken around them. When she did not reply, he added very softly, "I must speak to you or go mad."

For a moment she did not move. Then, slowly, she lifted her eyes to his. "Don't you understand?" Her eyes were filled with misery. Her voice was nearly inaudible. "There is nothing I can say to you. And nothing you can say that I should hear. I should not have walked with you, even so far as this." She pulled away from him, shivering. "Do not persecute me. Let me go."

But he couldn't let her go. He stepped to block her path. "Five minutes. That's not too much to ask, is it?" He saw refusal in her eyes and hastily revised his request. "Very well; three. Three minutes."

She was rigid with tension. Her gaze darted to the open doorway down the passage. "I cannot. Not even three minutes. Not here. Not now."

"Where, then? And when?"

"Derek, for pity's sake—"

"I'll meet you wherever you say, whenever you say."

"Nowhere! And never."

She tried to sidestep him, but again he blocked her path. This time he backed her slowly toward the wall. "You won't escape me," he told her, his voice low but forceful. "You know you won't escape me. I'll haunt you, Cynthia, as you have haunted me. You don't know what I have suffered, these three years."

She came up against the wall and, perforce, halted. "I do know," she whispered. Her face was white and drawn. "I suffered, too."

Her nearness was maddening. He wanted to crush himself against her body. He wanted it so badly he felt himself shaking from the effort to not touch her. "Meet me tonight." He loomed over her, his voice rasping from the tightness in his throat. "I don't care where."

He saw her eyes dilate. He could see her pulse jump in the hollow of her throat. Her lips parted. She whispered, as if in a trance, "At the top of the stairs. I'll meet you at the top of the stairs."

"When?"

"Midnight. No—a quarter to twelve. I'll meet you at a quarter to twelve."

"I'll be there." He took a breath and straightened, breaking the spell. Cynthia raised a trembling hand to her cheek, seeming horror-struck at what she had promised. Then she turned, ducked beneath his outstretched arm, and fled.

He smiled at her retreating form. Victory sang in his veins; he wanted to shout and leap and punch the air. "Which stairs?" he murmured aloud, but the passage was empty. Derek grinned. "Never mind," he told the absent Cynthia. "I'll find you."

Chapter Nine

Cynthia laid the seven of diamonds face up on the table before her, neatly covering all save the top half inch of the eight of clubs. Derek groaned aloud and Hannah cried, "Cynthia, you wretch!"

"Now, then, now then," chided Mr. Ellsworth, chuckling. "She's only playing the game, you know."

"Yes, but must she play the game so frightfully well?" Derek looked at his own cards with apparent disgust. "I shall never be rid of this lot."

Cynthia permitted herself a tiny smile. "It's only a game, Mr. Whittaker."

"One I am destined to lose, as usual. Have you done all the damage you intend to do, Lady Cynthia?"

She surveyed the pattern of cards laid on the table, carefully comparing them to the hand she held. It was difficult to concentrate on the rules of the game with Derek so near. She decided it was better to hazard a guess than to think it all out; everyone's eyes were upon her, and she could not bear close scrutiny tonight. "I believe so," she said, feigning a tranquillity she did not feel.

The play passed to Derek. He pretended to curse under his breath, comically moving his cards this way and that, as if they might magically change into playable cards when viewed in a slightly different order. Time passed. Twice he selected a card from the unwieldy stack fanned out against his palm and let his hand hover over the table as if about to drop it into place. Both times he returned the selected card to his hand, shaking his head and muttering furiously. Hannah eventually began to giggle, and Mr. Ellsworth ventured a good-natured protest: "I say, dear chap, play or draw. Play or draw."

Cynthia could not laugh. She dared not drop her guard that far. She watched Derek from under her lashes, her mask of utter calm firmly in place. Beneath her outward poise, she could feel her heart galloping. She was able to spend the evening at Derek's side, her knee a few inches from his beneath the card table, only because Hannah and Mr. Ellsworth were rounding out the foursome. She scarcely dared meet her mother's eyes tonight; she was deliberately trying to give the impression that it was Mr. Ellsworth she was encouraging. But she knew, in her heart, that her newborn rebellion was thriving. In fact, the urge to defy her parents and follow her heart seemed to grow hourly stronger.

She must nip this dangerous impulse in the bud. This, she told herself firmly, was the real reason why she had agreed to meet Mr. Whittaker tonight. Not for any illicit purpose. Merely to set matters straight, once for all. She would explain everything to him, and he would understand. And even if he didn't understand, he would leave her alone in future—once she had made it perfectly plain to him that he must. For his own sake as well as hers, she reminded herself. She would be doing him a favor by rejecting him plainly. Irrevocably. Hope was a deceptive emotion that led only to greater pain. She would spare him pain; she would leave him no hope.

Of course, she thought she had done that once before. It was terrible to have to do it twice. The first time, at the embassy ball, had been hard enough. She had wept until dawn that night. This night, she promised herself, there would be no weeping. She had no time for regret.

The porcelain clock on the mantel chimed ten. Derek gave no sign that he heard it, for which she was deeply grateful. Every tick, every chime, every reminder that their rendezvous inexorably approached, seemed to send a rush of sudden heat through Cynthia's veins. Was it fear or excitement that had her so on edge tonight? Both, she thought, and she could not decide which thrill dominated.

Not that it mattered. Both emotions were completely beside the point. More than irrelevant, they were inappropriate. She had nothing—*nothing*—to feel either excited about or fearful of. She was going to have a discussion with Mr. Whittaker tonight. A private discussion—but a discussion and no more. She would clarify a few points, gently but firmly, and withdraw.

Why did she have to keep *reminding* herself of that resolve? It was almost as if . . . as if her mind were not irrevocably made up. Which it was. Of course it was. It had to be. It *was*.

Cynthia suddenly became aware that she was clutching her cards in a death-grip. She forced herself to take a calming breath and loosen her hold. *Nothing to be afraid of,* she told her hammering heart. *Nothing to get excited about.* Still, her unruly emotions boiled and sang, rattled and hissed and hummed. Anticipation thrummed through her, making her feel as giddy and sick as if she were running a fever. Thank heaven it would soon be over. An hour and forty-five minutes from now . . . no, an hour and a half.

At that realization, she had to take another deep breath.

As far as she could tell, Derek was behaving in a perfectly normal, unconcerned fashion. She hoped she was matching his excellent example. She was never very chatty in a group, so perhaps no one noticed her preoccupation. Her mother would surely see something amiss, if given the opportunity to observe her, but the card game had removed Cynthia from Mama's orbit. And she had deliberately chosen a seat that turned her back to the rest of the room.

Under the cover of Hannah's playing her turn, Cynthia sneaked a covert glance at Derek. Every time she looked at him, another flicker of heat shot through her. To Cynthia, he was masculine perfection, beautifully displayed in a coat of blue superfine set off with spotless white linen. Nothing ostentatious, nothing extreme, just the simple, elegant cut of a London tailor that showed off his tall, well-formed person. Candlelight gleamed on the dark waves of his hair. His profile was perfect, his mouth well cut and firmly muscled. His cheekbones . . . the line of his jaw . . . the shape of his hands, strong and clean . . . everything about him made her dizzy with desire.

But handsome didn't begin to describe him, she

thought, her heart aching. He was so much more than a collection of fine features. There was strength and confidence in his bearing, an aura of command tempered with self-deprecating humor. Leadership came naturally to him, and he seemed unaware that his vitality was anything out of the common way. His modesty was as endearing as his strength. And, most important, most attractive to her, there was deep kindness in his warm, brown eyes.

Oh, this was torture. She dropped her eyes back to her cards, trying to ignore Derek's overwhelming presence. But it was like trying to ignore gravity; he pulled and tugged at her consciousness no matter what she did or where she tried to turn her mind. The more she knew of him, the stronger her conviction grew that he was exactly what he had seemed to be that long-ago night in London: the man of her dreams. And the harder it was to face her future . . . a future that would not have Derek Whittaker in it.

The clock ticked. The cards were laid and drawn and shuffled and dealt. Laughter and chatter surrounded her. Cynthia felt as if she were wrapped in cotton wool, suffocating beneath the duty of smiling and talking and following the game. Just as the last hand of their game was ending, eleven o'clock chimed. *Three quarters of an hour from now.* Cynthia's pulse rate kicked up another notch.

She sneaked another peek at Derek. It was a silly thing to do; had he been looking at her, their eyes would have met, and her carefully constructed wall of composure might have crumbled. However, he was not looking at her. He was looking across the room, an absent frown clouding his brow.

She followed the direction of his gaze and saw that he was watching his sister. She was still registering this fact when she heard the scrape of Derek's chair as he stood and tossed his cards down. He excused himself pleasantly from the table, promised he'd be back in time for the reckoning—"You will all have a chance to abuse me and tell me what an abysmal player I am"—and walked away, strolling casually up to the group surrounding Lady Malcolm. She saw him bend and whisper to Lady Malcolm for a moment. Lady Malcolm nodded, looking a little embarrassed. Derek straightened and caught his brother-in-law's eye, giving him an almost imperceptible signal, a tiny jerk of the chin to direct Lord Malcolm's attention. Lord Malcolm's gaze immediately swiveled round and fixed on his wife, a frown of concern gathering on his face. He lost no time in making their excuses and removing his wife. In less than a minute, Lady Malcolm was gone, ushered lovingly out of the room and off to bed.

Cynthia felt her throat grow tight with unexpected emotion. She must be more overwrought than she knew. Why would witnessing that simple little scene touch her so?

Derek returned to the card table. Cynthia dared not look directly at him for long, but she did glance up as he seated himself. "I hope your sister is not unwell," she ventured.

"She looked tired," said Derek. His swift smile

forced Cynthia to look away. It was painful to refuse to smile back at him—but Mama's eyes were on her now. She had felt them on her when she turned to watch Derek cross the room.

"You are a good brother." The words felt pulled from her. She hadn't meant to say them. She hadn't intended to say anything more than she already had. Cynthia bit her lip, staring wretchedly down at her hands. She could not lift her face.

"Natalie is a good sister."

Well. That wasn't so alarming. He had sounded perfectly offhand. She must try to match his nonchalance. Since she still could not look directly at Derek, she aimed her smile at Hannah and Mr. Ellsworth. "Lady Malcolm is fortunate, I think, to have two men guarding her with such care."

"She doesn't think so." Derek sounded amused. "Natalie calls it an embarrassment of riches. She often begs us to stop fussing over her."

Hannah giggled. "I think it would be lovely. You may both transfer your fussing to me, if you like. I shan't complain."

Cynthia thought it would be lovely, too. She could not imagine her own brothers noticing if she looked tired, let alone taking action on her behalf. Not even if she were in the family way. Would she, someday, have a husband who tenderly cared for her? The prospect seemed dim.

The thought made her glance automatically at John Ellsworth. She was struck again with how poorly he compared to the paragon across the table from him.

But she mustn't think about that.

She watched him for a moment, trying, for the dozenth time this evening, to ascertain the state of Mr. Ellsworth's affections. Irritation rose in her. He did not seem particularly interested in her, she thought. If anything, he seemed rather afraid of her. She had tried to moderate her natural coolness in his presence—especially when Mama was around to observe it—but Mr. Ellsworth was one of those souls who hid an innate shyness behind a genial, overly hearty manner. Such people were very difficult to read. She could not perceive any sure signs of attraction to herself but, on the other hand, he did not seem especially drawn to Hannah. He was, in fact, bafflingly unresponsive to any and all lures cast in his direction. And Cynthia hardly knew whether to feel glad or sorry.

Her mind would clear, she told herself, once she had rid herself of Mr. Whittaker's attentions. She could not concentrate with Derek distracting her.

Of course, he was scrupulously *not* paying attention to her tonight, and she felt more distracted than ever. She sighed and returned her attention to the new hand being dealt.

Ten more minutes crawled by. By a quarter past the hour, Cynthia's churning anxiety had tied her nerves into knots. Would the evening never end? But when the duchess finally rose from her place by the fire, signaling the party to break up, it suddenly seemed to Cynthia that the interminable evening had flown past in an eyeblink. She walked off with her mother, carefully keeping her eyes on the floor to prevent them straying to Derek.

Arm in arm, Cynthia and her mother mounted the stairs with a stately slowness that, tonight, Cynthia found excruciating. Mama's maid, Lucy, was asleep in her chair but jumped up when they entered. Mama and Lucy disappeared into Mama's room. Cynthia ducked into her adjoining bedchamber and checked her reflection in the glass, nervously tucking her hair into place and praying that her upcoming escapade would avoid detection. With luck, Mama would not even know she had gone.

Half past eleven. Still too early to slip away. Perhaps it was just as well; it would be awkward to encounter Lucy in the hall. She would wait and hope to put off her departure until Lucy was safely upstairs.

Twenty minutes to twelve. Lucy finished brushing Mama's hair and came, yawning, to Cynthia's room to offer her assistance.

"Thank you, Lucy, but I think I can manage for myself tonight." Cynthia hoped that her reassuring smile was convincing enough. "You may go to bed if you like."

Lucy looked mildly surprised, but dipped an obedient curtsy and scurried off. As the door closed behind her, Cynthia heard her mother's voice raised in anxious inquiry.

"Cynthia? Did you dismiss Lucy?"

Cynthia's heart sank. "Yes, Mama. Was there something else you wanted?"

"No, my love."

142

But Cynthia heard the bed springs creak and knew her mother was snatching up her dressing gown to come and check on her. *Lud!* She seated herself hastily at the little vanity table in her room. By the time Mama appeared in the doorway, Cynthia was digging aimlessly through the vanity drawers. She met her mother's eyes in the mirror, trying to appear guileless. Mama's eyes were cold with suspicion.

"What are you doing, Cynthia? You are not ready for bed."

"I'm not sleepy tonight. I thought I might read for a while."

Mama frowned. "What has that to do with—"

"And I think I've left my novel downstairs in the library. So vexatious! I shall have to go and find it."

"You should have sent Lucy for it."

"I couldn't, Mama. I am not entirely sure where I left it. And it is so late that I didn't like to keep her longer from her bed."

"And will you go alone to the library, in the dark, at this time of night? Everyone else has gone to bed. I do not like it."

Cynthia forced a little laugh. "Nonsense, Mama. I shall carry a lamp. What harm could possibly come to me?" She rose and picked up a lamp as she spoke, hoping to make her actions seem reasonable.

Her mother did not smile. There was wariness in every line of her face. "I do not like it," she repeated.

Cynthia tried to look exasperated. She didn't feel exasperated; she felt guilty. "Shall I take a dagger with me?" she asked, trying to make a joke without appearing disrespectful. "Really, Mama, you are being overly cautious. I don't think I will encounter many desperate characters at Oldham Park. None between here and the library, at any rate." She bestowed a light kiss on her mother's cheek. "Good night."

"I shan't go to bed until you return," said her mother grimly. "If you do not return in ten minutes, I shall ring for help."

Dismay shook her. Ten minutes! She couldn't say all she needed to say in ten minutes. And what if Derek came late to the rendezvous?

She patted her mother's sleeve coaxingly, as she used to do when she was a little girl. "Oh, pray, Mama. I thought I might read in the library for a while. It would be more comfortable there."

"No," said her mother with great finality. "Absolutely not. Come directly back, Cynthia Fitzwilliam, or I shall raise the entire house to search for you."

She would do it, too; Cynthia knew she would. She dropped her hand and gazed at her mother, appalled. "Pray do not do anything to make us look ridiculous," she begged. "I will try to hurry. But I may be back in ten minutes, or I may not."

"Ten minutes is more than time enough for such an errand."

"And what if the book is not where I think it is? Allow me twenty minutes, Mama."

"Fifteen. And not a second more."

" 'Tis a very large house. And I might have left it anywhere!"

"If you do not find it, come back without it. I give you fifteen minutes, Cynthia." The hall clock chimed faintly; it was a quarter to twelve. "Be back here by midnight."

She could not waste more time in futile argument. Cynthia carefully unclenched her jaw. "Very well, Mama. Midnight. Or shortly thereafter." She made good her escape before the anger she felt showed in her eyes, fearing it would lead to still more questions, still more restrictions.

A husband's rule could hardly be worse than this, Cynthia thought resentfully. It would almost be worth it to marry—to marry anyone—just to be rid of Mama.

The disloyal thought came unbidden, and immediately Cynthia was swamped with guilt. What a bad daughter she was: unfilial, secretive, disobedient, ungrateful! What was the matter with her? Why couldn't she be *good?*

She could be good, she promised herself, and *would* be good. Fifteen minutes from now, her dangerous feelings for Derek Whittaker would be over and done with. Or, at the very least—since she did not seem able to control her feelings where he was concerned—the temptation to encourage him would be over and done with. She was about to *dis*courage him, in no uncertain terms. And once she had done that, it would no longer matter what she felt.

The lamp was steady in her hand. Her head was high. Filled with virtuous resolve, Cynthia closed the door behind her and started down the passage toward the stairs.

She nearly jumped out of her skin when Derek fell into step beside her. She gasped, and he lifted a finger to his lips to warn her to silence. His eyes were laughing, but with mischief, not mockery. He placed his arm around her waist and pulled her farther down the passage, away from the door she had come through.

The touch of his hand did not help Cynthia's state of mind. "You nearly startled me out of my wits," she hissed, trying to sound more outraged than she felt. Her heart was leaping with gladness as much as fear. "Where did you come from?"

"The statuary niche." He grinned down at her, utterly unrepentant. The sight of that grin—a grin she found attractive enough at a distance, now only inches from her face—sent a flutter of joy and desire through her. She actually felt herself weakening. This was going to be harder than she had thought.

Meanwhile, the hand at her waist was guiding her, gently but inexorably, down the passage. "Much as I enjoy hunting you down," he remarked, "I couldn't take the chance that I might miss you. I decided the best course was to wait outside your door."

"Did you hear what was said?"

"No. Tell me." He led her to a window seat beneath a tall, gothic arch of many-paned glass. In daylight hours, the huge window lit the stairs and landing. In the darkness of near-midnight, the expanse of glass was opaque and black. She sank down onto the stone ledge and Derek sat beside her.

"I can only give you fifteen minutes."

"As many as that? You only agreed to grant me three."

Cynthia bit her lip. In her eagerness to discourage him once and for all, she had forgotten that. "I—I changed my mind. I wanted to give you more time because . . . well, it doesn't matter, since I can't. I promised Mama I would return by midnight."

His brows flew up. "Does she know you are with me?"

"Of course not. I told her I was going to fetch a book that I left downstairs." Cynthia shivered, suddenly dispirited again. "The glass is cold."

Derek moved immediately to warm her, placing his arm around her and pulling her close against him. For half an instant, Cynthia resisted. Then she surrendered. After all, this might be—no, *would* be—her last chance to nestle into the arms of the man she loved. Tears rose in her throat, and she swallowed hard to keep them from reaching her eyes. She must not cry. She had only fifteen minutes.

"Derek." She laid her head against his shoulder. It felt divine. "I have come to bid you good-bye."

She felt him go very still. She rushed into speech before he had time to recover and interrupt her. "There is no hope for us. They will never let me marry you."

"Are you telling me that you don't want to marry me?"

"I am telling you that I cannot. That my parents will never agree to the match. I suppose you will say that we ought to defy them—"

"Yes, I jolly well will!"

"—but I can't. It would be very wrong of me."

"What nonsense is this?" He took her by the shoulders and held her away from him, the better to see her face. "I know you feel the same things I feel." His eyes, dark and compelling, held hers. "I know it," he repeated softly.

Cynthia nodded miserably. "I suppose I do. But it doesn't matter."

"It's the only thing that *does* matter. And if you think differently," he added dryly, "I doubt that you can explain it to me in fifteen minutes."

"I must try." She took a deep breath. "Derek, pray listen to me. And try not to argue with me, or I'll get muddled."

His expression was grim. "Very well. Go on."

"I'm afraid I must confide some things about my family that I . . . that I hope you will keep private."

"You have my word."

"Thank you." She took another breath to steady her nerves and pressed her palms together, thinking. There was no easy way to say what must be said. The words that would convey the information quickly were, alas, blunt. She steeled herself and began.

"My father is, in many ways, a wonderful person," she said quietly. "But he is greatly addicted to sport. Racing in particular. And . . . and he is, perhaps, over-fond of drink." She could feel herself blushing. She dropped her eyes. "It is an unfortunate combination of traits."

"Yes, I can see that it would be," said Derek. Compassion sounded in his voice, but she sensed the wariness in him, too. She did not blame him. If she meant to bid him farewell, he was under no obligation to make it easy for her. "It's a common enough problem, one hears. Is he badly dipped?"

" 'Dipped'? You mean, have his losses been heavy? Yes, I think so. It's not the sort of thing one discloses to one's children, so I haven't been told in so many words. I don't know the extent of it. But I definitely have the impression that our straits are rather . . . dire. And have been for some years."

"There is no need to tell me the entire story. I can save you a little time." His voice roughened. "When you rejected me in London, I made a few inquiries, trying to understand what had happened. To make sense of what you had done. I learned enough to be sure of one thing: Your family's ardent desire is to auction you off in the marriage mart, and the sooner the better. You are, as I suppose you know, a valuable commodity."

Cynthia flinched, and Derek's voice gentled. "What is less clear to me, my love, is why you consent to be used in this fashion. Why should you sacrifice yourself to line their pockets?"

The endearment sent her emotions spinning. *I must not cry,* she reminded herself desperately. *No matter what he calls me.* "It's not so hard to fathom, surely," she said, but she was unable to keep her voice from quavering. " 'Tis the way of the world. It has been ever so. Daughters are given in marriage to advance the fortunes of their families."

She saw anger spark in his eyes and held up her

hand, palm out, in a gesture beseeching silence. "You did agree to hear me out and not to argue with me."

He clamped his mouth shut with a visible effort. "I did," he said through his teeth. "Pray continue."

"I can easily imagine what you thought of me," said Cynthia softly. Her throat tightened again at the memory. It was painful to recall the stunned expression on Derek's face that night at the ball . . . even more painful, to her, than the anger and bitterness he had shown when encountering her again. She could understand his bitterness against her; her conduct had been despicable. But she must have hurt him deeply for him to still be that angry with her after so much time had passed. She couldn't avoid hurting him, but she hadn't meant to hurt him deeply.

She closed her eyes for a moment, trying to hide the pain and shame she felt. "I am so sorry," she whispered. "I'm sorry for my coldness to you, but I am more sorry for—for the other." She opened her eyes again, forcing herself to meet his gaze. "It was wrong of me to encourage you."

"Hang it all, don't apologize for that!" He gave a strangled sort of laugh. "I liked that part."

She knew he was trying to make her smile, but she could not. "No. It was a mistake. I should have known better. I should have . . . resisted the temptation."

He studied her face, trouble in his eyes. "You're serious."

"Yes."

"Well." He took a breath and blew it out, seeming perplexed. "Having done so in the first place—

encouraged me, I mean—I do wish you had gone on as you began. Why drop me a hint to come to that wretched ball, for example, if all you meant to do was humiliate me?"

Cynthia winced. "It must have seemed very odd."

"That's not the word I would have used. But 'odd' will do."

She looked down, staring at Derek's knee rather than his face. It was a singularly attractive knee, large and well shaped. She looked back at her own lap instead. "I didn't mean to blow hot and cold. I wanted . . . Well, you must know what I wanted."

"It would still be pleasant to hear it from you."

She smiled faintly. "I wanted to dance with you."

"Is that all? Never mind. I shan't press my luck." The warmth in his voice would be her undoing. She dared not look up. He said softly, "What changed your mind?"

"I had to change it. That day in the park," she said hesitantly, "I was with the Hendersons. You remember that."

"Yes."

She glanced fleetingly at his face, then away again. "Mr. Henderson did not recognize you at first. It was only after we rode on that he remembered where he had seen you last and who you were. He told me . . . he told his wife and me . . . that you were Lord Stokesdown's secretary. At first he was a little offended that you had dared to approach him. And then he seemed to think it an excellent joke. Laughed at your audacity and tried to tease me, you know, by vowing it was my beauty that had lured you to overstep your bounds. That I had drawn you to the carriage and so forth. He didn't mean anything by it. He didn't really guess that we had met before. It was all in jest. But—" She could feel herself blushing, but she forced herself to meet Derek's eyes. "Derek, pray understand—" Her voice broke. "I was so frightened when I learned . . . when I realized . . ."

There was really no decent way to tell him. Why had she not foreseen this? Any set of words she chose would still convey the insult. And an insult, she saw now, it clearly was.

He finished the sentence for her, in a deadly quiet voice. "You realized that I was poor."

She pressed her palms to her flaming cheeks. "Oh, how vile it sounds."

"Truth is often ugly." He looked angry, but she knew it was injured pride that he felt. "How poor did you think I was, Cynthia? Too poor to support a wife? Did you take me for the sort of rogue who casts out lures to respectable females, with never a thought of marriage?"

"No, no, I never thought that!"

"At any rate, you have certainly explained the abrupt change in your behavior." Disgust turned down the corners of his mouth. "By the time I saw you at the ball, you had discovered that I was not the wealthy man you thought me. And you treated me accordingly."

"I had to do it, Derek. Don't you see?" She laid her hand on his sleeve and lifted pleading eyes to his.

"Can't you understand? I was trying to be *kind.*"

"Kind?" He recoiled from her. "Is that your notion of kindness?"

"Yes." The hand she had laid on his sleeve was trembling. "I knew I could not allow you to pursue me. I thought it would be easier for you, then, if I made you hate me." Her eyes filled with the tears she could no longer suppress. "It worked, did it not? Derek, pray tell me that it helped you. Tell me . . . tell me my suffering was not in vain." Her breath caught on a sob. "You don't know what it cost me to humiliate you."

He looked dumbfounded. She took a deep and struggling breath, fighting back her tears, furious with herself for betraying such weakness. She lifted her hands to her face and dashed the shameful tears away. "I'm sorry," she said, gulping. "I promised myself I wouldn't cry." Her fists clenched in her lap. "I never manage to keep my promises to myself, where you are concerned."

He immediately reached to take her in his arms. Cynthia shrank back, pressing her hands against his chest to keep him at bay. "No!" she said in a strangled voice. "Don't be kind to me. And whatever you do, don't touch me." She found she was laughing and crying at once. "You will only make matters worse."

Silently he pulled out his handkerchief and handed it to her. "Thank you," she said, trying for a little dignity. She mopped up her tears and took several deep breaths. "I have now wasted two precious minutes."

"You've wasted nearly ten," he told her softly. "If

153

what you meant to do was bid me good-bye, you have wasted all your time thus far."

She glanced apprehensively at him. "What do you mean? I have tried to explain to you— Oh, I see. You mean I haven't explained it."

"Cynthia, my love, you *cannot* explain it." He spoke with utter conviction. "The moment you admitted that your feelings matched mine, your cause was lost." A tiny smile played at the edges of his mouth. "I shall never let you tell me good-bye," he whispered. In his eyes was complete confidence—and infinite tenderness.

He took the handkerchief from her suddenly nerveless fingers, touched it lightly to her damp cheeks, folded it, kissed it, and returned it to his pocket. All the while, she stared helplessly at him, her thoughts tumbling chaotically. She had muddled it somehow. Somehow, she had failed to make matters clear to him. For surely, if he understood, he would let her go. It was the correct thing to do. It was the gentlemanly thing to do.

And if he did not? Her imagination balked. It was inconceivable. How *could* he not? If she told him to keep his distance from her, he had to honor her request. She thought she had said it plainly, but evidently she had not. She would say it even more plainly. They were running out of time.

She faced him squarely and seized both his hands, earnestly leaning forward in her eagerness to claim his full attention, to make him understand. "Derek, please. Don't make this more difficult than it already is. I hoped I had made it clear to you. I am bidding you farewell not because I want to, but because I must. I am heartily sorry if it pains you, but whether it pains you or no, you must accept it. As I have done."

"Cynthia, my love—"

"I am *not* your love. I can never be your love." Her eyes frantically searched his and found only refusal. And tenderness. She shook her head despairingly. "Don't you understand? I have a *duty*. Duty has a stronger claim than emotion. My parents gave me life. They gave me a home, an upbringing, an education. I would not even exist if not for them. And the Bible strictly admonishes us to honor our mothers and fathers. It would be *wicked* for me to disobey them in this. They have pinned all their hopes on me. Marrying where my duty lies is the sole way I can repay them for all they have done. If things were different, if I had a sister, perhaps, who might take my place . . ." Her voice trailed off, then grew strong again. "But I do not. And it is silly to repine. My life is what it is, and there's nothing to be done about it."

His brows had drawn into a troubled frown. "You realize, I suppose, that I am no longer the poor man I was three years ago."

She nodded, miserable. "I know that you have inherited Crosby Hall, although I am not quite sure how it happened. But . . ." Hope stirred in her heart. She caught her breath. Was it possible Mama was mistaken about Derek's estate? Was he, after all, wealthy enough to help her family? "How—how large an estate is Crosby Hall?"

He looked even more perturbed. "What an indelicate question, my dear," he said wryly. "But since you are so frank about what matters to you, I will answer with equal frankness. It is fairly large, and it is prosperous. It provides me with what the world calls a 'respectable' income."

Her heart sank. "Yes. That was my impression."

"What! So downcast? A respectable income is, I take it, insufficient?"

She had offended him. It could not be helped. "Derek, I wish there were time for me to tread lightly on the subject, but the clock may chime at any moment—"

"Yes, yes, I understand you." His face had set once again in grim lines. "You require great wealth, and will not marry for less."

"Cannot." She shivered. "I have more than myself to consider. More than my own wishes. My entire family looks to me. They depend upon me to mend our fortunes."

"I will ask you one question. And think before you answer, Cynthia; this is important." His eyes were very dark and serious, his expression unreadable. "Is it only your parents who want you to marry a rich man? I need to know, sweetheart, so tell me truly. Everyone wants a comfortable life. But how important is it to you, to have luxury at your command? Would you feel deprived if you could not have the best of everything? If you could not spend unthinkingly, buying whatever took your fancy?"

The idea was so absurd that it startled a laugh out of

her. She had never had a life of luxury. Her family had been financially strapped for as long as she could remember. Mama had gone to tremendous efforts to conjure up the appearance of wealth, merely to launch Cynthia upon the world. Cynthia had had habits of economy instilled in her at a very early age. Apart from the needs of her parents, she cared nothing for great wealth. Indeed, she wouldn't know what to do with it. She started to tell Derek so—and then stopped herself.

He had given her a way out.

All she need do was confess to having a mercenary heart. It would be a false confession, but perhaps God would forgive her this tiny lie. She would tell it in pursuit of a much greater good: forcing Derek to accept the inevitable.

Because if he did not . . . if he did not help her to turn her back on him . . . she feared she would not have the strength to do her duty. Her weakness for him was like Papa's weakness for drink. It would lead to ruin if she indulged it. The resentment she felt toward Mama lately, her increasing restlessness, her inner chaos—all were the result of her feelings for Derek Whittaker. These feelings were *wrong*. They didn't feel wrong, but they had to be; they were having a harmful effect. Not only were they making Cynthia miserable, they were leading her to rebel against her parents' God-given authority. Why, even now, as she contemplated telling this little white lie, this lie in an excellent cause, her heart was rebelling. Her traitorous heart was begging her not to lie to Derek, not for any reason, not ever.

She dropped her eyes and stared steadfastly at the knot in his cravat. "Well," she said cautiously, "I think you are right when you say that everyone wants to be comfortable. I suppose that some people are able to be comfortable with less than others. Some people require a—a great deal more than others, in the way of material goods, before they truly consider themselves comfortable."

"I am asking what you require, Cynthia."

She could already hear the hardness in his voice. Anticipating her answer, he was condemning her. *Good,* she thought wildly. *Good.* She wanted him to condemn her. She wanted to convince him, despite the myriad ways she had betrayed her feelings in the past day or two, that he had been right to begin with—that she was nothing more than a moneygrubbing harpy. That her heart was as cold as rumor said it was.

"I think I would like to be rich," she heard herself say.

"And how do you define 'rich'?" He sounded angry now.

She had no idea. She had never given it serious thought. Of course, a girl whose ambition was to be rich *would* have given it some thought, so Cynthia stalled for time. She turned her head sideways and tried to look vague. "Oh, I don't know," she said, deliberately conveying the impression that she had an income in mind but was too coy to voice it.

She was not looking into Derek's face anymore, so she failed to read his intentions. She gasped, startled, when she felt herself roughly pulled to her feet. Derek had lifted them both off the window seat in one smooth motion. Before she knew what he was about, he had taken her, willy-nilly, in his arms. She looked instinctively up into his face, and was lost. She could not look away. His eyes, filled with pain, bored into hers.

"There are all sorts of riches, Cynthia," he said hoarsely. "Wealth can be measured in many ways. Let me show you one of them."

He was going to kiss her. *Oh, no.* Panic surged through her. He would know . . . he would know everything. The way she felt. The fact that she had lied. But a strange lassitude was gripping her; she could not seem to move. Her eyes dilated with fear, but she did not pull away. And when his mouth closed on hers, her ability to think fled, taking all fear with it.

She went limp and pliant in his arms, loving the feel of him. The taste of him. *Derek.* There was room for nothing more in her mind; her racing thoughts quieted and focused. Her will to resist, consumed by a firestorm of pure emotion, vanished like smoke in a whirlwind. Chaos ended. Doubts faded to nothingness.

She belonged in Derek's arms. This was right. This was good. This was all she ever wanted. For a few blissful seconds, Cynthia was in heaven.

And then, inevitably, the clock downstairs began to toll midnight.

Chapter Ten

How could she kiss him like that if she didn't care for him? She must feel *something*. Some tenderness, some desire. Something.

He was dimly aware of bells ringing in the distance. Cynthia seemed to freeze in his arms. She tore her lips from his with a moan of frustration, then rested the top of her head against his lapel, staring at the floor and gulping air. "I must go," she said in a half-strangled voice.

Midnight. Of course.

He threw his head back; he was feeling the need to gulp a little air himself. "Very well," he said unsteadily, "Cinderella."

She gave a sad little choke of laughter, then raised her head and looked at him. "I shall have to tell Mama that I did not find my book."

"Good. Perhaps she will let you come back out and continue your search."

"Unlikely, I'm afraid." She gave him a wan smile. "I would not hang about in the passage, waiting for me to reemerge, if I were you."

Her lovely face was a portrait of pure sorrow, bravely but inadequately hidden behind that unconvincing smile. It was heartbreaking. He lifted her hand to his lips and kissed the tips of her fingers. "Cynthia," he said hoarsely. "I would gladly wait all night, if—"

"Hush." Her voice was tight with pain. "No more. I

must go, and quickly now. Good night."

"One kiss more." He bent his head, drunk with need, but she pushed him away as if panic-stricken.

"Derek, I cannot stay. She will pull the bell rope and wake the servants. I must go back." With a desperate little shudder, Cynthia pulled herself out of his embrace and picked up her lamp. The light wavered and danced in her trembling hand.

He extended his own hand, steadier than hers. "Give me the lamp. I'll escort you."

She hesitated, irresolute, then shook her head. "My mother might open her door and see you. Good night, Derek. Good—good-bye." Her voice quivered, nearly suspended with tears; he heard them plainly. But even as he reached for her again—to comfort her, to argue with her, to steal her from her wretched, greedy family—she was gone, her footsteps hurrying lightly down the passage.

He took a deep, rueful breath and blew it out, raking his hair with one hand. That had *not* gone as planned. His only consolation was that it hadn't gone as Cynthia planned, either. Tell him good-bye, indeed! And over money, of all things. He snorted with disgust. If there was one thing his up-and-down life had taught him, it was the treachery of money. People did terrible things to one another in pursuit of it, and for what? Neither love nor health nor luck, none of the things that truly enriched a man, could be purchased.

It occurred to him that Cynthia, on the other hand, appeared to be for sale. And there was no blinking the fact that Cynthia would enrich his life. So perhaps great wealth was desirable after all.

He jammed his hands in his pockets, scowling, and headed moodily for the bedchamber Cummings had assigned him. He had to admit, unpleasant though it was, that if Cynthia were truly mercenary he would be better off without her. He was, most would say, a reasonably wealthy man. But there were women for whom no amount of money was sufficient. A woman like that could wreak havoc in a man's life. Even if he won her hand, he might live to regret it. It clearly behooved him, then, to banish her from his dreams.

On the other hand, he had attempted that feat for three years without success. He had firmly believed then what he only *feared* was true now, and despite his long-held conviction that Cynthia Fitzwilliam was a mercenary jade, he had dreamed of her incessantly. What made him think he could forget her now, if he couldn't then?

She felt something for him, he was sure of that. Whatever her ambitions, however focused she was on her goals, he could certainly distract her. He had demonstrated his power to do so time and again. But should he? Was it wise? In the long run, was he better off standing back and letting her cast out lures to Ellsworth?

He needed more information, he decided. Stronger evidence, in one direction or the other. Cynthia seemed to have an odd mixture of priorities vying for dominance: filial duty, attraction to him, and greed. *Seemed,* he thought, because there was something wrong with that picture. He just wasn't sure what it was.

Ah, well. Time would tell. He'd sort it all out somehow. He had always considered himself a fortunate chap. People said he had been born under a lucky star, and he was inclined to believe it. Whenever things looked bleakest, somehow fate always intervened on his behalf. He had inherited Crosby Hall against nearly impossible odds. Perhaps he would win Cynthia, too, and live happily ever after.

Unless, of course, those two things were mutually exclusive. In which case he must trust his lucky star to *prevent* him from winning her, even if he tried. Because it seemed pretty clear that he was going to try, even against his better judgment.

He had to place his faith in something: God, or fate, or lucky stars. He obviously could not trust himself.

The next morning he set out to waylay Cynthia again, but something even more pressing reared its head. Natalie did not come down to breakfast.

Derek startled the housemaid carrying breakfast to Lady Malcolm's room by intercepting her in the passage and forcibly wresting the tray from her hands. He reduced her to giggles and blushes with a wink, a grin, and a promise that he would not spill Lady Malcolm's tea, and then carried the tray to his sister with his own hands.

He found her lying listlessly against a welter of pillows. She turned her head when Derek came in, and he saw her woebegone expression transform comically into one of pleased dismay. "Oh, no!" she uttered in tones of despair. "Not you."

"Yes, dear sister, it is I," intoned Derek, bearing the

tray into the room and depositing it on a low table beside Natalie's bed. "I have come to visit you on your bed of pain."

She glowered at him. "It isn't a bed of pain. It's merely a bed of discomfort. Get out, Derek, do! I look hideous."

"Nonsense," he said loyally. "Buck up, Natalie, and stop feeling sorry for yourself. Everyone tells me you are healthier than you think you are."

He hoped to high heaven they were right. She really did look terrible, poor girl. It wasn't just the hugeness of her distended belly; her color wasn't good, and there were dark circles under her eyes.

"Move over," he ordered. "I want to sit on the bed."

"There isn't room," she said glumly. "I'm enormous. Pull the chair over, if you *must* stay. Gracious, not that one! That's the commode."

"No. Is it?" He stared at it with interest. "Very clever."

"It's practical, at any rate. I daren't stray too far from it these days. There's a plain chair by the vanity."

The vanity chair was small and spindly. "The commode looks more comfortable," he complained.

"I told you, you needn't stay."

"Nonsense. How else am I to force all this tea down your throat?" He hauled the chair close to the bed and sat in it, facing her. "Give over, Natalie! If you didn't want me at Oldham Park, you shouldn't have sent me that affecting letter."

Her lips twitched. "I wanted you near," she admitted. "But not this near." She eyed the tray with misgiving. "What is that? Porridge?"

"Gruel, I think." He lifted the cover and sniffed the air. "Mmm."

Natalie shuddered and closed her eyes. "Take it away, for pity's sake."

"Careful," he warned her. "You'll hurt my feelings in a minute. I'm beginning to think you don't want me here."

She gave a strangled little laugh and then covered her face with a pillow, emitting a hollow moan. "It's not just you," she said, her voice muffled beneath the pillow. "I can't bear for anyone but Malcolm to see me this way."

"Well, why should Malcolm be the only one to suffer?" he said reasonably. "Share the burden, Natalie. Make us all take turns looking at you."

As he expected, Natalie removed the pillow from her face and threw it at his head. "That's better," he said smugly. "Now you're feeling more the thing, eh? And, by the by, where is Malcolm?"

"I made him go away. There's nothing anyone can *do* for me. I must simply endure this until it is over. If you wish to feel sorry for someone, feel sorry for Pippa. Malcolm and Sarah are old enough to understand, but poor Pippa thinks I have abandoned her."

"She'll recover. And so, of course, will you." He picked up a piece of toast and wagged it invitingly at her. "Toast? It's buttered."

"Oh, very well," said Natalie crossly. "Although, for once, I am not hungry." She took it from him and bit into it without enthusiasm.

"Excellent. While you are recruiting your strength, I shall distract you from your misery with a tale."

She looked askance at him over her toast, and he chuckled. "Well, it isn't really a tale," he admitted. "It's a true story. I need a little advice—for a friend," he added untruthfully. "You were always better at that sort of thing than I am."

Natalie looked mildly interested. "I hope it's a love triangle. Those are my favorite."

"Well, it's not a triangle, exactly, but it is definitely a romantic sort of problem. The very thing at which I'm hopeless."

She visibly perked up. "Fire away. I'll do my best."

Derek leaned back in the narrow chair and crossed his arms over his chest, thinking. "What would you tell a chap," he began slowly, "who has fallen in love with a girl—"

"Congratulations?"

"I haven't finished. A girl whom he suspects is a fortune hunter?"

"Oh." She thought for a moment. "Has your friend got a fortune?"

"No."

"I see. Congratulations, then, is a bit premature. How certain is he that the girl is a fortune hunter?"

"Fairly certain," Derek admitted. "She's told him she can't marry him because he's not rich enough."

Natalie choked on her toast and went into a brief coughing fit. "That's rather conclusive evidence," she said when she had got her breath back.

"Yes, but he's not ready to throw in the towel just

yet. He thinks the girl has feelings for him."

"Oh." Natalie absently reached for more toast. "Well, that does complicate matters a bit. For the girl, at any rate."

Derek quirked an eyebrow at her. "If he's right, doesn't that give him some hope?"

"Perhaps." She chewed thoughtfully. "It depends on what her feelings for him actually are, and why she wants to marry money. And, of course, whether your friend is facing serious competition. Is there a rich suitor waiting in the wings?"

"I believe there is," said Derek gloomily.

"Well, do not blame the girl too much if she chooses the rich man," said Natalie. She sounded, to Derek, depressingly chipper about it. "There are all sorts of reasons for fortune hunting. Some can be quite compelling. Without knowing what her reasons are, it's impossible to judge the situation."

He frowned. "What are you saying? That if she has a good reason to marry for money, there is nothing inherently wrong with that?"

"My dear Derek." Natalie looked amused. "It's the way of the world. Or hadn't you heard?"

"I've heard," he growled. He felt his frown deepening. "But it's repellent. Aren't some things more important than wealth?"

"Many things. But you don't need to convince me. You need to convince the girl. And if dear old Uncle Joe needs to be rescued from debtors' prison, or Papa's lands have all been mortgaged and the lenders are calling in the notes, or anything of that sort, you—

and your friend—will have your work cut out for you. That's all I am saying."

"What if her reasons are not so compelling? What if she just likes spending money and having beautiful things? A life of leisure and all that."

Natalie rolled her eyes. "Any sensible person, given a choice, would rather be rich than poor. But if she truly has tender feelings for your friend, I should think her desire for him would outweigh her desire for silk gowns and an army of servants."

Derek shifted uneasily on his chair. "And if it doesn't?"

"Then your friend is clearly mistaken about the lady's sentiments—or her sense—and ought to withdraw his suit."

This was not the answer Derek wanted to hear. "Don't you think he could change her mind about the importance of money? If she does care for him, that is, rather than the other chap. Perhaps she hasn't thought it through. If he pursues her ardently—"

"Then he's a fool." Natalie brushed the toast crumbs from her fingertips with an air of finality. "The girl is either in love with him or she is not. If she is not, he might try to win her heart. But you say she *is*. Or something near it. My dear Derek, in that case the girl is plainly a ninny, and your friend is better off without her."

He stared at her, taken aback. "Come, now! You told me a moment ago that it's the way of the world, that anyone would rather be rich than poor and all that rot."

She pointed imperiously at the teapot. He obediently poured her a cup. As he did so, Natalie went on. "Of course. But any female who would rather marry a rich man whom she does not love than a poor man whom she *does* love—"

"He's not poor. He's just . . . not as rich as she needs him to be."

"Worse and worse," exclaimed Natalie. "Then her choice is not between poverty and wealth, it is merely between rich and richer?"

"Something like that," admitted Derek.

She held out her hand, and he passed her the cup and saucer. "Your friend sounds like an idiot," she remarked, apparently disgusted. "What does he see in this harpy? She's obviously shallow and grasping. And probably trifling with your friend for her own amusement. I don't believe she cares for him at all."

"Well, what am I to tell him?" asked Derek, nettled. "I can't tell him that he's an idiot and his inamorata is a harpy. The chap wants advice, not invective."

"Here's my advice: Forget about her. Look elsewhere."

"He can't! He's in love with the chit. Been mad about her for years."

"My word." She swallowed a sip of tea. "How sad. I confess, I do not foresee a happy outcome."

Derek's feelings propelled him from the chair and sent him prowling around the room, muttering curses under his breath. Natalie watched these gyrations from the bed, her composure unruffled. "You seem to be taking this a bit hard," she observed.

"Well, I wanted to give him some advice worth having. Not "give up and go home." How can you be so sure of what you say, when you don't know the people involved?"

Natalie opened her eyes at him. "Why, then, give him your own advice. You asked for my opinion, and I gave it."

He had to acknowledge the justice of this. Still, it rankled. "I was relying on you," he grumbled. "You generally give excellent advice. But I think you're wide of the mark this time."

"Why? What do you think your friend should do?"

"Pursue her as if his life depended on it," replied Derek promptly. "Give her no peace. Thrust himself in her path. Force her to acknowledge what she feels."

"Well," said Natalie cautiously, "that might do some good. But not in the way you think."

"What do you mean?"

"I think it may, rather than force the lady to acknowledge her true feelings, force *your friend* to acknowledge her true feelings. Which he seems loath to do." She leaned awkwardly over to set her empty teacup back on the tray. "At any rate, if he chases her determinedly, her response—whatever it may be— will doubtless be revealing. One way or the other."

A peculiar look came over her face. "Derek, I need you to leave now. And pray take that chair out of my path."

170

Chapter Eleven

He was pursuing her. Cynthia felt it. She saw it. And she was terrified that everyone else would soon see it, too.

Gone was Derek's perfect, circumspect behavior that had so relieved her mind the previous evening. It was as if her words, her explanation, her farewell, had had the opposite effect from what she intended. He did not behave like a man who had been given his congé. He behaved as if she had encouraged him! What ailed the man? Was he blind? Was he dense? Or was he merely rude?

She was forced, all day long, to go to extraordinary lengths to avoid him. It wasn't that she minded spending time with Hannah. Hannah was her dearest friend. But she was keenly aware that the only reason she clung to Hannah's side like a burr was her fear that, if she did not, Derek would pounce and spirit her away somehow. And she dared spend no more time alone with him.

The Oldham Park party was to attend a subscription ball at public rooms in Rochdale tonight, and her mother decreed that Cynthia should wear the glacé silk they had been saving. By the time she went upstairs to don it, she was as cranky as a two-year-old who had skipped her nap. She felt mutinous and unsettled, and it didn't matter one whit to her whether her anger was rational or irrational. She was angry with Derek for ignoring her stated wishes, angry with herself for failing to resist his kisses, angry with her mother for ordering her about, angry with Mr. Ellsworth for comparing so poorly to Mr. Whittaker—why couldn't he be attractive and interesting? why must he be so *humdrum?*—and angry with life in general for placing her in a position she wished she were well out of.

She stared moodily into the mirror while Lucy dressed her hair. There was no easy way to get through what promised to be a wretched evening. She supposed her best course—the one that would simultaneously please her mother and thwart Derek—would be to flirt with John Ellsworth, although she shrank from the task. She was not animated enough to be an accomplished flirt, and Mr. Ellsworth was a difficult subject to target. Plus, she suspected that Derek would do everything in his power to get in the way. On top of that, she had no real desire to spend the evening in Mr. Ellsworth's pocket. And on top of *that,* she agonized over Hannah's probable reaction. How badly would Cynthia wound her friend if she finally attracted Mr. Ellsworth's interest? How angry would Mama be if she did not? She hardly knew which outcome she dreaded more: success or failure.

At last Lucy's ministrations were done, and Cynthia stood before the pier glass while her mother walked all round her, noting each detail with a critical eye. The pale blue silk, so pale it was nearly white, gleamed beautifully in the candlelight. It clung to every curve of Cynthia's slim body. Her mother tugged expertly on the tiny, puffed sleeves to lay the

172

dainty rosettes that bordered them perfectly flat, smoothed the delicate ridge of silk piping, and made an infinitesimal adjustment to straighten the single strand of pearls clasped round her daughter's throat. Mama's eyes sparkled with all the suppressed excitement that Cynthia wished she felt but did not.

"Perfect," said Mama at last, and she broke into a smile. "Looking at you makes me long to be young again, facing an evening of flirting and dancing. You will accomplish much in this gown tonight, Cynthia. I feel sure of it."

Cynthia forced herself to smile back. "You would handle this evening much better than I shall," she confessed.

"Nonsense," said Mama. "I was fair enough in my day, but I never had your beauty, my love." Still, she looked pleased, evidently thinking Cynthia meant to compliment her. Which she had . . . but now that she thought about it, Cynthia wondered why it was considered such a compliment, to be told, basically, that one could break hearts. Was the ability to hurt other people something to be proud of?

Something of this dark train of thought must have shown in her face, for Mama frowned at her. "What's amiss? You look lovely, Cynthia."

That was not what was troubling her. In the irritated state of her nerves, her mother's shallowness repelled her. It was, she thought cynically, characteristic of Mama that she assumed, when seeing that something worried her daughter, that it must have something to do with her appearance.

"Yes, Mama," she said automatically. Then, realizing how that sounded, she amended it. "I mean, nothing is amiss. Are these the gloves you wanted me to wear?"

Her mother's brow magically smoothed, her concerns vanishing as she addressed the all-important question of gloves. "Yes, I think the short gloves look well enough, don't you? The longer gloves would look well, too, if you prefer them. No? Then let us leave it as it is. If your arms are cold, you may drape a shawl over your elbows—the white silk, I think. The wool would be warmer, but its color would not complement that delicate blue you are wearing."

Her chatter continued, but Cynthia ceased to listen. Few of the things that struck her mother as important mattered to her. This rather depressing fact was reinforced when they gathered in the hall to board the carriages that would transport them to Rochdale. When Mama learned of the travel arrangements that had been made, she was visibly put out. It was obvious to Cynthia that Mama had hoped to be placed with the Ellsworths, but the Ellsworths were going in Lord Grafton's carriage. It was the largest and could seat six passengers, so Lord and Lady Grafton—and their daughter Hannah—were taking up Sir Peter and Lady Ellsworth and their son, John. The duke and duchess were not going, and neither, of course, were Lady Malcolm and the younger Chase girls. That left Lady Ballymere and her daughter to ride in Lord Malcolm's coach, with Lord Malcolm and his brother-in-law, Mr. Whittaker.

It was a logical arrangement. But Mama's mouth turned discontentedly down when she heard it, and Cynthia—although careful to give no outward sign—felt her heart beat faster with anxiety. How long would the trip to Rochdale be? Nearly an hour. Nearly an hour, confined in a coach with Derek . . . and Mama. She could scarcely think of a worse way to begin the evening.

And then Derek walked in.

The sight of him, resplendent in impeccable evening attire, struck her like a physical blow. She felt as if the breath had been knocked out of her. There had never been another man as handsome, as desirable, as Derek Whittaker. Not to her. He appealed to her on some visceral level she could neither control nor alter. Everything about him—the way he looked, and spoke, and moved—his smile, his voice, those magnificent shoulders . . . Oh, it was terrible! She felt drawn to him in some unfathomable, deeply rooted, utterly instinctive way. And the sight of him in full evening dress somehow made the attraction even stronger. What a catastrophe.

She could not let her eyes linger on him, much as she longed to. She wrenched her gaze, feeling dazzled nearly to the point of blindness, away from Derek and to his companion, Lord Malcolm. Looking at Lord Malcolm was not dangerous. She gave him a perfunctory smile, still too rattled by Derek's presence to react to the way Malcolm's brows had climbed. But then his lordship strolled over to shake her hand, remarking, "Lady Cynthia, you outshine the stars tonight. I am allowed to stare and pay you extravagant compliments, you know, because I am a safely married man."

She wished she had a talent for easy banter, but she did not. She knew Lord Malcolm was only being friendly. She *liked* Lord Malcolm. And still, from long habit, her Frost Fair persona immediately surfaced. Her face went blank and expressionless. "Thank you," she said in a voice devoid of emotion, and she pulled her hand from his.

A man had touched her and paid her a compliment, and Cynthia had frosted him the way one swats at a fly: automatically.

Her chilly reception of Malcolm's friendly remark seemed to embarrass him. Cynthia was heartily sorry for it, but she could not think how to salvage the situation. Beneath her vacant expression, she was horrified by what she had done. She could imagine other girls, less shy, more socially skilled than she, able to apologize to him, or to turn what had just happened into a joke. Cynthia, however, became petrified. She simply could not think what to do or say.

The last thing in the world she expected was that Derek would save the day—but he did. He laughed, drawing Malcolm's attention back to himself. "Safely married, my eye! Get back here, you rogue, or I'll call Natalie down to keep you in line."

Everyone laughed, and Malcolm returned to Derek's side, complaining in a jocular way about Derek's suspicious nature. Cynthia forced herself to smile, too, and pretend that her icy set-down had been part of the joke. How easily Derek had intervened! How did one think, so quickly, of the right thing to do? It was a talent she recognized and admired, but could not seem to cultivate in herself. *One more way in which you need him,* a treacherous voice seemed to whisper in her ear. She quashed the thought—with some difficulty—and returned her attention to the room.

The assembled persons made an elegant group. Mama wore a dark blue silk specifically chosen to create a suitable background for Cynthia's palest of pale blues, but despite her altruistic motives, Lady Ballymere was still an attractive woman and looked exceptionally well in dark blue. For their part, Lord and Lady Grafton resembled illustrations in *La Belle Assemblee* come to life. And Hannah looked much prettier than she usually did, dressed in yellow, the only pastel shade that actually became her.

The Ellsworths were dressed more conservatively than fashionably, but John Ellsworth had done justice to the occasion by combing his thinning hair into a fairly convincing approximation of the *coup de vent,* and at least there was nothing of the country squire about him tonight. Lord Malcolm Chase was a tall man and, like most tall men, looked highly distinguished in evening dress. Derek, of course, was simply the best-looking and most naturally elegant person in Creation, so gorgeous tonight that she could not bear to look directly at him.

Too soon, the carriages arrived. Too soon, she was seated beside her mother in the dark confines of a narrow coach, with Derek sitting across from her and

Lord Malcolm across from Mama. A lurch, a rumble, and the journey to Rochdale began.

Mama and Lord Malcolm carried on a desultory conversation; about what, Cynthia could not tell. She could neither speak nor follow what was said. She sat silent, as motionless as the swaying of the coach allowed, enduring a maelstrom of jumbled thoughts and bubbling emotions.

Derek's eyes never left her. She stared, unseeing, out the tiny window in the door beside her but felt Derek's unwavering gaze upon her whether she looked at him or no. His regard was so intense it seemed to heat her skin. She sensed that he was willing her to look at him, but she stubbornly refused to do so. It felt, to her, as if staring out the window were the last bit of defiance her wilting resolve could muster.

Occasionally the movement of the coach brought their knees into brief contact in the darkness. Every time it happened, a shock of sensation shot through her, hot and cold together, racing along her nerve endings. It made her shiver and burn. It curled her toes with some indescribable longing, an impulse to do . . . what? She hardly knew, but whatever it was, it was wanton and wild—and stronger than she was, for she could not control it.

She could not make the sensation go away. She could not make it stop happening. She could not avoid the intermittent touch, and she could not suppress the way it made her feel. It awakened a peculiar craving in her, a craving to experience that unsettling shock, that shiver and burn, over and over. At first, she could not prevent grazing his knee with hers from time to time. But before long, she realized that she was deliberately provoking it, angling her body ever so slightly to increase the chances that a random bump in the road would throw Derek's body into surreptitious contact with her own.

When she realized what she was doing, a thrill of heat flashed through her. Recognizing her wantonness should have caused her to repent of it. Perversely, it did the opposite. Her desire to touch him, once acknowledged, increased. And it instantly occurred to her that Derek must be doing the same thing: He must be touching her knee with his *deliberately*. Being Derek, he had doubtless been doing it deliberately all along. With her mother right there—and Lord Malcolm! How did he dare!

Why, it was . . . exciting.

She could not resist. She had to test his audacity. How far would he go? Still staring disinterestedly out the window, she eased one slippered foot an inch or two forward. It may have been a tiny gesture, but her own brazenness thrilled her; she had never known that so much boldness lurked, unsuspected, in her heart.

It was doubly thrilling when, almost immediately, she sensed Derek responding to her advance, shifting his weight on the seat bench across from her. At the next rock of the carriage she felt his knee insinuate itself between hers, and the inside of his leg, knee to ankle, pressed lightly along her own.

She had never guessed how sensitive her flesh was on the inside of her leg. The intimacy was shocking.

All that separated them was a thin barrier of cloth. She could feel the warmth of his flesh. She could sense the muscles in his calf. Her lips parted on a swift intake of breath, and her eyes, as if of their own volition, stopped obeying her will and surrendered to his. She turned her head and looked at him.

Their gazes met and locked. Cynthia felt her breath quicken. He was closer to her than she had thought. The divide between the two benches was narrow, and his limbs were long. His dark eyes were luminous in the dim, reflected light. His shirtfront glimmered in the near-darkness. He loomed across from her, as desirable as he was forbidden. Feverish fantasies scampered, unbidden, across her mind. Had they been alone, what might have happened? Her lips could almost taste the searing kisses promised in his eyes.

The horses slowed. Light bloomed outside the coach. They were arriving. And still Cynthia could not tear her eyes from Derek's. It was only when the coach rocked to a standstill that she woke from her trance, at least sufficiently to exit the vehicle and pick her way across the street to the assembly rooms. Once freed of Derek's spell, she took care not to look at him again. Even so, the lingering effects of what had passed between them in the coach left her feeling drugged and strange, as if nothing around her were real. As if reality waited behind her, in the darkness, with Derek.

Standing in the foyer, waiting for a servant to take her shawl, Cynthia felt her mother tug on her elbow. "Why, this is first-rate," Mama whispered, sounding pleased. "I had no notion we would encounter so much elegance here."

Cynthia, still feeling a bit shaken, murmured her assent. Her response had been automatic, but as she looked around her she found that what her mother said was true. The assembly rooms comprised most of the ground floor of a fairly modern-appearing building. It seemed to have been designed specifically to house such entertainments; the rooms were large and well lit, opening into each other in a way that lent itself well to a public ball. There were small rooms on one side of the entry hall for cards, refreshments, and cloakrooms, and on the other side of the hall was a spacious ballroom. A flight of stairs ahead led to a mezzanine; this apparently opened out into a balcony or gallery above the ballroom floor.

Mama craned her neck, then tapped Cynthia on the arm with her fan. "There is our party," she said triumphantly, nodding to where tall Lord Grafton's head could be glimpsed above the throng. "Come along." She began threading her way through the chattering people who crowded the hall, and Cynthia obediently trailed behind her. They were leaving Lord Malcolm and Derek behind, but she supposed that was, on the whole, a good thing.

As they traversed the narrow room, Mama turned her head to issue last-minute instructions in a lowered tone over her shoulder. "Bear in mind, my love, that this is not Almack's. We have no notion who most of these people are, and I daresay many of them are persons with whom we would not normally associate.

You must dance only with members of our own party, or those whom the Chases introduce to you."

"Yes, Mama."

"And no more than two dances with any one gentleman, mind you. Not even the married ones."

"I know, Mama."

"Unless, of course, Mr. Ellsworth should happen to ask you for a third dance—but I cannot imagine him doing anything so improper."

"No, Mama."

There was not time for more; they had reached the corner where Lord and Lady Grafton were holding court. The presence of members of the Chase family had, inevitably, caused a stir; they were the preeminent family in the area. By the time Lady Ballymere and Cynthia reached them, Lord and Lady Grafton were surrounded, busily greeting and renewing their acquaintance with a steady stream of the local gentry. Cynthia's mother lost no time in attaching herself to Sir Peter and Lady Ellsworth, who were standing to one side of the mob, and engaging them in conversation.

"Such a press of people," she remarked, smiling brightly at the Ellsworths. "I am glad to have a few *friends* among the crowd. I do not entrust my daughter into the hands of just anyone, you know; I insist she dance only with the men she has met at Oldham Park." She looked significantly at John Ellsworth, including him in her smile. "You are such a gallant group of gentlemen, I feel sure my Cynthia will not be left among the wallflowers."

Thus prompted, Mr. Ellsworth energetically agreed, voicing his opinion that it would be impossible for Lady Cynthia to be overlooked, even among their own small group. After a painful pause, during which Lady Ballymere stared expectantly at him, he solicited Cynthia's hand for the quadrille. Cynthia, naturally, accepted.

Apparently satisfied by the result of her labors, Cynthia's mother then drifted away, arm in arm with Lady Ellsworth, and left Cynthia to stand with Mr. Ellsworth and wait for the music to begin. It was rather awkward, Cynthia found. She had formed such a habit of ignoring men that it was difficult for her to unbend and converse naturally. And poor Mr. Ellsworth was, beneath his hearty bluster, as shy as she. They stood side by side, Mr. Ellsworth rocking on his heels and humming under his breath, looking about in a vague sort of way.

Cynthia cleared her throat and ventured a remark. "I suppose they will begin with the quadrille," she said.

"Eh? Oh, yes, yes. I fancy they will. It's generally done, isn't it? To begin with a quadrille."

In that case, our suffering will soon be over, she wanted to say. She didn't say it, of course. Another awkward pause ensued. Across the knots of people, Cynthia saw her mother's reproving eyes upon her. She knew she had to make more of an effort. She turned to her companion but could not catch his eye; he was looking elsewhere.

"Do you enjoy dancing, Mr. Ellsworth?" she said loudly.

He glanced sideways at her, in the manner of a skittish horse. "Dancing? Enjoy it? Enjoy dancing?" She had evidently caught him at a loss. He gave a kind of gulp, then found his tongue. "I don't mind it. One must dance, eh? Expected. I'm not a dab hand at it, mind you," he added. "Not the sort of chap who—that is, I'm not particularly— Well, I've never been fond of—"

"Dancing," she finished helpfully.

He appeared grateful. "Yes."

They were both palpably relieved when Hannah escaped the group that surrounded her parents and joined them. Her presence seemed to ease Mr. Ellsworth's awkwardness as much as it did Cynthia's; he visibly relaxed and his affect became less forced. Hannah took John's arm with one hand and Cynthia's arm with the other. She drew them from the foyer into the ballroom as if it were the most natural thing in the world that they should form a threesome.

"I know it is horrid of me," she confessed, "but I simply cannot *wait* to get away from here and back to London. I loathe being the center of attention, and every time we attend one of these local events we are mobbed."

"Ghastly," said Mr. Ellsworth sympathetically. Then he smiled the most natural smile Cynthia had yet seen him wear. "But I daresay you would be mobbed tonight in any event, Lady Hannah. Never saw you look so pretty, upon my soul."

Hannah looked startled, and so thrilled that Cynthia was afraid that even Mr. Ellsworth could hardly fail to notice the heart pinned to Hannah's sleeve. However, she had evidently underestimated the thickness of his skull. He gave no sign that he saw anything out of the ordinary in the glowing look Hannah threw him, nor in the pretty confusion his compliment cast her into. For a moment, Cynthia longed to box his silly ears. Then she remembered her role: She was not here for matchmaking. She was here to steal hapless Mr. Ellsworth from her friend. That meant she must be *glad* that Mr. Ellsworth was dense.

Depression settled on her spirits. Her only consolation was that Hannah, surely, could do much better for herself than to marry John Ellsworth. She had to believe that, at any rate . . . She would go mad if she did not. Marriage to Mr. Ellsworth seemed, to Cynthia, a fate so dreary that only she deserved it. If she allowed herself to believe that Hannah might actually be *happy* with the man . . . and that Mr. Ellsworth might, also, find happiness with Hannah . . . she would feel even meaner and more despicable than she already did.

A tingle of awareness along the back of her neck alerted her to Derek's presence before she actually saw him. She felt him approach the way one feels a thunderstorm approach; he seemed to exude a subtle charge of electricity that changed the weight of the air. She reflexively wiped all expression from her features and stared into the middle distance.

Hannah shifted to make room for him, and Derek joined them. "Hallo, you three," he said genially. "I'm glad to find a few familiar faces among the horde."

Hannah giggled. "These balls are always a frightful crush."

"I hope you ladies have saved me a dance or two."

It pained Cynthia to see the shy, hopeful glance Hannah shot Mr. Ellsworth. "I haven't promised a dance to anyone yet," she said. This was the perfect opening for him to claim a dance with her. But Mr. Ellsworth, as always, seemed oblivious.

Cynthia altered her posture to subtly imply that she was not standing with the group, but with Mr. Ellsworth alone. "I have promised the quadrille to Mr. Ellsworth," she said. Then, mindful of her mother's instructions, she remembered to smile at him. "I do not yet know if he will require more of me."

It was a statement, but she inflected it as if it were a question. Mr. Ellsworth blinked, evidently startled by her sudden brashness. "Oh, ah—certainly. Yes, I think I will, Lady Cynthia. Certainly I will. Who wouldn't, eh? Yes, if you'll do me the honor, I shall . . . I shall press my luck."

His response lacked enthusiasm, but passed the test of bare-bones gallantry. At any rate, she had successfully painted him into a corner. Whatever his intentions originally had been, he would, perforce, ask her for a second dance. That should appease Mama. The next trick she needed to perform, of course, was to effect an escape before Derek painted her into a similar corner—easy enough for him to do, since she could hardly refuse to dance with him. He was, as she was, a guest of the Chases.

The musicians in the balcony, mercifully, chose that

moment to begin tuning their instruments. The ball was about to begin. Mr. Ellsworth presented his arm and Cynthia gratefully took it, nodding a cool dismissal to Derek. Sensing Hannah's disappointment at her walking off with Mr. Ellsworth, she avoided Hannah's eye. She thus missed whatever took place between Hannah and Derek after she and Mr. Ellsworth took to the floor to find their places for the quadrille. She could guess, however, so she was glad when her partner led her to the last empty slot in a set. When Lady Hannah and Mr. Whittaker appeared among the dancers, as she had expected they would, they had to join a neighboring set.

The quadrille began. Cynthia wondered, not for the first time, why balls always seemed to begin with a quadrille. It was one of the more difficult dances to learn, and there were always a few people on the floor who forgot the sequence or danced the wrong steps. It soon became apparent why Mr. Ellsworth had moved with such alacrity to place them as fourth couple; he, alas, was among those who humbugged their way through the dance, waiting until someone else moved before venturing to guess which figure came next. As a result, he and Cynthia were slightly behind the time in any figure that was not danced by the other couples first. His concentration and anxiety were such that conversation was impossible; throughout the dance he counted the bars of music under his breath and stared nervously at others' feet, trying to anticipate what would be required of his own.

By the time the music ended, Cynthia was both

bored and annoyed. Mr. Ellsworth's preoccupation struck her as boorish. Why had he asked her to dance the quadrille, of all dances? His lack of skill had made them both conspicuous. As usual, she gave no indication of her feelings. She hid her irritation behind a bland and noncommittal smile and laid her glove upon his sleeve so he could escort her off the floor.

A familiar shirtfront stepped squarely into her line of vision, forcing her to halt or walk into its owner. Cynthia chose to halt. With her hand still on Mr. Ellsworth's arm, she lifted her eyes to Derek's face, one eyebrow delicately lifted in a carefully practiced expression of icy incredulity.

She had quelled many an advance with this lifted eyebrow. She had routed formidable opponents; she had reduced grown men to stammering, red-faced boys. However, her glacial glare had no effect whatsoever on the audacious Mr. Whittaker. His response was neither embarrassment nor apology nor dismay. Instead, he gave her a cheeky grin. That grin contained enough heat to melt the most frozen of hearts, and Cynthia felt her willpower turning to slush.

Inwardly berating herself for her appalling weakness, she straightened her spine and lifted the other eyebrow. "Are we in your way, Mr. Whittaker?" she inquired, her tone a perfect mixture of politeness and hauteur.

"It's the other way round," he replied promptly, with undiminished cheer. "I am in yours. I say, Ellsworth, did you happen to see which way Lady Hannah went?"

Mr. Ellsworth looked befuddled. "No, can't say that I did. Have you lost her?"

"Well, she isn't here," said Derek vaguely. His statement was true, as far as it went, but Cynthia knew a fib when she heard one. It was plain to her, if not to Mr. Ellsworth, that Derek was cutting a wheedle. She shot him an indignant look, but it seemed to bounce right off of him. He was busy trying an ingratiating, apologetic air upon her companion. "Be a good chap and find her for me, would you?" he begged with apparent sincerity. "I am unfamiliar with this place. I don't like to think of Lady Hannah wandering about unescorted."

Concern knitted Mr. Ellsworth's brows. "Certainly not. Most improper. All sorts of persons here; not a private ball. Pray excuse me, Lady Cynthia. I'm sure Mr. Whittaker will take good care of you."

"That I will," said Derek. His assumption of meek gratitude was highly suspect. Cynthia shot him her best affronted stare again, but it still had no discernible effect.

"Don't let Lady Cynthia wander off as well, eh? Ha! Ha!" Mr. Ellsworth was already scanning the crowd, as if he had completely forgotten Cynthia's presence.

"Oh, I have learned my lesson," Derek promised. He plucked Cynthia's hand off Mr. Ellsworth's sleeve and tucked it firmly in the crook of his elbow. "Lady Cynthia shan't escape me."

"Have I nothing to say in the matter?" demanded Cynthia, but Mr. Ellsworth was gone, shouldering his way through the crowd. She directed a fulminating glare up at Derek. "You, sir, are unconscionable."

"I don't know what you mean."

"Yes, you do. Pray do not try that wide-eyed stare on me. I shan't be duped by it. I know you too well."

"Done," he said promptly, as if they had just made a pact. "And you may stop blasting me with that arctic freeze of yours. I shan't be duped by it. I know you too well."

He started for the door leading back to the foyer, and Cynthia was forced to fall into step beside him or risk causing a scene. He still had her hand hooked in his elbow, and had covered it with his other hand to make sure she could not easily remove it. Cynthia was guiltily aware that she had no real desire to remove it, that some treacherous part of her was secretly glad he had taken this step. This knowledge ruffled her feathers even further.

"Where are you taking me?"

"Refreshments. You look thirsty."

"I am not thirsty, Mr. Whittaker. I am angry."

"What, at being separated from Mr. Ellsworth? I hate to be the bearer of bad news, Lady Cynthia, but he was remarkably easy to dispatch." He shook his head with mock sympathy. "Not a good omen for your ambitions, I fear."

Cynthia fumed in silence. She was so preoccupied with trying to find a suitable retort that she failed to notice where Derek was leading her. Her focus returned when he opened a door leading to the terrace behind the building.

She stopped short, staring in disbelief at the opened

door—and the cold darkness beyond it. "This is not the refreshment room."

"No, but you said you weren't thirsty. I thought you might like some air. To cool your temper," he added, words plainly chosen to do the opposite.

Cynthia immediately snatched her hand away and turned on her heel. She had not taken two steps before she felt his hand at her waist, pulling her sharply back against him. She froze, terrified that people would see him holding her. His warm breath tickled her ear as he murmured, close to her head, "Don't try to escape me, Cynthia. I've told you before, you won't succeed."

"Let go of me at once," she hissed.

"I will, if you agree to dance with me."

She gasped. "For shame! Will you *force* me?"

"If I must." But she felt his hand loosen and then, with obvious reluctance, release her. "I had hoped there would be no need."

This was too much. Exasperated, she whirled to face him. "I don't know what to do with you," she exclaimed. "You seem to willfully disregard my wishes. You hear only what you choose to hear. How can I make it clearer? There is no hope for you, Mr. Whittaker. Your suit will not prosper. I have told you so time and again."

"Yes, you have." He looked completely unperturbed. "And yet I fail to retire from the lists. Odd, isn't it? I wonder why I don't give up? Other men would. Call me foolish—"

"I shall call you worse than foolish! You are utterly pigheaded. I know perfectly well why you continue to harass me. You are too stubborn to admit defeat."

He rubbed his chin thoughtfully. "Well, that's possible," he admitted. "I own I can be remarkably tenacious at times."

"Tenacious? That's a polite word for what you are."

"On the other hand, I'm a fairly good dancer," he offered. "Which brings us back to the point of our discussion. Will you do me the honor, Lady Cynthia, of standing up with me?" He held up one finger in a warning gesture. "Be careful! You mustn't read too much into my invitation, or I will begin to think you conceited. I have asked you to dance with me, not marry me."

He was so ridiculous she found herself fighting an impulse to laugh. "You *have* asked me to marry you," she muttered resentfully. "Conceited, indeed! I am no such thing."

"Well, then, let me point out that the invitations were issued separately. Consent to one does not bind you to the other."

What an attractive smile he had. One could not help returning such a smile, however reluctantly. "Very well," she said. "One dance." Inspiration struck. She felt her smile turn sly. "The pavane, if they play it."

"The pavane!" For an instant he looked dismayed, but he recovered quickly. "I feel sure they will play it. I have an instinct for such things." There was a cunning gleam in his eye; obviously Derek would not hesitate to bribe the musicians. Cynthia had to look away to keep from laughing aloud.

"Pray take me back to Lord and Lady Grafton. You

may come and find me when you hear the pavane. *If you hear the pavane.*"

"Oh, I may come and find you long before that," he assured her.

She tried to look stern. "I beg you will not. You have a most unsettling effect upon me, Mr. Whittaker. You made me lose my temper—something that has happened so seldom in my life that I nearly failed to recognize it just now."

"It's good for you." His face was alight with mischief. "Even the iciest of ice queens must have someone in her life whom she cannot frighten."

"How absurd you are! I don't frighten people."

He looked skeptically at her. "What would you call it?"

She bit her lip. "It's unkind of you to tease me about my shyness," she said with dignity.

He threw back his head and gave a delighted yelp of laughter. "Touché! I apologize, my lady."

"Then you will take me back now?"

"Your wish is my command." He lifted her hand and laid it on his sleeve, covering it with his own.

The dynamic between them subtly shifted when he touched her. She looked pointedly down at his hand covering hers. "You are too familiar, sir," she said, but not convincingly. The words came out high-pitched and breathless.

"Ah, Cynthia, don't frost me," he murmured coaxingly. His voice was low and intimate, sending shivers through her. "Let me touch you while I may."

Her heart seemed to flutter in her chest at these provoking words. Before she had time to think better of the impulse, her eyes had lifted to his—a fatal error. The maidenly protest she was preparing to utter died, unspoken, on her lips. Instead, she heard herself say, in a broken whisper, words that seemed to bubble up out of nowhere.

"Derek, you will be the death of me. I don't know whether I am on my head or my heels when I am with you."

She saw his eyes darken with understanding. The rest of the room seemed to fade and float away, leaving the two of them utterly alone in some sweet and private place.

"You keep trying to follow the rules," he told her softly. "But, Cynthia, my darling girl, the rules do not apply to us."

His words made no sense, and yet they rang utterly true. She felt in the depths of her soul that he was right.

Cynthia shuddered and looked away, trying to regain her poise by breaking their eye contact. They were still, after all, at the edge of a foyer near a crowded ballroom. "Take me back," she said faintly. "I cannot think when I am with you."

"You know that I am right."

"It seems to me," she said wretchedly, "that I know absolutely nothing anymore. And the older I get, the more certain I become that everything I once knew is wrong. Take me back, Derek. Please."

Chapter Twelve

Half in a dream, Cynthia watched Derek disappear, heading purposefully toward the stairs. The stairs led to the mezzanine. The mezzanine led to the musicians. She smiled to herself, guessing his errand; he was going to ensure, by fair means or foul, that the pavane was played tonight. And Cynthia, rightly or wrongly, felt a flutter of giddy pleasure at his persistence.

She almost laughed, trying to picture the scene that was doubtless about to take place above her head. The pavane was an ancient, courtly dance, neither romantic nor fashionable. She imagined it was not among the pieces frequently requested by amorous young bucks.

She felt a sharp rap on her forearm and spun, startled. Her mother had walked up behind her and tapped her with her fan. Mama's eyes were glittering with wrath. Cynthia went cold with fear at the sight.

"Where have you been? Mr. Ellsworth is dancing with Lady Hannah."

"Well, Mama, I cannot dance every dance with him," Cynthia hedged, trying to sound reasonable.

"I saw you walk off with Mr. Whittaker after the quadrille. Cynthia, for heaven's sake, what are you about? Why did you not ask Mr. Ellsworth to bring you a glass of punch? You might have kept him by your side another quarter of an hour."

Cynthia's control frayed. "To what purpose? It's absurd! I cannot *force* him to like me."

For an instant, Mama looked stunned. Then her eyes narrowed in fury. "I disagree," she hissed. "And who, pray, are you, to set up your will against mine? How dare you flout my authority, you ungrateful little snip? I have shown you every indulgence, Cynthia—more than most parents would have done. Did you not promise me after Filey died, that if I let you rebuff all suitors for a twelvemonth, you would then marry at my bidding? Well? Did you not?" Her fingers dug painfully into Cynthia's arm.

"Yes, Mama," said Cynthia faintly, feeling utterly intimidated. How she loathed being scolded! "Mama, pray—pray let go of me."

Her mother did let go, flinging Cynthia's arm away with an angry huff. "The idea!" she exclaimed. "'I can't force him to like me,'" she mimicked in an exaggerated, high-pitched whine.

"Oh, Mama, *pray*—"

"My point is you haven't tried properly! Why shouldn't he like you? You are the most beautiful girl in the room tonight. Any man present would leap at the chance to enjoy your favor. But you show no interest in Mr. Ellsworth. You barely smile at him. You stand aloof and silent, rather than trying to ingratiate yourself with him. I have warned you, Cynthia, that you will get nowhere unless you adopt a more conciliatory manner. You simply must be more *approachable*. Is that so difficult?"

"For me, yes, it is," said Cynthia, agonized. "I don't

know why. I don't mean to flout your authority, Mama. I know what I owe to you—to my family."

"I'm glad to hear it," her mother snapped, fanning herself in an agitated manner. "I believe you mean to be a good daughter, Cynthia. I merely ask that you *act* on it a little. Follow through, for heaven's sake. The ten thousand Filey gave us is all but gone."

And whose fault is that? Not mine. Resentment, thick and black, bubbled up in Cynthia's heart again. It was unstoppable, like oil seeping from the depths of the earth. And she felt she would never be rid of it now that it had oozed out of whatever cranny had bred it, that her heart would never again be wholly clean, never be free of its sticky filth. She would never love her mother the way she had in childhood. That trust, that purity, had been sullied forever by her growing anger.

She had to clamp her mouth shut to keep from saying words to her mother she knew she would regret. It did no good to lay blame, she reminded herself, fighting the ugly feelings. Ten thousand pounds was a great deal of money, but it had not been enough. It didn't matter why. Her family had counted on thirty thousand but had received only ten. She must marry a man with sufficient means to make up the difference. A hefty marriage settlement and, with luck, a yearly stipend for the bride's parents; this was what Mama dreamed of. This was what her parents needed. And Cynthia was their only hope of securing such a windfall.

The music ended with a flourish. Mama darted back

to Lady Ellsworth's side to pursue her portion of the campaign: flattering and fawning upon Mr. Ellsworth's parents. Cynthia was left alone to observe Mr. Ellsworth and Hannah leaving the floor.

Hannah was in a visible glow of spirits. As Cynthia watched, Mr. Ellsworth leaned in to her, with an indulgent smile, to hear her chatter. Cynthia knew she must detach her friend from Mr. Ellsworth. It was her duty to do so, and quickly. Mama was watching. She braced herself to tackle the distasteful task, but was spared—for the moment. The couple suddenly veered to the left, heading away from her and toward the refreshment rooms. She knew she shouldn't feel so relieved . . . but she did.

And then Derek materialized at her side again, the deviltry in his grin causing her heart to do somersaults. She smiled, almost against her will, and felt the knots of tension in her shoulders mysteriously loosen. Just being with him made her feel better. And that made no sense at all, because she knew perfectly well that being with him increased the danger she was in.

"You look pleased with yourself," she remarked.

"I'm a clever, resourceful sort of chap," he agreed. "I think you owe me a dance, my lady."

As he spoke, she heard the musicians starting up again. They were beginning, unmistakably, the pavane. She had to bite her lip to keep from laughing. "What an odd coincidence, that they would play the pavane. And so soon!"

"Well, as it happens, the musicians didn't intend to play it at all. They seemed to think no one would expect it. Tried to tell me it wasn't danced anymore."

"Fancy that," murmured Cynthia.

"Hard to believe, isn't it? Fortunately, I was able to convince them that the pavane is danced at all the best balls, and to leave it out would be shockingly remiss." He offered his arm. "I'm a persuasive fellow, in my way."

"I know you are." She let him lead her on to the floor, still struggling to suppress a bubble of laughter. "But if they did not intend to play it at all, you must have been eloquent indeed. They changed their minds so completely as to play it immediately."

"There was some talk, originally, of simply tacking it on to the end of the programme," he admitted. "But I scotched that."

"Oh?" She dipped in the customary curtsy, then stepped to his side with a graceful swirl and took her position for the dance. "Why?"

He actually had the cheek to *wink* at her. "Couldn't bear to wait that long," he explained, lifting his hand to accept hers.

Something had happened while he was upstairs, greasing the musicians in the fist. He had known immediately, by the tense set of her shoulders and the storminess in her eyes. But he also noticed that her unhappiness, whatever its cause, melted away shortly after he arrived on the scene. He was glad of that. His experience of Cynthia was still limited, but it seemed to him that she was subtly different when he was around. Even when ripping up at him she seemed to be enjoying herself. And Cynthia did not have the look of someone who generally enjoyed herself.

He stole another glance at her. She was so lovely in the pale blue silk that he could scarcely believe she was real. It was obvious she had chosen to grant him the pavane out of pure perversity, believing that it would not be danced. But now that he had thwarted that bit of mischief, he had to own that she looked exceedingly beautiful dancing it. She glided demurely along beside him, arms daintily upheld in the traditional manner, her hand laid so lightly on the back of his that he could barely feel it. The courtly pose had been invented to show off the flowing sleeves of a Renaissance costume, but it served equally well to display Cynthia's pretty arms, bared in a way that the pavane's original dancers would have found shocking. The infinitesimal sleeves and low neckline of today's fashions exposed much of her soft, gorgeous skin, and the sight of it almost made his mouth water. He had to look away again, swallowing hard.

They were not the only dancers on the floor, much to Derek's amusement. The pavane was the sort of dance everyone had been taught at one time or another, whether they had ever danced it publicly or no. And the steps were so simple and stately that the floor soon filled with couples—including those too infirm to dance more energetic dances and those too unsure of their dancing skill to attempt more complex dances.

"We seem to have scored a hit," he observed.

"Naturally."

He cocked an eyebrow at her. "Oh, did you expect it?"

She looked amused. "Everyone likes the tried and true. When dancing, at any rate."

"The safety of the familiar."

"Precisely."

"I forget what to do when we reach the end of the floor. Do we hit the wall or continue on out the door?"

A little choke of laughter escaped her. "I shall pass in front of you, and we then promenade down the floor in the opposite direction."

"Ah, yes. It all comes back to me now."

"Why, Mr. Whittaker, anyone would think that you rarely danced the pavane." Her tone sounded almost flirtatious. Was she teasing him? He devoutly hoped so. If he did nothing else for his lady love, he hoped, at least, to bring a little fun into her life.

He looked down his nose at her in a comical way and drawled, "Lady Cynthia, you wound me. We have established, have we not, that the pavane is danced at all the *best* balls? What do you take me for—a bumpkin?"

She actually laughed out loud, although she immediately covered her mouth with her hand to stifle it. "Pray do not make me laugh," she begged, glancing apprehensively toward the wall. He followed her gaze with his and saw that Cynthia's eyes had gone to where her mother stood, ostensibly conversing with Lady Ellsworth but, in reality, watching her daughter. The coldness in her gaze was so pronounced that even Derek felt its chill.

"What do you fear?" he asked Cynthia, suddenly serious. "Does Lady Ballymere not allow you to laugh?"

"Not in public," she said hurriedly. "Not out loud. And I never do laugh in public, so if she sees me— Here, let me pass before you; we are near enough the wall."

It was obviously not a good moment to tease her about which partner was supposed to lead and which was supposed to follow. She had interrupted herself before she could tell him what it was she truly feared. But he could guess. He passed Cynthia before him in silence, and they led the procession back down the floor. She seemed to breathe easier once she was on his other side, where her mother's eyes would find it difficult to monitor her every move and expression.

He chose his words carefully. "It strikes me," he said at last, "that you live your life on tenterhooks. You seem to especially fear that your mother will discover our—"

"Oh, hush!" Her eyes darted wildly about, as if dreading that spies lurked everywhere. "Do not say it."

"Very well, I won't finish my sentence." He lowered his voice. "But I have hit the mark, have I not? If your mother sees that I make you laugh, she might conclude that you enjoy my company." He could not keep the dryness from his voice. "And we can't have that, can we?"

"No," said Cynthia, lifting her chin at him. "We can't. As I have told you more than once."

"Why hasn't she noticed anything yet?" he demanded. "Does she know you so little? I can tell from across the room what you are feeling."

She looked at him strangely. "You are the only person who can," she said softly. "Don't you realize that? I am generally thought impossible to read."

His eyebrows flew up. He was about to pooh-pooh the notion as preposterous and tell her she was transparent as glass—when he remembered her reputation. He had heard from more than one source that Lady Cynthia Fitzwilliam was the coldest fish in nature. He had heard jokes to that effect—had even, in the depths of his heartbreak, repeated them.

"Egad," he muttered. "You're right." He digested this revelation in silence for a few seconds. It struck him as further proof, had he required any, that he and Cynthia were meant for each other.

Cynthia spoke, sounding thoughtful. "I do wonder, however, why she hasn't voiced more distrust of you. Not that she doesn't view you with suspicion." Ironic amusement lit her voice. "But she seems no more hostile toward you than she is toward every other personable man who crosses my path."

"She hasn't noticed my fascination with you?" He chuckled. "That's because it doubtless strikes her as no more than your due. Are you not aware, my love, that I am presently the envy of every man in the room?"

A tiny frown appeared between her brows. "Ridiculous."

"Not at all. We have escaped detection for two reasons: No one can tell what you are feeling, and my admiration becomes lost in the crowd. My single-minded focus on you does not stand out, my lady, because so many other men stare at you with their mouths agape."

She looked startled, and not at all pleased. "That's an exaggeration at best, and utter nonsense at worst. Stare at me, indeed! I would hate that. I am exceedingly careful to draw no attention to myself."

Fascinating. She seemed really to believe that circumspect behavior—never laughing out loud, for example—would keep people from noticing her. Was she really unaware that she could cause a sensation simply by walking into a room? Come to think of it, the way she floated through social events, withdrawn and blank-faced, indicated that she might honestly be too detached to feel the stares.

Why, then, did she react immediately when *he* looked at her?

He glanced again at the angelic face beside him, now averted in a futile attempt to avoid his scrutiny. "You always seem to know when I am looking at you," he said quietly. "All this time, I thought you were uncannily sensitive. Aware of every set of eyes that fastened upon you."

"Only yours," she assured him, then bit her lip. A faint pink suffused her cheeks. "Oh, I am so vexed with myself," she exclaimed, clearly rattled. "Lately I seem to blurt out every rash thought that passes through my brain."

"These are trying times for you," he said sympathetically, but his eyes were laughing. "It's difficult to chase after money when your heart is leading you in a different direction."

She must have heard the laughter in his voice, for she looked indignantly at him. "Is everything a joke to you?"

"Many things. Not all. And never this. But it's better to joke than to weep." The tempo of the music slowed slightly, indicating that the piece was drawing to a close. Derek was forced to drop Cynthia's hand, face her, and bow.

She curtsied, her expression still stormy. He immediately offered his arm to escort her off the floor, but she ignored it and turned away. He fell into step beside her.

"I have angered you again. I am sorry for it."

She glanced fleetingly at his face and seemed to relent a trifle. "I am oversensitive these days," she acknowledged stiffly. "It must be the *trying times*."

"You thought I was joking about that? I wasn't."

"Never mind." She spoke in a low tone, but she did not sound angry anymore. They were nearly back to where their group had clustered, Lady Ballymere, Lady Ellsworth, and Lady Grafton all seated on spindly chairs while Lord Grafton and Sir Peter lounged nearby. Mr. Ellsworth, Hannah, and Lord Malcolm were nowhere to be seen.

"Stay a moment." He touched her arm, and she halted, turning reluctantly to face him. "Grant me another dance, Cynthia," he whispered, his eyes searching hers with utter seriousness. "Please."

She shook her head. "I cannot be seen to favor you over Mr. Ellsworth."

"If I ensure that Mr. Ellsworth stands up with you again, will you give me equal time?"

Her lips twitched in a reluctant, nearly invisible smile. "I suppose I must," she said softly. "Mama told me I must dance only with the men of our party. But that includes you."

She turned to go, but he stopped her again, leaning in for one more word. "Cynthia, do not marry a man who cannot tell what you are feeling," he urged her softly, with utter seriousness. "That's a recipe for misery."

"On the contrary." She lifted her chin, gazing defiantly straight ahead. "It's a recipe for privacy. Something I have learned to value highly, Mr. Whittaker." And she walked away from him to join the group by the chairs.

Chapter Thirteen

Cynthia was beginning to understand why being angry was sometimes called being "mad." The more Cynthia's resentment toward her mother grew, the more she felt as if she were losing control of her own thoughts.

A dim sense that her dear family was, in reality, taking shameless advantage of her, seemed to be coalescing into a firmly held and unshakable opinion— despite her frantic efforts to suppress and discourage the notion. A near-mutiny boiled beneath her calm facade, and its rising pressure threatened to blow the lid off her carefully lived, dutiful life. Thank goodness she was kept busy tonight, smiling and dancing and making polite, meaningless conversation. She had a strong suspicion that if she were given five minutes alone in which to think, she might very well run screaming into the night.

She had quashed her rebellious feelings and forced herself to dance a second time with Mr. Ellsworth. And during this second dance, she had determinedly set out to charm him. She had smiled. She had flattered. She had made a concerted effort to draw him out and get him to talk about himself.

And the man was dull. There was no way around it. He was a boring little man who led a boring little life, and in ten minutes on the dance floor they could find not a single subject on which to have a sensible conversation. They had no interests in common. They had no experiences in common. She felt no spark of attraction or interest in him whatsoever, and if he felt attracted to her, he certainly hid it well.

And then, by lucky chance, Cynthia mentioned Hannah. Immediately Mr. Ellsworth's eyes lit with enthusiasm. "Now, she's what my old Scottish nurse would call a grand lass," opined Mr. Ellsworth, beaming. "Not a selfish bone in her body."

Cynthia sincerely seconded this and congratulated him on his ability to see it. "For Hannah is so modest, you know, that she never puts herself forward."

"No, very true, by Jove. Very true. She never does,

does she? But that's one of the things one particularly admires in her. A very quiet, modest spirit, upon my soul! A grand lass."

Cynthia still wasn't sure what he meant by a "grand lass," but she was happy to hear her friend spoken of so warmly. They spent the remaining minutes of their dance sharing anecdotes that illustrated Hannah's goodness and loyalty, and eventually left the floor much more in charity with each other than Cynthia would have thought possible half an hour ago. For several seconds, she felt almost optimistic.

And then she saw Hannah. Hannah was standing stock-still near the ballroom entrance, staring at her friend with a stunned, tragic expression that sent a chill down Cynthia's back. Cynthia had never seen such a look on Hannah's face. She knew at once that Hannah had guessed, at last, what Cynthia was trying to do. Her poor face was a study in hurt feelings and betrayal. Before Cynthia could say one word, Hannah turned and bolted out of the room.

Something inside Cynthia suddenly snapped. Hannah's stricken face was the first thing, she felt, that she had seen clearly all night. Perhaps in years. Seeing her friend so hurt, and by *her* actions—her witless, heartless, unthinking actions—was a revelation. She had feared this, had she not? Well, she had been right to fear it. Right to fear it, and wrong to ignore her fears. *Wrong* to obey her mother. She had chosen obedience over her own better judgment.

She had only herself to blame. It was not Mama who had flirted with Mr. Ellsworth. The behavior had been hers, and hers was the responsibility. She saw, in a flash, that it was high time—long past time—that Cynthia Fitzwilliam grew up.

She forgot her duty. She forgot decorum. She forgot where she was and who she was with and what she was supposed to be doing. Nothing mattered but Hannah, and Cynthia's overwhelming need to wipe that look off her friend's face and make sure it never came back. Without a word to the oblivious Mr. Ellsworth, still at her side and in the middle of a sentence, Cynthia picked up her skirts and ran.

She was vaguely aware of Mr. Ellsworth's startled "Bless my soul!" behind her and the astonished stares of the people she dashed past. Their curious gazes followed her—surprised, disapproving—but she didn't care. "Hannah!" she called, desperate. She halted in the foyer, looking frantically about, craning her neck. She did not see her friend anywhere.

Seemingly out of nowhere, Derek appeared at her side. "What is it?" His voice, though concerned, was perfectly steady. "Can I help you?"

She looked up and her control crumbled further. Had she been wrong about Derek, too? She would address that later; Hannah came first. As for now, she saw beside her a rock of salvation. Derek Whittaker was exactly the sort of man one turned to in an emergency. Instinctively she seized his wrist and clung to it.

"Hannah ran out here," she said, her voice quivering. "I don't know where she is."

He asked no questions. He simply did as she knew he would do: He helped her. "We'll find her. Come along," he said calmly and led her toward the stairs to the mezzanine.

His air of certainty was a balm to her agitated spirit. "Thank you," she gasped, with real gratitude, and hurried to keep up with his longer legs. They started up the stairs. "You saw where she went?"

"No, but there are only a few places in this building where she might have gone."

She glanced at him, confused. "How do you know?"

He looked nonplussed. "I—ah—" He cleared his throat. "Let's just say I have an instinct."

Puzzled, but intuitively trusting him, Cynthia hurried up the stairs at his side. When they reached the top, the wide balcony stretched to her left, overlooking the ballroom below. She saw the musicians out of the corner of her eye, clustered in a niche. Her heart pounded when she heard the sound of muffled weeping; she could not tell from which direction it came. But Derek strode unhesitatingly to a narrow door on the opposite side of the landing and tapped gently on it.

The weeping stopped. Derek leaned closer, listening. "Lady Hannah? Are you in there?"

A pause ensued, during which, evidently, the weeper on the other side of the door considered her options. She eventually said, with every sign of embarrassed reluctance, "Who's there?"

"Derek Whittaker."

Another pause. Then Derek added, "And your friend, Lady Cynthia."

More silence, thick and ominous. Cynthia could

bear it no longer. She stepped to the door and tried the handle. It turned easily, and within seconds she had flown into the room and hugged Hannah, who immediately burst into fresh tears.

Hannah had evidently been indulging her bout of weeping while pacing, for there was nothing to sit on. The room was small and dark, its only illumination coming from French windows that opened onto a tiny balcony. It seemed odd to have tall windows and a balcony in a storeroom, which was what this evidently was, but the windows had probably been designed more for exterior ornament than any practical use. Spindly chairs, similar to the ones lining the ballroom, were stacked neatly along one wall. Everything else was under holland covers.

Cynthia was dimly aware that Derek had closed the door behind them for privacy. Her focus was on her unhappy friend. She held Hannah at arm's length, her own eyes filling with tears as she beheld Hannah's misery. "Oh, Hannah, how could you think I would serve you such a trick?" she exclaimed.

Hannah gulped. "I'm sorry. It looked . . . it looked as if . . ."

Guilt struck anew as Cynthia realized that her last remark, although heartfelt, had been a bit misleading. "Well, it was," she said, in a burst of candor. "It was exactly what it looked to be. But, Hannah, I'm so sorry! I won't do it anymore."

Hannah's face started to crumple again. "I can't compete with you, Cynthia. You're so beautiful and I'm so plain—"

"You're not plain," said Cynthia fiercely.

Derek coughed discreetly. "I'll just wait outside the door, shall I?" he said mildly.

Hannah gave a little gasp; she had apparently assumed that she and Cynthia were alone. "Oh, pray—pray do, Mr. Whittaker!"

Cynthia threw him a grateful glance, and he stepped outside to the mezzanine, closing the door quietly behind him. Hannah, meanwhile, was pulling herself together. She had found a handkerchief somewhere about her person and began mopping her face with it. "I'm sorry to be such a baby," she said shakily.

"You're not. And it's my fault," said Cynthia remorsefully. "This is all my fault. I've been thoughtless and wicked."

"Oh, Cynthia, no! You mustn't say such things."

Cynthia held up a warning hand. "Do not defend me, Hannah! Do not even *tempt* me to forgive myself, or I shall very likely do so. And I mustn't go on as I always have. I see, now, that I desperately need to mend my ways."

A faint smile lightened Hannah's features. "Do you? You seem perfect to me."

"Too perfect," said Cynthia bitterly. "Too dutiful." Doubt shook her. "Is that possible? Can one be too dutiful? Too obedient?"

Hannah thought for a moment, then nodded, still sniffing a little. "I suppose any virtue, carried to an extreme, becomes a vice. I've heard it said that love taken too far becomes idolatry. Modesty taken too far becomes prudery. What does obedience become?"

Cynthia had never pondered the question before. She hugged her elbows, thinking hard. "Laziness," she said glumly. "Moral laziness. Certainly mental laziness. I haven't . . . haven't *thought* properly." She frowned, struggling to find the right words. "My obedience has made me passive. In submitting to the will of others, I have suppressed my own judgment. I have actually tried *not* to think, often and often. And that's wrong, isn't it?"

She did not wait for an answer but began pacing, her tumbling ideas pouring themselves out to Hannah's sympathetic ear. Excitement was welling in her. She was on the verge, she felt, of a momentous discovery. "Of course it is wrong! Why, just now, it was my stupid devotion to duty that led me to injure my friend—and I knew better, all along. I simply wouldn't listen to myself. I obeyed my mother rather than follow my heart."

Hannah looked amazed. "Do you mean it was your mother, not you, who wanted you to—"

"Yes, of course it was." Cynthia waved that off as unimportant. "That can't surprise you, Hannah. Have I not always yielded to Mama? With increasing reluctance, I must admit! But I have always believed that submission, in and of itself, was virtuous. So I tried, even against my better judgment, to submit. And now I think . . . I think submission may be a child's virtue. I think I may have a higher duty, as an adult. To think for myself. To form my own judgments."

"Of course you do," said Hannah warmly. "Why shouldn't your opinions be as valid as anyone else's?"

Cynthia laughed, feeling almost giddy with relief. "It's like you to support me, whatever mad thing I say! But I can think of several reasons why my opinions might not, in fact, be particularly valid. I have exercised my own judgment so little; I might be foolish to start relying on it now."

Hannah smiled. She seemed to be feeling better. "You might be a bit rusty," she acknowledged. "Perhaps you should move slowly at first. But I don't believe that lets you off, Cynthia. You still must try to use your head. We all must."

"I shall," she promised. "I shall try to think for myself. I shall try to—to stand up to Mama." Her first qualms assailed her. She sternly quashed them, aware that, for the first time in memory, it was her meekness she was suppressing—not her rebelliousness. An interesting switch. She took a deep breath, then smiled at Hannah. "I am utterly certain of one thing. Setting my cap for your Mr. Ellsworth was wrong."

Even in the semidarkness, she sensed Hannah's flush of embarrassment. "He is not 'my' Mr. Ellsworth."

"Even so," said Cynthia firmly. "He may very well be your Mr. Ellsworth one day. And I had no right to interfere with that, once I knew how you felt." In another surge of remorse, she crossed swiftly to her friend and took her hands in hers. "What a *ninny* I have been! There is no excuse for me, Hannah—none. I can only beg your forgiveness."

"Don't be silly. You were only doing what you thought was right." Hannah's shy smile broke through again. "Although, I must own I am glad you decided to rethink it."

Amity restored, Hannah announced that she was ready to return to the ballroom. She had promised to dance with her uncle Malcolm and was afraid he might be looking for her. Cynthia urged her to go down ahead of her, and Hannah slipped out the door. Cynthia wanted a few moments alone to collect her thoughts—and to brace herself for what lay ahead.

She was seldom alone. Despite her rioting thoughts, the solitude felt wonderful. She moved to the French windows and opened them. Fresh air poured into the stuffy room, cold and bracing. She drank in the chill and the silence. The quiet of the night was somehow emphasized by being laced with distant music. She rested her head by laying her temple against the door-frame, looking out at the stars and thinking.

There was a great deal to think about.

Before she had got very far, she heard the faint sounds of the door opening and closing behind her. She knew, without turning to look, who had come through that door.

"It's cold in here," said Derek.

"I like it." She still did not move or turn her head, but went on looking at the stars. Soft footfalls crossed the room behind her, and she felt the prickle of electricity that seemed to flash in the air around him.

"As you know, I heard a little of what passed between you and Lady Hannah." His voice was quiet, in deference to the night's stillness, and very near. "It seems she was able to achieve what I could not."

She turned her head and looked at him. His face was only inches from hers. The silvery light from the night sky wrapped them in a faint shimmer, adding a magical, intimate quality to what was already a dangerously private meeting. When their eyes met, she felt her pulse flutter and jump.

"What do you mean?" she whispered. She hadn't intended to whisper. Her voice simply failed her.

His voice did not sound much steadier than hers. "If I heard aright, you agreed to stop setting traps for John Ellsworth."

"Oh. That."

"Did I hear you right?"

His closeness, combined with his intensity, was too much. She dropped her eyes. "Yes," she said softly. "It was wrong of me. I see that now. I hope"—she glanced fleetingly back up at his face, then dropped her eyes again—"I hope you aren't offended. That Hannah could convince me, when you could not."

"Offended? I'm delighted."

The optimism of his words was premature. She shivered. "Do not be. The news is not as delightful as you may hope."

"What do you mean? Cynthia, this changes everything." His voice was low and urgent.

"I am sorry to disappoint you," she whispered. "Sorrier than you know. But it changes nothing, where we are concerned. At least—" She broke off, searching for the right words. He waited in silence for her to continue. "I suppose the truthful thing to tell you is that I don't know. I haven't thought it all out. And I need to consider, very carefully, exactly what has changed and what has not." She sighed. "The only thing that has certainly changed is that I shan't try to attach John Ellsworth. On that, at any rate, I am resolved."

Derek stared very hard at her, looking perplexed. "You know, Cynthia, I am a patient man." He seemed to be choosing his words with care, as if hanging on to his vaunted patience by the slenderest of threads. "But this would try the patience of a saint. I thought you had come to your senses. I was evidently mistaken. If you have *not* decided to make me the happiest of men, then why, pray, are you letting Ellsworth wriggle off the hook?" An answer immediately seemed to dawn on him. He cocked an eyebrow at her. "Has it something to do with Lady Hannah?"

Of course he would guess that Hannah cared for Mr. Ellsworth. But at least she had not told him. She shook her head, smiling a little. "I cannot betray a confidence."

"Never mind, then. You needn't. A blind man could see what is happening." He thought for a moment, a frown gathering on his features. "On the whole, I honor your decision. It shows a tenderer heart than the world gives you credit for. But if you are sacrificing your ambition for your friend's sake, I daresay it is only Ellsworth you have agreed to let alone. Your intent to marry a man of vast wealth has not altered."

"Correct. And that, alas, is why I cannot give you hope."

He looked disgusted. "You're very frank."

"It's useless to prevaricate," she said bleakly. "You deserve to know where you stand. I owe you that, at least."

"At the very least," he agreed, giving her a wintry smile. He had withdrawn from her. And why shouldn't he? Isn't that what she had told him to do? Once again, she had no one to blame but herself. She had held her ground, even though she was no longer sure of her ground.

Confusion swept through her. What was real, and what was not? She had told him she must marry money. She had told him she *wanted* to. The first was true, but not the second. If she allowed him to believe that she was mercenary, was that dishonest—or merely a kindness, to spare him from false hope? How honest should she be? Would it truly make everything worse, if she told him the truth? She had thought so, only an hour ago. But now, having formed a determination to think for herself, shouldn't she question that belief? What, really, had it been based on?

Trembling, she stared at his face. He looked aloof. Hurt. A little angry. And it was all her doing. She hated it when people were angry with her. She longed to apologize and make it up to him somehow, but the new Cynthia did not trust that impulse. Her aversion to conflict, she realized, had been a major component of her unhealthy docility—the timidity she had resolved to overcome. She must not replace her morbid fear of Mama's displeasure with a morbid fear of Derek's displeasure. That would bring her no further along in her quest to grow up.

What should she do? In another moment, it would be too late to decide. He had stepped back from her and was bowing. "There seems little point in my staying longer," he said flatly. "I wish you a pleasant evening."

He was nearly at the door before she found her tongue. "Derek," she croaked, hoarse with tension. "Wait."

He stopped but did not immediately turn. When he did, it obviously cost him something. Gratitude flooded her heart, so sharp and sweet that tears stung her eyes. "Thank you." She blinked to clear her vision. "I can't . . . I can't let you go. Yet. I can't let you go until I . . . until I tell you something."

He did not move toward her. "What is it?" he asked quietly.

There was no time to ponder every angle. She had to choose, rightly or wrongly, on instinct. She followed her heart. She chose honesty.

"I lied to you."

His head recoiled slightly, as if she had struck him. Cynthia covered her mouth with her hand, wishing she could call back the words. But having chipped a hole in the dam, the pressure of suppressed truth forced more words out of her. She gave a little gasp, then let the torrent take her.

"It was stupid and cowardly. I knew it was wrong the instant I did it. I never want to lie to you again. I hope . . . I hope you can forgive me." Her voice threatened to break. She cleared her throat, lifted her chin, and went on. "I told you I wanted to be rich. That was a falsehood. It is my family who desires that for me, because they need funds and they see no way to obtain them except through me. You guessed that, but I led you to believe that you were wrong. I told you I wanted money for its own sake. I told you— Well, I don't remember exactly what I told you. I just know that whatever I told you was a lie."

He still said nothing, but he walked back to the window and placed his arm around her. She leaned against him, wilting with relief. *Just for a minute,* she promised herself. It wouldn't do, to stay like this for long. It was scandalous enough, just being alone with him.

With her cheek against his chest, his voice rumbled in her ear when he spoke. "Every time I think I understand you at last, you trip me up somehow. Of course, in the present instance, I'm glad to be mistaken."

"Derek, I'm sorry. I'm so sorry. The truth is I'm rather a— Well, I'm rather a mess, I'm afraid. I'm so confused lately. I don't seem to know who I am, so how can anyone understand me? Even you."

"Even I." He placed his finger beneath her chin and lifted her face off his chest, tilting it up so he could smile into her eyes. "If that means you believe I have a special understanding of you, I'm glad."

She had spoken without thinking, but he was right; that was exactly what she had meant. A sense of wonder filled her heart. "I do believe it." She felt her lips curve as she pondered this absurdity. "Daft, isn't it? I don't know *why* I believe it."

The faint, silvery light lent sorcery to his smile. "I grant you, it's mysterious," he said softly. "But it's

220

real. We both felt it, that first night. A certain . . . connection to each other. Remember?"

That night, and ever since. She nodded, speechless, then ducked back into his arms and once more laid her cheek against his chest. "I remember." Her voice came out a bit quavery again. All these emotions were difficult to weather. One began to tremble, she thought, from sheer exhaustion.

He held her quietly for a few moments. She closed her eyes, listening blissfully to his heartbeat. She felt silent laughter shake him. "So you're not entirely mercenary, after all."

"No," she murmured. "Not entirely."

"I've been wrestling with the notion that I'd be better off without you. Trying to convince myself that you were a coldhearted jade. But I've been finding it a hard row to hoe, convincing myself of that. No matter the evidence." His arm tightened around her. "I knew you were not," he said, softly but with conviction. "What is it the French say? The heart has reasons which reason knows nothing of."

"Mm." She could not resist burrowing her nose into his waistcoat for a moment. He smelled wonderful.

"I hope you will explain to me exactly why you lied. And, for that matter, why you confessed just now."

"Oh, that's easy." She was starting to feel a little tipsy. All this truth-telling was going to her head. And snuggling Derek in the starlight wasn't helping her equilibrium, either. "I was afraid I could not resist you, and I thought I must," she said recklessly. "So I lied. Hoping that you would then dislike me. Or, at the very least, stop hanging about. And that, of course, would have helped me resist you."

"And the confession?" Laughter quivered in his voice.

"Once again, I was motivated chiefly by fear. Do you see a pattern emerging?" Her light tone took on a self-mocking edge. "This time, I was afraid I had gone too far and that you really *would* stop hanging about. And I am no longer quite as certain as I was—" She stumbled, suddenly appalled by her own frankness. And then she realized that if she stopped now, she would, yet again, be allowing fear to dictate her conduct. Anger at her own cowardice swept through her. She took a deep breath, and defied it. "I am no longer certain of much, Derek, but I do know what I feel. And the last thing in the world I want is to drive you away before you've had a proper chance to . . . to change my mind. It may be selfish of me—"

His kiss interrupted her, scattering her thoughts like feathers in the wind. *Heaven.* She let her lips cling to his, almost delirious with desire. This would be her undoing. She knew it, and despaired—but even the despair felt too good to resist. How could she be virtuous, while Derek Whittaker tempted her with his kisses? She was only human.

His mouth lifted from hers. She tilted her chin higher, blindly seeking more, but he kept his face out of reach. "Marry me, Cynthia," he said hoarsely. "Must I kneel and beg? I will, if you want me to."

"No." She opened her eyes, dazed. "No, don't do that."

"But you will marry me." His arms went possessively round her. "You will."

"No," she said desperately. "Derek, I can't promise that. A hundred things may prevent it. My mother—"

"*Hang* your mother! Sorry," he added, as Cynthia stiffened. "I mean no disrespect. But it's bad enough, letting Lady Ballymere decide your future. Now she's deciding mine as well." He took Cynthia's shoulders, holding her gently away from him so he could look into her face. "Don't you realize, sweetheart, that if you agree to marry me, I can protect you from her? From all of them. No one shall lecture you or scold you ever again. Does your mother really have the power to say us nay?"

It sounded wonderful, but it wasn't real. Cynthia sighed. "Yes, actually, she does. I shall be one-and-twenty in two months' time, but—"

"Then we'll marry in three months' time. June's a lucky month for weddings."

"Derek, stop it! It's not that simple." She pulled herself out of his grip and turned away, feeling flustered and depressed. "There is more at stake here than your happiness and mine. It's not simply a matter of flouting my parents' authority and forcing them into genteel poverty for the rest of their lives—although that is bad enough. I *love* them. And I love Ballymere. I love the land on which I was born, and all the dear people . . ." Her throat constricted with emotion. "Everyone is depending on me. If I marry well, I replenish my family's fortunes. By saving my father's land for him, I rescue everyone who depends upon that land." She turned back to him, pleading. "Derek, don't you understand? It's an awesome responsibility. I shall feel *terrible* if I fail at this. It's too important."

He studied her face, his expression troubled. "Well. In that case, we shall have to contrive a little. There must be something we can do. How much does your family need? Do you know?"

She shook her head miserably. "I've no idea. Not in any real terms."

"What had Filey promised them?"

"Thirty thousand," she said reluctantly, and saw his jaw drop in disbelief.

"Thirty thousand *pounds?*"

"Yes." She bit her lip. "I know it sounds utterly mad. And that was just in marriage settlements, mind you. I have the impression they expected he would offer additional help from time to time, as the need arose."

"Good God." He looked stunned. "I can't possibly match that."

"No. Scarcely anyone could."

A new thought seemed to occur to him. He looked skeptically at her. "You know, the Ellsworths may have pots of money, but I can't picture them handing over a cool thirty thousand just to secure a bride for their John. Not even if the bride were you, my love. Why should they? If Lady Hannah is carrying a torch for him, he can't be as hopeless as you and I think he is."

"Oh, I don't think Mama expects to receive another offer like Sir James's. Those circumstances were"—

she swallowed hard—"unique." She didn't like to think of those days. Her engagement to Filey had been extremely unpleasant.

Was Derek guessing her thoughts? She steadfastly regarded his topmost waistcoat button, but she could feel his eyes on her. "He must have wanted you very badly," said Derek softly, compassion in his voice. "Could he not have you for less?"

"No," said Cynthia numbly. "He could not. Mama is a skillful negotiator. And, as you say, he wanted me badly." She took a deep breath and leaned against the door frame, trying not to show the agitation that churned in her whenever she thought of her first Season. "Sir James had a well-known weakness for young girls—the virginal sort, you know, with pale hair and pale skin and no experience of life. At seventeen, I fit the bill perfectly." She was trying to speak lightly but could not keep the bitterness from her voice. "Mama exploited this weakness of his. She chose her target very well. Sir James was exactly what she wanted, and I was exactly what he wanted." She gave an almost hysterical little gulp of laughter. "I have no idea why I am telling you this."

"Because I asked," said Derek steadily. "And because you trust me. Am I right to feel deeply angry on your behalf?"

Unexpected tears stung her eyes. She shook her head, trying valiantly to smile. "You know perfectly well that this sort of thing is commonplace. Traps are set every day for wealthy men, and they generally walk into them willingly enough."

"I asked if I should feel angry on *your* behalf, Cynthia. Not his."

She crossed her arms in front of her and shivered. "No one has ever asked me that before." Her smile wavered. "I have heard people express sympathy for the fish wriggling at the end of the hook, but no one thinks how much worse it is for the bait."

"And you were the bait. My poor sweetheart." He took her back in his arms, cradling her against his body. Her arms went around him and she clung, feeling comforted even as she sensed the peril in letting him hold her like this.

She felt a craven impulse to tell him everything, to tell him exactly how degrading it had been— appearing publicly in nearly transparent clothing to entice Sir James. She wanted to confess how humiliated she had felt, seeing the slack-jawed lust in Filey's face as his eyes followed her everywhere, rarely looking at her face even when he spoke to her. Mama had taken care, at first, not to let Sir James get her alone, and for that Cynthia had been stupidly grateful—until it became clear that it had all been part of the plan, to withhold what he wanted in order to tease him into offering marriage. The first time Mama had allowed Sir James to spirit Cynthia away and paw her was the night at the opera house, when Cynthia had met Derek. Within a fortnight, her engagement had been announced and her doom sealed—or so she had thought. That had been the worst period of all.

No. She would not tell him. She would not unburden herself at the expense of causing Derek pain. Sir

James was dead and buried, and Cynthia must look forward, not back. She was safe, forever, from Sir James Filey. She would not let hideous memories poison this moment. It was Derek's arms that encircled her now. And they would not always, she reminded herself. This was a stolen moment. Derek Whittaker was not hers to keep. Not if she fulfilled the bargain she had struck with Mama.

"I am still the bait," she told him quietly. "But my mother has promised me that we will try to hook a different sort of fish." She leaned back against the circle of his arms, trying to smile. "It was worth trying to snag John Ellsworth, you know. At least he was young. Young rich men are hard to find."

"No doubt." He looked grim.

"The ten thousand we received from Sir James relieved the worst of Papa's obligations, so that enabled us—briefly—to be more choosy. And it made my parents feel generous toward me, so they stopped pressuring me about marriage altogether. Again, briefly." Those days were ending. Cynthia did not want to think about that.

Derek's brows climbed. "You received ten thousand from Filey even though you hadn't married him?"

"Yes. And, luckily, his death did not obligate Papa to repay it."

He emitted a low, thoughtful whistle. "Ten thousand pounds. I must say, my love, that I think your parents have wrung a sufficient sum from your charms. After landing a fish of that size, you ought to be—to continue the analogy—let off the hook."

She wrinkled her nose at him. "Ugh."

"Sorry." He smiled at her, his features softening as he studied her face. He lifted one finger and traced her cheekbone, as if marveling at it. The tenderness in the gesture tugged anew at Cynthia's heart. "I can't give you up," he whispered. "Don't ask it of me."

"I'm afraid I must." A lump had formed in her throat, making it difficult to speak. "But I haven't thought it all out. Give me time, Derek. Just a little time. If I can find a way—" Emotion choked her. She knew perfectly well that, absent a miracle, no way would present itself.

His expression was both grave and tender. "You don't believe there is a way."

Cynthia shook her head, not trusting herself to speak.

He pulled her to him with one arm, turning her to face the sky, and held her close. "Do you see those stars out there?" he murmured, nuzzling her ear. She smiled, shivering at the touch of his mouth, and nodded. "One of them is my lucky star."

Amusement brought her voice back. "Which one?"

"That, I have never been able to determine. But one of them most certainly is."

He sounded so confident. Cynthia had to laugh. "It seems a rather flimsy plan, to rely upon an unknown star."

"It has never yet let me down."

She turned her face up to his, smiling in spite of her heartache. "I have never had a lucky star. Do you think you could share yours with me?"

"Stand closer," he suggested, "where it can shine on both of us at once."

She was already touching him, but she nestled closer somehow, fitting herself snugly against his body. "Like this?"

"Closer," he whispered. His face was so near hers it looked out of focus.

Smiling, she let her eyes drift shut. "It must be shining on me now," she murmured. "I can feel it. Like the sun."

His lips felt hot against her chilled skin as he trailed them softly across her cheekbone. "Trust me, love," he murmured. "A lucky star is better than money in the bank."

I hope so, she thought wistfully, praying he was right. Then his lips took hers and she stopped thinking at all.

Chapter Fourteen

Lady Ballymere stood, half hidden behind a tall column, and watched her daughter walk composedly down the stairs with Mr. Whittaker. Cold rage seized her. Cynthia's demeanor was completely unruffled, but Lady Ballymere was no fool. Her sharp eyes took in the slight disarrangement of Cynthia's hair and the fact that her pearls no longer lay quite so neatly against her collarbone. Mr. Whittaker's cravat was a bit askew as well. The telltale signs might be invisible to the casual observer, but

Lady Ballymere was no casual observer.

She had noticed twenty minutes ago that the two of them had gone missing. Heaven only knew how long before that they had actually disappeared. Seeing them together now, and remembering Cynthia's ridiculous suggestion that she be allowed to set her cap for Mr. Whittaker, Lady Ballymere felt almost sick with anger. She had never before known Cynthia's head to be turned by a handsome face, but the dreaded day had evidently arrived.

Her hands had clenched into fists so tight that, even through her gloves, her nails were digging grooves into her palms. She made a conscious effort to relax, breathing deeply to ease the tension in her muscles. Cynthia was not the only member of the Fitzwilliam family who could hide her emotions beneath a bland exterior. She would smile and behave pleasantly, bide her time while she thought of a plan. For this budding romance, or whatever it was, must be killed.

She gave no sign that she had noticed anything untoward. She managed to be civil to Mr. Whittaker and affectionate with Cynthia, and even allowed her daughter to sit across from him again during the return to Oldham Park—although it stuck in her craw to permit it. She wanted to move cautiously. There was nothing more certain to go awry than blatant attempts to keep them apart. She even pretended to believe Cynthia the next morning, when Cynthia told her that she and Mr. Ellsworth were going to explore Saddleworth Moor on horseback—in company with Hannah and Mr. Whittaker.

Lady Ballymere perceived the true nature of this outing at once but forced herself to smile and acquiesce, pretending she was well pleased with the plan. Sick at heart, she even watched the foursome depart, riding sedately down the drive with Cynthia's mount beside Mr. Ellsworth's and Hannah bringing up the rear with Mr. Whittaker, just as Cynthia had led her to believe it would be. She knew, of course, that the instant they were out of sight of the house, the party would regroup.

She returned to her rooms, where she paced restlessly, thinking. No matter which way she looked at the problem, the best solution to all their difficulties was Cynthia's marriage to John Ellsworth. She simply *must* bring it about. He was young and rich and kind and, frankly, rather simple—all advantages in a husband. And a swift betrothal effected here would save the expense of yet another London Season, a Season the Fitzwilliams could ill afford.

A plan occurred to her. She halted her pacing, pressing her fingertips to her mouth as she turned it over in her mind. Oh, it was devious—actually underhanded, if truth be told. But would it work? If so, the end would clearly justify the means. She was prepared, at this stage of the game, to overlook her moral qualms. Decency wouldn't pay the bills. What good was honor when the wolf was at the door?

No, there was no point in being squeamish. There was only one important question, only one she need consider at all. She stood frozen in her tracks, her mind working feverishly on that one overriding question.

Would it work?

Cynthia was wearing her cranberry-colored riding habit again. She looked good enough to eat. The sunlight sparkled in her hair, strands of which had worked themselves loose in the fresh wind and were now flying about her face like glittering ribbons. Her cheeks were rosy. Her face glowed with laughter. Every time he looked at her, Derek felt his spirit soar in a kind of amazed delirium. When she smiled at him, which was frequently, he thought his heart might burst and kill him on the spot. Could a man die of love? If not, and he survived this day, he would never forget it.

By tacit agreement, they soon left Hannah and Mr. Ellsworth in the dust. Hannah was a nervous rider and too unskilled to leave the bridle path. Ellsworth seemed glad to have an excuse not to pit his horsemanship against Derek's; he accepted, with alacrity, the role of Hannah's companion. By contrast, Cynthia rose instantly to Derek's challenge, her eyes flashing with the delight of competition. She had willingly raced him across the moor—and she had *really* raced him, neck or nothing, lying nearly flat against her horse's mane and heedless of danger. In fact, she had damn near won.

He pulled Max up barely a second before Cynthia arrived at the rock formation they had designated as the finish line. She pulled her own mount to a stop, laughing and crying out, "Unfair!" Her mare skidded slightly in the mud and danced beneath her, snorting and tossing her head. Cynthia patted the animal's neck and held her together with no fuss and seemingly no effort, still laughing. "Max knows you too well. This poor little mare doesn't trust me yet. If I were riding my Westwind, I would have given you a race. You must come to Ballymere one day and give me a rematch."

"Gladly! But you gave me a race today, all right and tight." He grinned at her in undisguised admiration. "Lady Cynthia, you are a marvel. I hesitate to admit this, but honesty demands it. You are the first female who has ever raced me this well. Most ladies have too much regard for life and limb—and an equal anxiety about their hair."

"Pooh! Who cares for that?" She tossed her head, her eyes sparkling with mischief. Another few strands fell out of her coiffure and danced ecstatically in the wind. "I wouldn't have missed that gallop for the world."

"Where is your hat?"

She gave an airy wave. "Back there somewhere. With the pins still in it, I hope. Did you expect me to check my horse for such a trifle?"

"Lud, no. What's a hat, when all's said and done? A good gallop is much more important."

"My sentiments exactly."

He had never seen her appear so relaxed. They turned their horses and started leisurely back the way they had come, eyes peeled for Cynthia's hat among the scrubby vegetation that covered the moor. She sat beautifully in the saddle, her posture graceful and natural. The glint of the sun on her platinum hair, bared to the blazing light, was nearly blinding. The tendrils that had escaped their confines streamed like gold spun on the wind. To Derek, she was dazzling.

She tilted her face up to the sky, closing her eyes and smiling. "Oh, it's glorious," she murmured. "Spring is nearly here."

He lifted an eyebrow at her. "Another few days of this weather and the roads will be decent again. How soon will your mother whisk you off to London?"

She lowered her chin and opened her eyes. It seemed his words had brought her back to an unwelcome reality. "Not too soon, I hope."

"Amen to that."

"I don't believe she can." A slight smile disturbed her gravity once more. "After all, I haven't won Mr. Ellsworth's heart yet. At least, not as far as I know."

"Well, well, don't despair. Still waters run deep. Perhaps he's carrying a torch for you in secret."

She laughed out loud at that, throwing her head back with delight. It warmed Derek's heart to see her laugh so unabashedly. He grinned at her. "What's so funny?" he demanded. "Why shouldn't a chap carry a secret torch for you? I did, for years."

"And yet, you know, not everyone does." Her voice quivered with amusement. "Difficult as that may be for you to believe."

"Dashed difficult," he agreed.

She smiled at him in a way that made it hard for him to breathe. "When Hannah told me— Oh, dear." She covered her mouth with one hand for a moment, catching herself as she nearly spilled a secret.

234

"Never mind. I already guessed, you know. When Hannah told you what? That she fancies Mr. Ellsworth?"

Cynthia nodded, apparently resigned to her breach of confidence. "Yes. When she told me that, I thought she had run quite mad—since I knew she was acquainted with you."

Derek puzzled over that for a moment while Cynthia's cheeks grew visibly pinker. Then, realizing what she meant, he laughed, shaking his head. "By Jove. That's the best compliment I've ever received."

"Take care it doesn't go to your head."

They smiled at each other then, in perfect accord. Derek felt a besotted urge to blurt out another marriage proposal. He sternly quelled it. Any mention of marriage would send them into another rehashing of all the obstacles in their path, and he was determined that nothing so lowering would be allowed to intrude upon this day. They would have one day—or at least one morning—of unalloyed happiness together. He thought they would need the memory of this blissful ride on the moor to sustain them during whatever battles lay ahead. Dragons, he knew, lurked round the next bend.

"View halloo!" He pointed. "Is that your hat?"

"Oh, excellent! It is indeed." She turned her mare so skillfully that the creature seemed to move as an extension of Cynthia, scrambling down a steep little incline to where the bright splash of cranberry red lay against the brown and green of the moor. It was caught on a prickly bush, the feather that adorned it fluttering like a trapped bird.

He followed her into the shallow ravine and swung out of the saddle. Max stood quietly while he took Cynthia's reins. She bit her lip as she looked down at him, her face alight with mischief. "I shouldn't permit you to hand me down. I should ask you to simply give me my hat."

He extended his hand in invitation. "Come down off that horse, Lady Cynthia," he said, a purr in his voice. "And I will help you with your hat."

She gave a soft little laugh and placed her hand in his. He pulled her off the mare and she slid, deliciously, down the length of his body. She landed, as they both had known she would, in his arms. The ravine protected them from the wind and gave the illusion of privacy—and the horses wouldn't tell. So he kissed her, taking his time and savoring the precious, stolen moment. And she, bless her, relaxed against his arms and kissed him back with a wanton disregard for the possibility that they might be discovered.

"I think I'll pull a few more pins out of your hair," he murmured eventually.

"Don't you dare." She didn't seem very worried. She nuzzled his chin, eyes closed.

"I'd love to know how it looks unbound. Even more, how it feels." He played with a few escaped tresses, trying to imagine what it would be like to run his hands through that mass of warm, sun-shot silk.

She opened her eyes then and leaned languidly back, studying his face with sleepy amusement. "It feels like baby hair, if you must know. Very soft. We haven't been able to do anything about the fine texture, unfortunately, and it will never have the natural curl that yours has, but Mama and I have worked diligently to improve whatever we could. I brush it one hundred strokes every night."

Now, there was a picture to make a man's mouth water. Derek growled and held her tighter. "Someday," he vowed, "I want to take over that task." A shadow seemed to cross her face at his words. He hastened to change the subject before she could remind him that they had no future together. "I imagine it's hard work, being one of London's accredited beauties."

That made her laugh, as he had hoped it would. "You've no idea," she assured him with mock earnestness. "The constant application of Denmark lotion alone is exhausting. And the expense! Quite shocking. I am forced to consume it by the quart."

He pretended to study her features. "You will never convince me," he said softly, "that you owe this face to Denmark lotion."

He bent to kiss her again, but she tossed her head, laughing. "If it's not the Denmark lotion, it must be the strawberries."

"Strawberries?"

"Crushed," she said primly, "and applied to the face, to brighten the complexion. With cucumber slices laid on the eyelids to prevent puffiness. Oh, and oil of cacao for the hands— Why, you could feed an army on the wasted foodstuffs I have slathered on my skin."

"Let me see if it worked," Derek suggested, tugging

on her gloves. They were buttoned securely at her wrists or he would have had them off of her before she could object. The buttons delayed him sufficiently to let her laugh and exclaim, pulling her hands back, and a brief tussle ensued. At the end of it her hands were pinned behind her back and Derek and Cynthia were pressed tightly together, chest to chest.

Her eyes were wide with laughter and alarm. "What are you doing?"

"Teaching you something worth knowing." He grinned and waggled his eyebrows at her. "Sometimes, my lady, it's fun to lose a tug-of-war." She started to make a laughing protest, but he stifled it with a kiss. It was gratifying to witness how easily she was distracted. Within seconds, her body softened against his as she gave herself up to pleasure. She was a fast learner, however, on how to win a tussle. He kissed her so hungrily that he dropped his guard, relaxing his grip on her hands, and she immediately pulled neatly out of his grasp. He lifted his face from hers, growling in mock anger, and she laughed and swatted at him until he captured her hands—and lips—again. Her playfulness warmed his heart; he suspected that it was a side of her few others had seen. But he was soon forced to admit that it was time he fulfilled his promise to help her with her hat.

He retrieved it from the bush, grumbling comically about the prickles he endured during this exercise, and presented the hat to her with a flourish. She turned it about in her hands, examining it, lips pursed. "Hm. I don't suppose you have a mirror."

"Sorry, no. Shall I act as lady's maid?"

She eyed him with misgiving. "Entrust you with my hat pins? You must think me a ninnyhammer."

In the end, however, she had to trust him with them. Derek drove the wicked-looking hat pins through her coiled hair with great relish. Cynthia then tried, in vain, to tuck her hair back up under the reanchored hat. It was too small and fashionable to serve any useful purpose and she had to give it up, letting the escaped strands continue to blow free. Derek assured her that she looked charming—and although she pulled a face and laughed at this assertion, she truly did.

And then it was time to go. Derek laced his fingers and prepared to accept her boot, to toss her back up into the saddle. It was Cynthia who hesitated. She tugged insistently at his arm, and he straightened, gladly, to take her back in his arms for one more kiss.

When the kiss ended she sighed, a mournful sound that tugged on his heartstrings. "Don't be sad, Cynthia," he whispered. "This will not be our last kiss. I promise you that."

She looked up at him, sorrow in her eyes. "I wish I could be as certain of that as you are."

"That's easily accomplished." He lifted her wrist to his mouth and planted a kiss on the tiny space of skin between her glove and her sleeve. She shivered at the contact, closing her eyes as if in pain. "Let me speak to your mother," he urged softly. "Let me, sweetheart. Today."

A tiny crease appeared between her brows. She shook her head. "No."

"Cynthia—"

"No!" She opened her eyes. "I need time, Derek. Please."

"For what?" Exasperation sharpened his voice. "There's nothing to wait for. We love each other. That can't be changed; it's too late. At some point, my darling heart, your parents are going to have to face it— as we have done. You can't keep what's between us a secret."

She did not immediately reply. Her gaze seemed to be fastened on his cravat, as if she were afraid to meet his eyes. She clutched the lapels of his coat, a gesture that simultaneously allowed her to cling to him and hold him at bay. When she answered him her voice wavered slightly, and the color drained from her cheeks as she spoke. "Derek, I don't know what to do." Her expression was anguished. "I would give you an answer if I could. I can't. And until I can, there is no point in your approaching Mama. You must accept that. It *is* progress, you know—of a sort." She tried to smile. "Only yesterday, I was quite certain that I would never marry you. Now . . . I don't know."

His mouth turned down wryly. "I am tempted," he muttered, "to make the decision for you."

She gave a shaky little laugh. "Everyone wants to make my decisions for me, it seems."

"Yes," he said with grim humor. "That is what stops me. I've a strong aversion to replacing your parents' tyranny with my own."

Cynthia smiled with relief. "Thank you. I know how difficult this must be for you. It's torture for me as well. I suppose you will say I have the power to end it," she added hastily, seeing the spark of ironic agreement in his eyes. "But I dare not rush things. I am not accustomed to making my own decisions. I must take care to decide aright."

There was a hint of severity in his expression. "You realize, I hope, that I am unlikely to take no for an answer."

She looked anxious. "What do you mean?"

He cupped her chin in his fingers and held her eyes with his. "You have already tried to deny me, Cynthia," he reminded her. His voice was soft but merciless. "You have bade me farewell more than once, yet here we are. You cannot banish me, my love, because you cannot convince me that you truly want me to go. I will acknowledge defeat on the day you wed another man, and not one day sooner."

Her expression was a strange mixture of fear and exultation. "At this moment," she whispered, "I am glad of it. Whatever the future may hold, I will cherish the memory of these days with you."

He frowned. "You will have a lifetime with me."

Sadness flitted across her face. She pulled herself out of his arms and forced an unconvincing little smile. "Time will tell. I hope you are right."

"Never doubt it," said Derek steadily, but the words suddenly sounded hollow.

They had to go back at some point, so there was nothing necessarily sinister about Cynthia's abrupt withdrawal. Still, it bothered him. He had the distinct impression that she had brought the conversation to a

close because she could not bear to disappoint him—
but the sadness in her face told him that she felt she
had merely postponed, not ruled out, disappointing
him. Which meant that, despite everything, she anticipated handing him some very bad news one day soon.

He helped her onto her horse, and she disposed her
skirts while he swung back up onto Max's broad back.
"Now take off that Friday face, my lady, or Ellsworth
will think I have abused you," he said with mock
sternness. This sally won him a wan smile, but Cynthia's gaiety had vanished.

It did not take long to come upon Lady Hannah and
Mr. Ellsworth, still riding tamely along the bridle
path. As they approached, Lady Hannah's eyes
widened in innocent surprise. "How windblown you
are, Cynthia! What kept you so long?"

"I lost my hat, and we spent some time retracing our
race to find it."

Her poise was amazing. Derek looked sideways at
her, wondering how she did it. Despite the straggling
hair, she looked as cool and collected as if she and he
had spent the past half hour cantering side by side and
making small talk.

Hannah looked envious. "I wish I could ride well
enough to race."

"You ride very well," lied Mr. Ellsworth manfully.
"A very graceful seat, by Jove."

Hannah looked so pleased that Derek bit back the
jocular rejoinder that occurred to him. She bent her
shy smile on Derek and said gratefully, "It was Mr.
Whittaker who taught me. I had always been afraid of

horses before. *You* know, John."

"Oh, aye, I remember." Mr. Ellsworth chuckled. "Plough horse came and snatched an apple from her hand one day. One of those Clydesdale brutes, you know, seventeen or eighteen hands at the withers. Enormous. Lady Hannah was just a wee bit of a thing, younger than Sarah is now. Nearly frightened the wits out of her."

"Fancy you remembering that!" exclaimed Hannah. "Why, I barely recall it myself."

"Made an impression. Never saw you run so fast, before or since. And my word, what a screech you let out!" He chuckled again, shaking his head.

Hannah looked embarrassed. Cynthia smoothly intervened, saying in her calm way, "At any rate, Hannah, you are not afraid of horses now. I think you deserve great credit. It takes courage to overcome a long-held fear."

Derek slanted a glance at Cynthia. She appeared serenely unaware of his scrutiny, but he was not fooled by her show of indifference. "The prejudices we pick up in childhood are often the most difficult to unlearn," he said urbanely, as if agreeing with her. "And sometimes adults make it their business to instill fears in children—fears that may protect us while we are small but must eventually be outgrown."

Hannah wrinkled her nose. "What do you mean? Fear of the dark and things like that?"

"That, and other things. For their own safety, children must learn to obey adults, for example. But sometimes the adults in a child's life instill such a rigid regard for authority—"

"That's so. I had a tutor once who caned me," Mr. Ellsworth remarked, interrupting. "He was a frightful old screw. Drank, too, as I recall. Tsk! He didn't last long."

So much for communicating with Cynthia obliquely. Mr. Ellsworth and Lady Hannah fell into a reminiscent mood, chatting and laughing about their old tutors and governesses. Since neither Cynthia nor Derek had been acquainted with any of these persons, they were unable to contribute further to the conversation and fell silent.

It was difficult for the foursome to stay together. Lady Hannah was mounted on a fat little slug of a mare, an animal that dawdled along in a way that plainly irritated Max. He tossed his head and snorted, trying to communicate to Derek that a morning on the moor should not be wasted. Derek tended to agree. He leaned over to address Cynthia, who was riding along beside him. "Care for another gallop?" he murmured provocatively. "You said you'd like a rematch."

Cynthia ducked her head, smiling, and looked up at him through her lashes. "I said I wanted a rematch at Ballymere. But I'll give you one here as well, if you like."

Unfortunately, Hannah had overheard. "Oh, no!" she cried in patent dismay. "Do not go off without us again. And besides, shouldn't we turn back? We've been riding for simply ages."

"Very well." Derek straightened and pulled Max to a halt. The others reined in around him. "We'll turn round and race back to the top of the last rise. Who's with me?"

"I am," said Cynthia staunchly, as he had guessed she would. But to his surprise, Mr. Ellsworth chimed in.

"Let us all do it," he suggested. "Hannah, you said you wanted to try, did you not? Daresay we can't give these two much of a race, but you and I could race each other."

Hannah shrank with alarm—but she did look tempted, even so. "Oh, dear me. I couldn't, could I? Do you think I could?"

"Be good for you," opined Mr. Ellsworth. "Give you a bit of fresh air."

"I don't think Lady will toss me," said Hannah brightly. "She's very gentle."

Derek had to hide his laugh in his sleeve. It seemed unlikely, to him, that Lady would be coaxed into anything faster than a trot. "She won't have time, between here and the rise. It can't be more than a quarter of a mile."

The rules were quickly decided, and the foursome took their places on the narrow bridle path, Derek and Cynthia in front and John and Hannah well behind— to avoid, Mr. Ellsworth jocularly said, having to eat too much of Derek and Cynthia's dust. When she actually had to turn her mount and face a racetrack, of sorts, Hannah was visibly nervous. She gamely said nothing, however, and prepared to urge Lady into the closest approximation of a gallop that the placid animal would give. Hannah was allowed to give the signal, and when she cried "Now!" everyone sprang into action.

Derek and Cynthia flew toward the rise as one, low over their horses' necks and laughingly urging their mounts to greater and greater speed. The wind in their faces and the pounding hooves beneath them masked whatever sounds emanated from the other couple. It was only when they pulled to a stop at the top of the rise and turned, laughing, to beg Mr. Ellsworth and Lady Hannah for a verdict on who had won the race, that they saw what had happened behind them. Cynthia's eyes made sense of it before Derek's did. With a startled exclamation, she headed her horse back to where Hannah lay in the dust beside the path, with Mr. Ellsworth hovering helplessly over her.

Derek rounded up Lady, who had confusedly wandered off onto the moor, and led her back to the group. He dismounted and took the reins of all four horses, listening quietly while Cynthia questioned her friend.

"No," Hannah was saying as Derek rode up. Her voice was high and gasping with pain. "So stupid of me! I don't quite know what happened."

" 'Twas my fault," declared Mr. Ellsworth, wringing his hands in distress. "I should never have let you try it. Why did you not tell us, dear girl, that you had never ridden at anything faster than a walk?"

"Well, I didn't think it mattered. I didn't know how *different* it would be," wailed Hannah. "How could I?"

"Never mind that now." Cynthia took Hannah's hand in hers and bent over her, her eyes anxiously searching her face. "It doesn't matter how it happened. Where are you hurt?"

"She slid sideways. Slipped right out of the saddle," exclaimed Mr. Ellsworth. "There was nothing I could do. Happened before I knew it."

"Yes, yes, Mr. Ellsworth," said Cynthia patiently. "We shall discuss how it came about later. Pray let Hannah tell me what is amiss."

Hannah looked cautious, as if taking mental inventory of her body. "I landed quite hard," she admitted. "In a—in a sort of sitting position." She seemed loath to name the body part she had bruised. "And I did something to my knee when I tried to catch myself. I had hooked it, you know, on the saddle horn."

"Can you move your knee? Go slowly," Cynthia warned as Hannah winced.

"Not very well. It hurts."

Cynthia looked up at Derek. "She can't ride back. That's certain."

He nodded. "I'll go."

"Go?" Hannah glanced dazedly up at him.

"Back to the stables," he said. "I'll bring back a carriage of some kind."

"Oh, dear. How mortifying." Fresh tears streaked the dust on Hannah's cheeks. "I am putting you all to so much trouble, and I've ruined everyone's morning. I'm so sorry."

"No trouble at all," said Derek cheerfully. He gave her a wink and a salute. "Be back in a trice." He tossed the rest of the reins to Ellsworth, jumped lightly onto Max, wheeled the gelding around, and set off at a canter. That nincompoop, Ellsworth, was a useless creature, but it was clear that Cynthia had matters well in hand.

Really, the more of her he saw, the more he found to like. An excellent horsewoman *and* a cool head in an emergency. All in all, she would make some lucky man an excellent wife.

Chapter Fifteen

Cynthia was thoroughly annoyed with Mr. Ellsworth. He had been worse than useless; he had actually increased Hannah's pain by awkwardly trying to help her sit up. Hannah's knee was swelling rapidly, and Cynthia finally begged Mr. Ellsworth to let her lie. "And, if you know how, pray unsaddle Lady," she added, hoping to distract him with a task to perform. "We can place the cushioned portion beneath Hannah to elevate the injured limb."

Thus adjured, Mr. Ellsworth stopped wringing his hands and blaming himself, over and over, for Hannah's fall. He took Lady aside and eventually managed to get her saddle off. Cynthia stayed by her friend, shading her face from the sun and talking to her in a soothing, cheerful tone that helped to keep her calm. Hannah was a fearful little thing, and Mr. Ellsworth's carrying on had all but convinced her she would be crippled for life.

Cynthia gently helped Hannah raise her legs while Mr. Ellsworth, delicately averting his gaze, shoved the saddle beneath her calves. Hannah soon declared that the elevation of her knee had relieved her pain a bit. Cynthia thought this was probably just a brave lie, but she squeezed her hand in approval. Hannah's attempt to be strong would, Cynthia thought, help her more than indulging the fears Mr. Ellsworth seemed all too ready to encourage.

Unfortunately, the instant that his appointed task was done, Mr. Ellsworth plunged back into his mournful litany of sympathy, remorse, and alarm. Hannah bore it very well, seeming to like the attention, but it soon set Cynthia's teeth on edge. Mr. Ellsworth seemed to enjoy having his chivalry appealed to, so Cynthia finally turned to him with a display of helpless entreaty, begging him to walk the horses. "For I cannot leave Lady Hannah," she reminded him, a sentiment with which he instantly concurred.

By the time Derek returned, they seemed to have been stranded there beside the path for hours. The sun was warmer than it had been earlier, and Cynthia was exhausted from her efforts to simultaneously support Hannah's flagging spirits and tactfully keep Mr. Ellsworth at bay. Her heart lifted with relief at the sight of Derek's tall form appearing at the top of the rise and walking toward them. He was carrying something, but he was on foot.

"Bless me!" exclaimed Mr. Ellsworth. "The bridle path is too narrow for the carriage. Why did we not foresee this? Oh, dear, oh, dear."

"There is no carriage?" cried Hannah on a rising

note of panic. From her vantage point on the ground, she could not see Derek's arrival. "But I cannot walk. And I cannot *possibly* ride."

Cynthia's patience was wearing thin. "Hannah, hush. And Mr. Ellsworth, pray be calm! I am certain Mr. Whittaker has thought of something."

"Holloa!" called Derek, giving a cheerful wave as he approached. His confident air was balm to Cynthia's flayed nerves. She rose to her feet and greeted him with relief. He walked up and tossed his burden on the ground. "I'm glad I thought of this," he remarked, indicating the object he had thrown down. It was two long poles with a length of canvas strung between them. "It's a litter, for moving an injured person," he explained. "Mr. Ellsworth and I shall have to do the honors."

"Oh, no." Hannah raised herself on one elbow, her face a study in dismay. "You can't be serious."

"It won't be as bad as all that," Derek assured her, smiling. "There's a two-wheeled trap on the other side of the rise. Couldn't get it any closer, but at least you shan't have to loll about like Queen Cleopatra all the way to Oldham Park. Bear with us, my lady! We shall jostle you as little as possible."

Hannah looked only marginally reassured. Cynthia felt a twinge of sympathy; it would be, she imagined, extremely embarrassing to be carried on a litter. More so, if one were secretly in love with one of the men doing the carrying. And even more so, if one were sensitive about being plump. Poor Hannah!

The two men stretched the litter out on the ground

beside Hannah, and Cynthia helped her maneuver herself onto the thing. It wasn't easy. Mr. Ellsworth seemed shocked by Derek's suggestion that the gentlemen offer their assistance, and Hannah was too embarrassed to contradict him once he had made his feelings known. So, for propriety's sake, the two females had to manage the task without help. Hannah's skirts and injuries hampered her movement enough that she had to be half-lifted over the pole and onto the canvas. It was a struggle for Cynthia, but she accomplished it at last, and after disposing Hannah's torn and dirtied clothing appropriately, she announced that they were now as ready as they would ever be.

Hannah looked frightened. "What must I do?" she asked anxiously.

"Just lie as still as you can," Derek told her. His tone indicated that there was nothing extraordinary or difficult in what they were about to do. "We'll keep you perfectly safe, Lady Hannah. Won't we, Ellsworth?"

"Heavens! I hope so." Mr. Ellsworth looked nearly as nervous as Hannah. "We will certainly do our best." He leaned over Hannah, where she lay stretched out like a body in a coffin. "Hannah, my dear, we shall try very hard not to drop you. But if you should happen to fall off the litter for any reason, do try to break the fall with your hands," he begged her earnestly.

"She will *not* fall off the litter," said Derek firmly. "And we most assuredly will not drop her." He strolled over to help Cynthia remount her mare. "What a fellow that Ellsworth chap is," he muttered disgustedly, for her ears only. "He'll frighten Lady Hannah to death."

Cynthia tried to reply without moving her lips. "I was never more glad to see you than when you arrived just now," she murmured, placing her boot in his laced hands. "Thank you, Mr. Whittaker," she added aloud, as Derek tossed her into her saddle and handed her her reins. He threw her a speaking glance before turning back to the others, but the instant he was facing Hannah once more, his air of cheerful confidence returned.

"Well, Ellsworth, I suggest you relinquish the rest of the reins to Lady Cynthia now," he said, briskly rubbing his hands together. "Can't carry her ladyship and lead two horses at the same time. Are we ready? Lady Hannah, are you quite comfortable? Well, well, never mind. Just wait until we get you off the hard, cold ground; you'll be amazed at how much better you'll feel. Lady Cynthia, pray bring up the rear. You can supervise from there and shout out advice and encouragement as we go along." He caught Cynthia's eye and she gave him an amused nod. She perceived, of course, what he was doing: maintaining a flow of chatter to keep the atmosphere light and prevent Mr. Ellsworth from interjecting any more prophesies of disaster. Very clever.

She was even more impressed when they reached the two-wheeled pony cart—without mishap, just as Derek had promised. He had piled the back of the vehicle with pillows and bolsters, anticipating that they would need to shield Hannah from the bouncing of the cart as much as possible. The horse drawing it had been tied to a stout bush, since trees were lacking, and was waiting quietly. The two men laid the litter, with Hannah on it, tenderly in the back of the trap. The bed of the vehicle was narrow, and, unfortunately, the litter poles stuck out on either side of it. Derek deemed this dangerous, so Hannah scrambled off the litter and onto the cushions as best she could, and Derek stashed the folded litter in the underboot.

"I am so glad you thought of pillows," exclaimed Hannah gratefully.

"I sent for a surgeon, too," said Derek. "I hope he'll be there by the time we return."

"Excellent," exclaimed Cynthia. "Mr. Whittaker, you think of everything."

"A surgeon?" Hannah bit her lip. "But I don't think I need medical attention. A day or two of rest—"

"Now, Hannah, be brave," said Cynthia firmly. "We shall all feel better when we know you have been seen by an expert. A surgeon will be able to advise you what's best to be done, and how to care for your injuries."

Hannah looked dubious, but fortunately Mr. Ellsworth chimed in. "My dear Hannah, you cannot be too careful," he admonished her. "Lady Cynthia is quite right. I, for one, shall not rest until I know you have received the best care available."

This evidence of Mr. Ellsworth's concern seemed to perk Hannah up, so Cynthia bit back the crushing set-down she longed to give him. It was odd, she reflected, how differently Hannah was affected by Mr. Ellsworth's demeanor; it seemed to strike her in almost the opposite way it struck Cynthia. Hannah seemed to find Mr. Ellsworth's zealous solicitude comforting, where Cynthia found it exasperating. It would have driven Cynthia mad, had she lain injured while someone fussed about, glumly expected the worst, and made a point of reminding her of every dreadful thing that might occur.

She stole a glance at Derek Whittaker. Now, *there* was a model of knightly behavior. No nonsense, no fuss, no empty words of sympathy, no unnecessary precautions. Just action. Efficient, decisive action. What an excellent husband Derek would make for some lucky lady. She wished she believed that the lucky lady would be herself.

She stifled a sigh as she turned her attention back to her own appointed task: leading Mr. Ellsworth's horse. Mr. Ellsworth was insisting on riding in the back of the cart with Hannah, supposedly to catch her if she started to slide. So Cynthia, on her mare, was to lead his horse while Derek drove the pony trap, with Lady tied to the back of the vehicle.

The strange little procession, rumbling along at a snail's pace, would have made an interesting sight had anyone seen it. They did not encounter a soul, however, until actually approaching Oldham Park. Derek pointed with his whip at a shiny black gig being led toward the stable yard.

"Is that the surgeon's gig, Lady Hannah?"

She barely had time to crane her neck and reply, "I believe so," when two stableboys came flying toward them, followed by the head groom. The massive doors to the ducal palace were thrown open as well, and

Cummings emerged, two stout footmen with him. All was bustle and confusion for a few moments as Hannah was unloaded and carefully carried up the steps and into the front hall, Cynthia was handed down, and the animals and equipage were transferred to the stable hands. Mr. Ellsworth stayed at Hannah's side, hovering and exclaiming and warning the footmen at every step. Cynthia heard his voice recede into the distance—"Take care! Do not jostle her. Mind the furniture!"—as the footmen carried Hannah into the library.

Cynthia was the last to climb the steps to the entrance. As she entered the hall, stripping off her gloves, she saw Cummings pull Derek aside and whisper something to him that made his face go taut with excitement and tension. Derek immediately left Cummings and came to her. She could not help noticing, with a pang compounded of joy and regret, that his instinct was to include her in whatever was important to him.

"That *was* the surgeon's gig," he told her in a lowered tone. "But he did not come for Lady Hannah. He was already on his way when I sent for him—and he has brought the midwife with him."

"Oh! I am so glad. Lady Malcolm's time has come upon her?"

Derek nodded, then gave a short laugh. "I'm glad as well, if it means her ordeal will soon be over. Can't help feeling a bit anxious, though."

"Of course. But I'm sure all will be well. Will the surgeon have an opportunity to look at Hannah, too?"

"Oh, aye, babies take a great deal of time—from what I hear—and, of course, the midwife will be with Natalie. Malcolm, too."

Cynthia was startled. "Lord Malcolm! Oh, you must be mistaken. No man would stay with his wife at such a time."

Derek laughed, shaking his head. "You don't know Malcolm. He'll refuse to leave her side. When Pippa was born, he was nearly as exhausted as Natalie by the end of it."

"I've never heard of such a thing." Cynthia stared at him, amazed. "Most men won't remain in the house while their children are being born, let alone in the same room. And I imagine most wives would prefer they go off to their clubs or their stables or wherever they go, rather than hang about. Why does the surgeon permit it? I would think a husband would be very much in the way."

"Not Malcolm. He evidently makes himself useful. Talking to Natalie, rooting her on and so forth. Wiping her face. Fanning her. Whatever she needs."

"Gracious." Cynthia bit her lip. She could not imagine wanting her husband near her during the ordeal of childbirth. From what she understood, which was not much, a woman neither looked nor felt her best at such a time. And everything she knew about men—which, again, was probably not much—had led her to believe that, to them, a woman's appearance and demeanor were so important that it would be impossible for a man's love to survive the sight of his wife in labor.

But as the day wore on, she found herself wondering if this was yet another long-held belief she must question. The list, she reflected bitterly, was growing rather long.

An expectant hush permeated Oldham Park, punctuated with the occasional sound of running feet and doors slamming overhead. Housemaids carrying towels and basins hurried up and down the stairs, their young faces shining with a sense of their own importance. The surgeon did come in to take a look at Hannah's knee, in company with Lady Grafton, but his examination was fairly perfunctory and neither he nor Hannah's mother stayed long. He recommended elevation, which was already being done, and cold cloths—"Ice, if you have it; fifteen minutes on, then fifteen minutes off"—to take down the swelling. He promised to look at her again in twenty-four hours or so, but apologetically bowed himself out in record time. Mr. Ellsworth was indignant at the surgeon's evident haste, but Hannah seemed relieved. She confessed that she had been terrified that he would recommend old-fashioned cupping, a procedure she dreaded.

Cynthia remained with Hannah and Mr. Ellsworth in the library, making sporadic conversation and feeling herself very much a third wheel. Derek had, understandably, disappeared for the afternoon. He came down to the library near teatime, looking drawn and rather pale.

Cynthia rose to her feet, wishing she could smooth the worry from his brow. "Mr. Whittaker, we are so glad to see you. Is there any news?"

He shook his head ruefully and took the cup of tea she handed him. "Thanks very much," he said absently, sinking onto a chair. "No, no real news. I'm told that Natalie's pains began near daybreak, but she said nothing until she was certain—and by then, you know, we had left for the moor."

"It does seem to take a frightful amount of time," said Hannah sympathetically. "But, as I suppose you are aware, that's not unusual."

"Right." He stared down at the teacup in his hands. He did not drink from it. "I've been hanging about in the second-floor passage—near her room, you know, but not too near." He gave a short, mirthless laugh. "It's bad enough, even at a distance."

Mr. Ellsworth looked horrified. "I should think so, dear chap. A frightful business! Why not wait here, with us? Daresay they'll send up a shout the instant the child is born."

He shook his head. "I must be there. In case Natalie needs me."

"Well!" snorted Ellsworth, looking simultaneously sympathetic and nauseated. "Nothing you can do, Whittaker. You're only her brother, you know."

"I know." Derek's lips tightened. He set his tea down, untasted, and rose to his feet. "I've no appetite, I'm afraid. Sorry. I'll come back when I'm feeling more human." He gave Cynthia a strained smile, sketched a brief bow, and was gone.

Ellsworth folded his arms across his chest. "Bless me, what good does it do for Whittaker to lurk about in the passage?" he exclaimed. "He'll drive himself mad."

For a moment, Cynthia itched to tell Mr. Ellsworth what a booberkin he was. She folded her hands in her lap instead, and forced herself to speak politely. "He did not like to say it, Mr. Ellsworth, but you know that Lady Malcolm sent for him last week because she has been feeling poorly. It would be a sad thing, indeed, were he to miss the chance to tell her good-bye."

Mr. Ellsworth looked shocked and Hannah gasped, then covered her mouth with her hands. Cynthia blushed. "I should not have said it aloud, perhaps," she admitted. "And naturally one assumes that the danger is slight. But I think that is why he is hovering as near her door as he can bear."

"Oh, poor Mr. Whittaker." Hannah's eyes filled with quick tears. "What a terrible thought."

"Do not distress yourself, my dear Hannah," said Ellsworth earnestly. "As Lady Cynthia has said, the danger is surely very slight. And whatever becomes of Lady Malcolm, you must devote your energies to getting well."

"I am perfectly well," declared Hannah, waving her hand dismissively. "A sore knee is merely a trifle. Poor Aunt Natalie! I can think of nothing else."

This was doubtless a noble sentiment, but Cynthia had to turn away to hide her smile. It did seem that Hannah's mind was fully occupied, but not in thinking of her aunt's travails. Despite her lingering discomfort, she visibly glowed as she basked in John Ellsworth's undivided attention.

Hannah's helplessness had evidently made her an object of interest. Mr. Ellsworth sat at her right hand, in a chair drawn very close to the sofa where she lay, and scarcely took his eyes from her. Cynthia was amused to see how intently his gaze fastened on Hannah's face, and how alive he seemed to be to her every need as he waited on her, hand and foot. Was the ice making her cold? He jumped up and stirred the fire. Was she too warm now? He removed the rug that covered her legs. Cold again? Back came the rug. The sun, traveling across the sky, eventually slanted through the windows and struck her face. He hurried to the window embrasure and drew the draperies to her precise requirements—enough light, but not too much. And every quarter of an hour, like clockwork, he alternately took the cold cloths from her or handed her fresh ones, to make sure the surgeon's orders were followed to the letter.

It was really a remarkable performance. Cynthia remembered what Hannah had told her earlier, of his assiduous attentions when she was a child with measles, and had to stifle a laugh. If illness and injury brought out the best in John Ellsworth, he'd turn Hannah into an imaginary invalid within a decade.

If, of course, he married her. That thought ran a chill of depression down Cynthia's spine. If Mr. Ellsworth continued to dance attendance on Hannah, Mama would eventually notice it—and she would be beside herself with anger.

There was not a doubt in Cynthia's mind that her mother would blame her for this turn of events. Mama was utterly convinced that all Cynthia need do to attract any man alive was crook her little finger, and whoever he was, he would come running. No amount of evidence to the contrary seemed able to shake this belief; Mama was supremely confident of Cynthia's superiority to every other marriageable female. She supposed it was a mark of her mother's love for her, in a way . . . but these unrealistic expectations were wreaking havoc.

She frowned and stared out the window at the darkening sky, thinking. The best way to avoid a scene would be to think of some other gentleman, equally acceptable to her family, whose name she could immediately suggest as a substitute for Mr. Ellsworth. But who? There were so few truly wealthy men . . . and those she had already met had shown admiration but little serious interest in her. Except, of course, for Sir James Filey. And, come to think of it, one or two others in his circle. Older men, still clinging to the trappings of the last century. Men with dissipated faces and drawling voices and languid gestures and cruel smiles. She shuddered, remembering. They had all been horrid.

She looked again at Mr. Ellsworth, almost wistfully. Of all the men that Mama had ordered her to encourage, he truly was the best of the lot. What a pity that Hannah loved him. And, of course, that Derek had shown up.

On the whole, since Derek *had* shown up, she supposed she must be glad that Hannah loved Mr. Ellsworth. It would be harder to justify giving him up, if she had no other excuse to offer Mama than her own feelings. She watched, smiling a little, as Mr. Ellsworth shook out Hannah's pillows for the umpteenth time. It seemed plain to her that someday—perhaps not this year, nor the next, but someday—Mr. Ellsworth would marry Hannah. And believing that, plus knowing Hannah's feelings, gave her a perfectly respectable reason to look elsewhere.

She did wish that looking elsewhere allowed her to look at Derek Whittaker. But she did not share his sanguine belief that everything would work out, nor his trust in lucky stars. Her smile faded as she contemplated this unpleasant truth. She would have a week or two, at most, in which to indulge her dreams. Then it would be on to London, and another suitor selected from the ranks of the obscenely rich. Unless a miracle happened . . . but Cynthia feared that she had already used up her portion of divine intervention. The sudden death of Sir James Filey had been her miracle. She dared not expect another.

Darkness settled in, and the party scattered to dress for dinner. A walking cane was brought to Hannah, and she proudly demonstrated how well she could hop about with its assistance. Nevertheless, Mr. Ellsworth insisted that she be carried up to her bedchamber and that she have her dinner sent up on a tray. She wrinkled her nose at him and laughingly told him that he worried too much. Still, it was clear that his concern pleased her, and although she hobbled along the passage on her own she did allow the footmen—supervised by Mr. Ellsworth—to carry her up the stairs.

Lady Malcolm's interesting situation was not deemed sufficient to upset the smooth running of the household. Dinner was served at the usual hour. Lord and Lady Malcolm, Mr. Whittaker, and Lady Hannah were absent, but the rest of the party gathered as if nothing unusual were occurring upstairs. The duke and duchess's sense of decorum dictated that no one mention what was uppermost in everyone's minds, so conversation was intermittent and a bit random.

The suspense was nerve-wracking. Everyone at the table seemed to have one ear cocked for the approach of any news on the other side of the dining room door. They were politely listening, with the other ear, to one of the duke's sporting anecdotes when His Grace abruptly fell silent in the middle of a sentence. Firm, rapid footsteps could be heard crossing the hall outside the dining room. A low voice spoke briefly to the footman outside, and the door was flung open.

The surgeon entered, beaming despite his evident fatigue. He bowed very low to the duke and duchess. "Your Grace," he said, aiming his speech neatly at the air between the two. "It's a boy."

Pandemonium broke out. Hannah's fourteen-year-old sister, Lady Elizabeth, actually tossed her serviette in the air and cried, "Hurrah! Well done, Aunt Natalie!"

"Oh, Betsy, hush," protested sixteen-year-old Lady Jane, laughing with delight even as she pretended to be scandalized by her younger sister's outburst. The duke rested one elbow briefly on the table and covered his eyes with his hand for a second or two, hiding the strong emotions that naturally seized him, but he swiftly regained control. Not even the birth of the first male Chase in thirty-six years could unman the Duke of Oldham. He took a deep breath, straightened, and calmly inquired after the infant's health.

"He's a fine, healthy child, Your Grace," the surgeon assured him, his eyes twinkling. "Large, well formed—and exceedingly loud."

Even the duke laughed at this. Among the congratulations and exclamations that broke out, the duchess raised an imperious hand. "Pray tell me, Mr. Turner, how is my daughter-in-law?" she asked.

"Lady Malcolm is resting comfortably, Your Grace."

"All went well?"

"Very well, Your Grace."

The duchess's shoulders relaxed, and she nodded. "Thank you," she said quietly. Her eyes sought her husband's, and she smiled. "Congratulations, William."

"Thank you, my dear." The duke's countenance was warm with pleasure. It was the softest expression Cynthia had seen him display.

Emotions ran high, not only at the head and foot of the table but around the entire room. Under the cover of Jane and Betsy's impetuous hugging and Lady Ballymere's more temperate offer of felicitations to the duke and duchess, Cynthia's eyes were drawn to Lady Grafton. She saw the marchioness surreptitiously slip her hand into her husband's, and witnessed the twinge of sadness in the smiles Lord and Lady Grafton exchanged.

Cynthia felt a pang of sympathy. It must be bittersweet, for them, that Lord Malcolm had sired the anxiously awaited heir after all their years of failure. Lord Grafton was next in line and would inherit the dukedom in due course, but his nephew, not his son, would follow him. Cynthia had observed how hard it was on Lady Malcolm to carry the weight of the Chase family hopes. Lady Grafton, as she produced daughter after daughter, must have seen her children awaited with the same bated breath—only to have them greeted, at least initially, with disappointment. How heartbreaking, how devastating, that must have been for her. It would be, for any mother.

Seated at the duke's elegant dinner table, with candlelight sparkling in the crystal and gleaming mellowly on china and silver, Cynthia sat, untouched by the rejoicing that surrounded her, and brooded on the poverty of her sex. Why was it, she wondered, that the snowy linens, the china, the crystal, the silver, the servants, the palace itself and all its contents, should pass to the squalling infant upstairs rather than to his sisters or his aunts? For the first time, the ancient system of passing wealth through the male line struck her as inherently unfair.

She frowned down at her plate and gave herself a mental shake. Everything seemed to upset her these days. What was the matter with her? It must be her new mood of rebellion, or her newborn determination to think for herself. Or perhaps she was merely suffering a touch of the megrims. If she continued on like this, questioning every established rule of life, she would likely end her days in Bedlam.

Chapter Sixteen

Malcolm could not be torn from Natalie's side, so Derek strolled downstairs alone. Happiness and relief made him feel almost giddy with contentment. He had seen both mother and child—for a space of perhaps twenty seconds—and could now confirm to anyone interested that Natalie was safe and the Chases had their baby boy at last. He hoped they would take his word for it. Anyone who wanted to see for themselves would jolly well have to wait for morning. He had achieved his own glimpse by ducking in unannounced, but Malcolm was now closely guarding his wife and son's slumber.

Humming, he headed past the drawing room and continued down the next flight of stairs, hoping Cynthia would have returned to the library after dinner. To his disappointment, the room contained only Lady Hannah Chase, stretched out on a sofa and morosely leafing through a slender volume of sonnets. Cynthia must have retired, very correctly, to the drawing room with the rest of the crowd. For a lady supposedly engaging in an illicit romance, she certainly was difficult to separate from the pack. He was going to have to explain the rules of the game to her: When everyone else gathers in the drawing room, make some excuse to go elsewhere. Give a chap half a chance to see you alone. Follow the example of . . . Lady Hannah.

Hm. This was interesting. What the deuce was Hannah doing all by herself in the library?

"Hallo, my lady," he said cheerfully, leaving the door very properly open behind him as he entered. "Am I interrupting you?"

She closed her book hurriedly. "Oh, no, Mr. Whittaker. Certainly not. How is Aunt Natalie? Have you seen her?"

"I have, and I am here to report that your aunt and your new cousin both seem to be in excellent health. They have been through a hair-raising experience, however, and are sleeping it off together." He dropped into a wing chair across from her and filled her in on the few details he knew. Hannah seemed glad enough to see him, but Derek sensed that she had been hoping for someone other than himself to walk in the door.

He inquired after her health and she told him, with great relish, of the terrific pain she had endured, the palpitations of fear she had suffered when the surgeon examined her, the misery and inconvenience of icing one's injuries in March, and the horrific colors her knee had turned. She was illustrating with her hands the diameter of her swollen knee, modestly hidden beneath a lap rug, when John Ellsworth walked in. Hannah's face visibly brightened. She interrupted herself in the middle of her recitation to greet him, seeming to forget everything she had been about to say.

Ah, yes, Derek knew the feeling well.

He watched with some amusement as Mr. Ellsworth hurried to Hannah's side, scolding her gently for placing herself too far from the bell pull and for going off alone. "For what if you should need something?" he reminded her anxiously. "A cane will not safeguard you against further injury. Indeed, it may *add* to the danger you are in, by giving you a false sense of independence. You could very well fall a second time, trying to cross the room to summon assistance! Really, it is most imprudent. You must not run unnecessary risks."

Lady Hannah looked pleased by all this rubbish. She seemed about to speak when Mr. Ellsworth startled her into silence by seizing her hand and patting it. "And I must say, my dear girl, I think any idea of your leaving the house and actually walking abroad, particularly in the dark, must be abandoned at once. I have come here to beg you—to persuade you, if I can—that you must not do such a thing."

He seemed quite agitated. Hannah stared at him, her color fluctuating. "Why, I—that is, certainly, John. If you think it unwise—"

"Indeed I do." He spoke vehemently, dropping into the chair closest to the sofa and still retaining her hand. "Will you promise me, Hannah? *Promise* me you will not do anything so foolhardy."

Hannah glowed. "I promise," she breathed, starry-eyed. Derek felt almost as if he should tiptoe away rather than witness this scene; it had taken on a distinct note of intimacy. He wasn't sure exactly what Hannah had just promised and would have bet a monkey Hannah didn't know, either. It didn't seem to matter. From the look on her face, she would have promised John Ellsworth dashed near anything.

Ellsworth looked relieved. He patted her hand one last time and released it. "Thank you. You had me very worried, you know."

"Did I?" She looked a bit lost.

"Well, of course you did." He leaned earnestly toward her, lowering his voice. "I would be happy— honored—to speak privately with you at any time you desire. Anywhere you say. Why wouldn't I?"

She blinked at him. He seemed to expect a reply. "Why, indeed?" she murmured obligingly.

"We can talk about anything you like."

"Can we?" She still looked confused. "Thank you."

He beamed. "No need to leave the house and tiptoe about in the shrubbery, eh? Hah! I daresay Whittaker will excuse us here and now, if you like. Or not," he added hastily. "If you'd rather do it another time."

They both turned to Derek, Ellsworth looking expectant and Hannah apprehensive. He coughed. "I've no objection. Shall I go away, Lady Hannah?"

She was slowly turning pink. "Well," she hedged. "I—I hardly know. What do you think, John?"

Thus appealed to, Mr. Ellsworth puffed his cheeks and looked uncomfortable. "Why, my dear Hannah, it is entirely up to you. I am at your disposal. You have promised not to walk more than you should on that injured knee of yours, and I can ask nothing more than that. I really have no other stipulation."

Hannah glanced dubiously from John to Derek and back again. "Well," she said hesitantly, "if you really do not care one way or the other, I think—I think I had rather go upstairs now. Will you take me? I do not think I need be carried, if you will give me your arm."

"Of course. Delighted. Happy to be of assistance." Ellsworth jumped up with alacrity and, seemingly, relief. He handed Lady Hannah her cane. "Take my arm on your injured side, dear girl, and use the cane on your uninjured side. Yes, yes, that's right. Excellent."

And so, with Hannah leaning heavily on Mr. Ellsworth's arm and balancing with the cane on her other side, the two of them bade Derek good night and progressed slowly toward the library door. Ellsworth kept up a steady stream of gentle admonitions and instructions, seeming completely focused on guiding Hannah's faltering steps.

Courtesy dictated that Derek remain on his feet while Lady Hannah was still in the room, so he was in an excellent position to see what happened when they reached the threshold. Mr. Ellsworth, muttering something that sounded like "And we shan't need this any- more, shall we?" pulled a piece of paper from his pocket and, in one motion, crumpled it with his fist and tossed it into a wastepaper basket. He then returned his attention to begging Hannah to mind her step: "For the floor out here is quite slick, I am afraid. Very highly polished, upon my soul."

Derek's curiosity, already roused by the peculiar scene he had just observed, instantly got the better of him. The moment Ellsworth and Lady Hannah were out of sight, he nipped over to the basket.

"I've missed my calling in life," he muttered rue- fully as he rummaged among the bits of paper in the bottom of the basket. "Should have been a spy. I've a gift for it. Heigh-ho, what's this?"

He spread out the wadded-up sheet. It appeared to be notepaper, and of the finest quality, folded neatly in half. Inscribed on the outside in flowing, feminine handwriting were the initials "J.E." What Mr. Ellsworth had tossed away was a note—a note from a lady. Interesting.

Derek took the sheet of folded paper back to the center of the room, where the lamp was. He sat on the sofa recently vacated by Lady Hannah and stared at the note, turning it over and over in his hands. Should he open it? Probably not. Whatever it was, it was clearly intended for eyes other than his.

On the other hand, it was more than human nature could resist. He reminded himself that the message couldn't possibly be private or important, since Ellsworth had thrown the thing away. His conscience was only moderately appeased, but moderately appeased would have to do. Having retrieved the note, he was dashed well going to read it.

He flicked the note open with his thumb and smoothed out the creases. The message was short, and the handwriting beautifully clear.

I must speak privately with you on a matter of grave importance. I rely upon your discretion and your chivalry, and beg you to come to the orangery at midnight tonight. Pray do not fail, for my need is urgent and I know not where to turn if not to you.

He read it once. Twice. His mind could make no sense of it at first. The note was unsigned. Except for the "J.E." on the outside it might have been addressed to anyone. And yet, oddly, he was finding it difficult to breathe, as if all the air in the library had been sucked out by some malevolent spirit, leaving him choked and dizzy. It was as if his body understood the meaning of the note before his brain did.

Eventually, of course, his brain caught up.

John Ellsworth had received this note and had assumed that it came from Hannah Chase. That much was plain as a pikestaff. Apparently, modest Mr. Ellsworth could not conceive of any other lady sending him such a note. But it seemed to Derek, from Lady Hannah's evident confusion a few minutes hence, that Hannah had *not* sent the note. And the list of ladies other than Hannah who might have sent it was woefully short. In fact, he could think of only one other lady whose name could reasonably appear on that list.

Derek felt as if a leaden weight had descended on his chest, making it difficult to breathe. He stared at the note, unwilling to believe the evidence. He felt nearly as sick as he had felt that long-ago day in Lord Stokesdown's town house, reading the notice of Cynthia's engagement to Filey. For some minutes he tried desperately to think of an innocent explanation for the cryptic message he held in his hands. Why, apart from the obvious, would Cynthia seek a midnight rendezvous with John Ellsworth? He cudgeled his brain, but to no avail. No innocent explanation occurred to him. Whatever was afoot, it was anything but innocent.

Was it possible . . . was it *remotely* possible . . . that Cynthia had been double-dealing? That the reason why she was so elusive was that she had somehow managed to carry on romances with Ellsworth and himself at the same time?

He flinched from the very idea. No, no. Surely that was impossible. Even had she been able to achieve such a feat at the house—and he had to acknowledge that that, at least, was possible, albeit unlikely—one only had to consider her conduct at the ball to discard the notion. She had gone off alone with him for half an hour or more. And she had danced with him twice.

But she had also danced with Ellsworth twice.

Derek scrubbed his face with one shaking hand. Oh, this was nauseating. He should be ashamed to have such thoughts. It was lunacy to entertain, for even a moment, the notion that Cynthia was capable of such a monstrous thing. She loved him. He *knew* that, knew it on some bone-deep level that could not be gainsaid.

But she had consistently told him she would not marry him. And she had refused permission for him to address her mother.

Was it possible that Natalie's interpretation had been right, and Cynthia was merely toying with him? Using him to explore feelings she knew all along she would, in the end, set aside forever? Was that what Cynthia had been trying to tell him—that he was her last fling, her attempt to experience a grand passion once in her life, before marrying a man for whom she felt nothing?

If that was so, it was probably unfair for him to blame her. She had tried, over and over, to tell him things that he had refused to hear.

And yet, unfair or not, he did blame her. He blamed her bitterly.

Cold rage rose in him. So he was to be used and tossed aside, was he? A handful of kisses, a few whispers in the dark, a dance or two, and then farewell. That had been her plan all along. Looking back, remembering the things she had said and done, honesty forced him to admit that she had been consistent. She had never once promised him anything more than she had already given. It was his own stubbornness, his refusal to accept reality, that had given him false hope. Not Cynthia.

This stark truth failed to cheer him up.

Cynthia had assured him, only yesterday, that she would set no further traps for Mr. Ellsworth . . . but she had told him, the day before, that she longed to be rich. She had later assured him that that was a lie. Which was the lie, and which was the truth? His heart gave him one answer, but the evidence gave him another.

He read the note again, his lip curling in disgust. What a melodrama! The orangery at midnight. Faugh. It was the sort of assignation a child might make, playing at spies or ghosts. He screwed the paper into a ball and hurled it with great violence at the wastepaper basket, returning it where it belonged.

He was halfway up the stairs, heading for his bedchamber, when it occurred to him that Cynthia was about to spend a long, cold hour in the orangery, waiting in vain for John Ellsworth to arrive. A bark of mirthless laughter escaped him. Well, let it be a lesson to her. She should have known better than to send an unsigned note to a simpleton. Her misguided attempt at discretion had backfired.

Of course, there was another way in which Cynthia's little intrigue had gone awry. She didn't know that Derek had intercepted her note. She didn't know that her secret perfidy had been exposed. He'd be willing to bet that he was the last man on earth she would have chosen to show that note to.

He paused, one hand on the banister. An interesting idea had occurred to him. Ellsworth didn't know that Cynthia was waiting in the orangery . . . but he did. And Cynthia didn't know that he knew. He could surprise her by unexpectedly showing up in Ellsworth's stead. Should he do so? It might be highly instructive. Painful, perhaps, but instructive.

The possibility was intriguing. He strolled into his room, rubbing his chin thoughtfully. What would happen if he walked in on her, suspiciously alone in the orangery at dead of night and obviously waiting for someone? Would she try to pretend that her motives were innocent? Would she be defiant, reminding him that she had told him all along she would never be his? Would she weep and beg his forgiveness? Would she try to turn the tables on him, demanding to know what *he* was doing in the orangery? Or would she enact him a scene that somehow incorporated all those elements?

There was one way to find out.

He caught sight of himself in the wardrobe mirror and frowned, studying his appearance. If what he wanted to do was expose Cynthia's game, his best chance of doing so was to come upon her unawares. But how? The most conspicuous feature of an orangery, the thing that made it an orangery, was the enormous windows that ran the length of it on both sides. She would be watching his approach through those windows, no doubt. And he looked nothing like John Ellsworth.

Still, people generally saw what they expected to see. Under cover of darkness and muffled in a great-coat, he might just pass for Ellsworth—since Ellsworth was who she expected to see.

His build was more powerful than Ellsworth's, and he was considerably taller. But when he put the great-coat on, he discovered that it hid these attributes reasonably well. Beneath its bulk, he might be any shape at all. And the coat was long enough that he could walk with his knees slightly bent, thus taking a few inches off his height. He pulled a hat low on his forehead. He looked more like a highwayman than a lover on his way to a tryst, but perhaps that was all to the good. He hoped he looked intimidating. In fact, he hoped he looked terrifying. Cynthia evidently needed a good scare.

Filled with grim determination, he slipped downstairs and out into the night. It was much colder than it had been the night before. The gravel crunched beneath his feet as he strode down the neat paths that traversed the duchess's rose gardens, bare-stemmed and bleak in the moonlight.

The orangery topped the next rise. It was a romantic structure, built to resemble—vaguely—a Greek temple. The effect was heightened by the fact that it stood in splendid isolation, and one must approach it via a gently winding path. The irony struck Derek forcibly as he approached; it reminded him strongly of a drawing he had once seen, a fantasy of ancient worshipers approaching the Parthenon. Trying to shorten himself by walking with bent knees added to the illusion. He almost felt he should be carrying a stick of incense or a sheaf of wheat as he climbed the low hill to where the orangery waited, its tall, arched windows glittering blackly against pale stone walls.

The last third of the path was lined with some sort of shrubbery. There was no sign of life as he approached the door. The proportions seemed to dwindle as he arrived; the orangery's situation, isolated at the top of the rise, had made it appear larger than it was. When he reached the actual building, he saw that what had appeared to be a temple was really just a single room, long and low and lined with as many windows as the architect thought the building would bear.

The latch turned quite easily when he touched it. Derek stepped noiselessly inside and closed the door softly behind him.

The air was unexpectedly warm. It was nearly as warm as if the place housed people rather than plants. In fact, it was so much warmer than the wintry night outside that his face tingled with a pleasant flush of heat.

And then the perfume hit him, taking him completely by surprise. A fragrance like heaven itself filled the room, so delicious and heady that he instinctively lifted his nose to it, like a spaniel tasting the wind. None of the potted trees that lined the walls were large, but there must have been dozens of them; lemon and lime and orange after orange after orange. Some of the perfume was from their fruit, and some from flowers, for, incredibly, many of the trees were bearing both at once. He had never seen anything to equal it. Or, rather, he had never smelled anything to equal it.

There was a glass dome in the orangery's ceiling. Silvery light poured down through it into the center of the room, faintly illuminating the marble floor and a small, well-banked stove from whence the heat radiated. And, adding to the perception that he had accidentally wandered into paradise, Cynthia stood within the pool of spectral light, warming her hands at the stove. Her back was to him, and she had not heard him come in.

Derek felt pain constrict his heart. She was, of course, a vision of pure loveliness. The hood of her cloak had fallen back, and the moonbeams caught in her hair shimmered like a halo. She looked every inch the angel of his dreams. And she was waiting for another man.

He tiptoed up behind her and placed his hands over her eyes. She gasped and jumped, startled, then gave a breathless little laugh.

"Guess who?" he growled, in a voice that might have been anyone's.

She did not even hesitate. With his hands over her eyes, he could feel the smile lift her cheeks. "John Ellsworth," she replied, her voice warm with delight.

And she turned in his arms and kissed him full on the mouth.

Chapter Seventeen

Derek felt his body go rigid with denial. He pulled away from her at once. "Wrong," he said, his voice rasping with anger and grief. "Guess again."

She laughed. He could hardly believe the evidence of his ears: She *laughed*. "Well, let me see," she said, tilting her head to one side as she considered him. "How many guesses may I have?"

He stared at her. Something was amiss. His galloping emotions lurched to an abrupt halt, as if someone had just pulled the brake on a runaway carriage.

In the uncertain moonlight it was difficult to read every nuance of her expression, but he could have sworn . . . he could have sworn she looked perfectly relaxed. She was smiling at him. She seemed neither startled nor dismayed. And yet she must know, now, that it was Derek Whittaker who faced her, not John Ellsworth. Her reaction made no sense whatsoever. Unless—

"Cynthia, you know it is I," he blurted.

Now *she* looked surprised. "Of course."

Of course? What the deuce? He frowned at her,

bewildered. "Why, here's a riddle," he exclaimed. "Why did you say you thought I was Ellsworth?"

Her eyes widened with further surprise. "I was joking you." Sudden laughter lit her face again. "Don't pretend you thought I was serious! As if I could mistake you for poor Mr. Ellsworth." She shook her head, still laughing.

So she had said it as a joke. That's exactly what he had thought—after the initial shock. It was the only explanation that tallied with her demeanor. But it made no sense. "Were you not expecting Mr. Ellsworth?"

A strange little pause ensued. Her laughter faded. She seemed to be as puzzled by his behavior as he was by hers. "Why would I expect Mr. Ellsworth, of all people? Unless—did you bring him?"

"*I?* Why would I drag Ellsworth out here in the middle of the night?"

"I've no idea. Derek, what on earth . . . ?"

He took a deep breath. "Let's begin again, shall we?" He paced back toward the door, then turned around and approached her for a second time. "Now. Who am I?"

She stared at him in the liveliest astonishment. "Unless I am much mistaken, you are Derek Whittaker."

"And who were you expecting to meet here?"

"Derek Whittaker." Her expression and tone were amused, but also exasperated. "Are you not Derek Whittaker after all? Is this what we are here to discuss—the fact that you are an imposter?"

He rubbed his chin. "I'm beginning to wonder," he remarked, baffled. "Cynthia, my love, if you intended to meet me, why the dev—why the deuce did you send your note to John Ellsworth?"

"I beg your pardon?"

"Why did you—" he began again, slowly and distinctly, but she interrupted him.

"I heard you. I simply didn't understand the question. Derek, I sent no note."

"To me. You sent no note to me."

"I sent no note," she repeated patiently. "At all. No note to you. And certainly no note to Mr. Ellsworth. Derek, what are you talking about?"

"My dear girl, if you sent no note, what are you doing here?"

"Meeting you," she exclaimed. "As you asked me to do."

Her confusion seemed completely genuine. His definitely was.

"The perfume in this place evidently casts some sort of spell," he informed her. "One or the other of us has been bewitched. May I take off my coat? It's too warm for this room."

"By all means," she said politely. "Perhaps you are suffering from heat stroke."

"That would explain it," he agreed, pulling off his gloves and stuffing them in his coat pocket. "Hallucinations." He tossed his hat and muffler aside and started to work on the buttons of his greatcoat. "I could have sworn you sent a note to Ellsworth, begging him to meet you in the orangery at midnight.

281

Silly of me, wasn't it?"

"Very silly." She crossed her arms. "Especially since, if the note went to Mr. Ellsworth, you would not have seen it."

"I—uh—found it among the wastepaper. Never mind about that," he added hastily, seeing that she was about to question him on this point. "I wish now that I had brought it to show you, but I naturally returned it to the wastepaper basket. Are you saying you never wrote it? You must have written it." He looked doubtfully at her. "You are here, precisely where the note said you would be. At midnight, which is when the note said to meet you."

"Yes. Because this is where *your* note said to meet *you*. What game is this? It is a game, isn't it?" She looked puzzled again, and a little hurt. "You know perfectly well I would not send such a note to Mr. Ellsworth. And why would I want to meet him at the time and place where I had already agreed to meet you?"

"Hold a moment." He ran his fingers through his hair, distracted. "You received a note from me." It was not a question. The picture still was not clear to Derek, but he felt it becoming clearer every moment, like a foggy landscape once the wind starts to blow. "Do you have the note with you, by any chance?"

She shook her head. From the anxious expression she wore, it seemed that Cynthia, too, was guessing that she and Derek had stumbled into something strange. "It said to write yes or no and then return it. So I wrote yes—to tell you I would be here—and then slipped it under the corner of the rug outside the drawing room."

"Is that what the note said to do?"

"Yes," she said, almost inaudibly. "Was the message not from you? How—how could that be? There is no other 'D.W.' who could have . . ." Her voice trailed off, and her eyes went wide with a stricken expression. "Oh, this is dreadful. It means—it means someone *knows* about us."

He frowned. "Does it? There is some sort of deep game being played, but I haven't quite figured it out. Cynthia, are you certain that the note you received purported to be from me? And are you certain you were the intended recipient?"

"What do you mean?"

"Did it say, specifically, that it was from me to you? Or did you just assume it was?"

She stared at him as if he were a lunatic. "It was addressed to 'C.F.' and signed 'D.W.' So unless you can tell me of another couple whose initials match ours—"

He gave a short laugh. "No; it seems the note you received was fairly specific. The note I saw was not. It was addressed to 'J.E.' but it bore no signature. Ellsworth thought it had been penned by Hannah; it was I who deduced that the note was from you."

"This is all rather complicated."

"I agree." He folded his greatcoat in half and dropped it neatly beside his hat and muffler. Then he slipped one arm around her waist. "Sit with me," he murmured, "and we'll puzzle it out together." He guided her toward a stone bench placed between two potted trees. After the wild swings of emotion he had endured in the past few hours, it was a relief to end with unlooked-for happiness. Alone with Cynthia, and in such a setting!

"You don't seem very worried," she complained.

"I'm not." He grinned. "I didn't plan this meeting, and apparently neither did you. But now that we're here, I'm inclined to think it was a jolly good idea. Once we've concluded who is responsible, I think I'll send the chap a bottle of something rare. With my compliments."

"Derek, pray be serious. This is a highly alarming turn of events." In the tricky light he sensed, rather than saw, her blush. "You should have seen the message I was sent! It was extremely loverlike. Someone has deduced that I have . . . feelings for you. Whoever wrote that note believed that I would respond to it. And I did. If there were any doubt in the sender's mind, I erased that doubt." She bit her lip. "I replied with yes, did I not? And here I am."

"Here you are," he agreed. He sank down onto the marble bench, pulling her down beside him. "And I must tell you, sweeting, that I am, on the whole, glad of it. And I am *profoundly* glad to learn that you did not write that note to Ellsworth."

"What did it say? Oh, Derek." She sighed as his mouth grazed the top of her ear. "I can't think properly when you do that."

"Good," he murmured, then bent to seek her lips.

"But this is important." She sounded gratifyingly

breathless. "Someone has gone to great lengths to set a trap for us."

He paused. "A trap was set," he admitted. "But not for us. I was not meant to see that note to Ellsworth. I read it only by chance." Reluctantly, he straightened his spine and tackled the problem at hand. It was difficult to bend his mind to serious subjects with Cynthia in his arms—in a moonlit bower of orange blossoms, no less. Conversation seemed a ridiculous waste of time. He compromised with his protesting libido by holding her with one arm, encouraging her to nestle against him. "Very well, you are right. We must think it through. There's something dashed smoky about all this."

"Yes. Someone has been exceedingly busy. But who?"

"I imagine if we determine the object of the game, it will be obvious who is playing it." He laced his fingers through hers. "A note to you and a note to Ellsworth," he mused. "Contrived to get the two of you alone in the orangery. What would the object of that game be?"

Cynthia suddenly went very still. Half a heartbeat later, his mind made the same jump hers had obviously made. And, as he had idly suggested, the instant they realized what the object of the game must be—to force Cynthia and John Ellsworth into a compromising position—they also knew who had written the notes. There was only one person who stood to gain from this gamble: Lady Ballymere.

Derek's reaction was a peculiar mixture of shock,

contempt, and pity—but most of his pity was reserved for Cynthia. He could only guess at the jumble of emotions she must be feeling. He did not move to stop her when she jerked to her feet and walked away from him. She wandered aimlessly through the shadows as if she knew not where to go or what to do, then halted on the other side of the room, by the window across from where Derek sat. He watched her, compassion in his eyes. She seemed to be staring out into the blackness, but he knew she saw nothing. Poor girl.

She shivered and clutched her cloak tightly around herself. "It is my mother who has done this," she said in a low tone.

"Yes," he said quietly. "I'm afraid it is."

She threw her head back, inhaling sharply, then sighed. As the breath sighed out of her, she lowered her chin and sagged forlornly against the windowpane. "It almost defies belief," she said, as if to herself. "Almost." Her voice took on a brittle edge. "And yet, when I consider the source, I find I am not surprised." She shook her head slowly. "What a sad commentary on my mother's character."

Derek could stand it no longer; he rose and went to her. He opened his arms wordlessly and, with one convulsive sob, she flew into them. His arms closed around her, and he cradled her gently, rocking her and murmuring soothing nonsense while she clung to him and wept.

Almost immediately, however, he felt her fingers tugging at his breast pocket. He smiled into her hair when he realized she was unearthing his handkerchief.

She gave one great gulp and lifted her head.

"I will *not* cry," she announced. She swiped fiercely at her eyes with Derek's handkerchief. "I will not."

"Excellent." He took the handkerchief from her and carefully dried her cheeks.

"I seem to be crying a great deal lately." She sniffed, looking annoyed with herself. "I don't know why."

Derek smiled a little. She was so adorable. "Your life is changing rapidly. Or hadn't you noticed?"

She gave a choked little laugh. "I have noticed, thank you."

"Change is always unsettling. Even changes for the better knock one off balance a bit." He ran his finger lightly along her cheekbone, his smile fading. His heart ached for her. "And in this case, my poor darling, you are having to adjust to a rather unpleasant revelation about someone you have always trusted."

"Yes. But I mustn't turn into a watering pot"—she took a shaky breath—"just because my mother is behaving like a criminal."

"Oh, now, tsk. It's not as bad as that." He hated to see her so distressed.

But Cynthia refused to be comforted. "It's every bit as bad as that." The corners of her mouth drooped dispiritedly. "I can hardly believe it. It's monstrous. She wrote me a note—disguised her handwriting very cleverly, too—pretending to be *you*. And then wrote one to Mr. Ellsworth, pretending to be me. That is forgery, is it not?"

"Well, not really," he hedged. "Not in any legal sense. Forgery is only a crime if it is committed in pursuit of monetary gain." He paused, seeing Cynthia's ironic look. "Oh." He pursed his lips wryly. "You will say that it was, in fact, done in pursuit of monetary gain. But you know, my love, matchmaking mamas are often guilty of unscrupulous tactics. Your mother is not the first to do something a bit . . . unethical."

She stared up at him, incredulous. "This is more than a silly trick. It's *entrapment*. Why, if this stunt became known, Mama would be ruined. Disgraced. There's not a decent hostess in London who would receive us."

He could not argue with her. She was right.

"I suppose this does go rather beyond the line," he admitted. "I wonder why she ran such a risk? What did she hope to gain? It wouldn't accomplish anything to simply spirit the two of you off to the orangery. Ellsworth isn't the sort of chap who would take advantage of you." He was about to tease her by adding a sly remark about his own intentions, but stopped when he saw the look on her face.

Cynthia looked sick and stunned for a fraction of a second, and then her face went completely blank. All emotion, all expression, vanished. He knew her well enough to know that this was her instinctive defense when faced with something she did not like to face. His brows snapped together in a frown of concern. "What is it?" he said sharply.

She pulled herself out of his grip and moved like a sleepwalker back toward the door. She looked ghostly in the ethereal half-light, her flaxen hair colorless in the bleached, blue moonlight and her cloak falling from her shoulders like a shroud. When she reached the door he saw her hand, pale against the gloom, reach out and touch the handle.

"Locked," she said softly. "I thought it would be."

"What!"

Derek knew he had not locked the door. He crossed swiftly to where Cynthia stood. Her expression had taken on a dreamy, faraway look. She was almost smiling. Derek rattled the door handle, trying it this way and that, but she was right. The door was locked.

"Well, here's a pretty kettle of fish," he said disgustedly. "That's what comes of trying to disguise myself as Ellsworth. I never fooled you, but it seems I fooled someone else."

"She must have been hiding behind the hedge," said Cynthia. Her voice sounded as faraway as her expression. "How undignified."

"Stand back a little," ordered Derek. "I can break this thing in a heartbeat."

But Cynthia did not stand back. She slipped in front of him and pressed her back against the door, flinging her arms out to prevent him touching it. She was laughing a little, but her face still had that strange, dreamy look. "No," she said softly. "I don't think you should."

The atmosphere in the room subtly altered. Derek looked at Cynthia—really looked at her. Her eyes were luminous. Her mouth was soft. She seemed completely unguarded; the walls that had been up just a few moments ago were down. Something profound had happened when she touched that door handle and discovered that she had been locked in with Derek. Something had changed her. It was as if this final attempt by her mother to manipulate her had taken her beyond anger, to some moment of bright mental clarity that had lifted a burden from her soul. She seemed . . . liberated.

She gave him a smile that took his breath away. "Your lucky star came through after all," she whispered, her heart in her eyes. "Don't refuse the gift."

Chapter Eighteen

Elation filled her heart to overflowing. She knew he'd been longing to kiss her—and very likely more. Even when he laughed or talked nonsense to her, desire burned in the depths of his gaze. And he wasn't laughing now. He wanted her. And now he could have her. She was done with doubts. Farewell, hesitation. No more vacillation. No more wavering.

She swayed toward him, everything she felt written on her face. "Derek," she breathed, aching with love for him. "Derek."

He emitted a sound somewhere between a gasp and a growl, muttered some broken, unintelligible exclamation, and swept her into his arms. She clung to him, giddy with feelings. Waves of pure emotion pulsed in her veins, overwhelming her. He plundered her mouth, and she gloried in it. This was exactly what she had wanted, exactly what she had hoped for. *He* was exactly what she wanted. He was hers, and she was his. And from this day forward, that would be all that mattered.

He lifted his mouth from hers long enough to say, in a hoarse whisper, "You will marry me."

"Yes."

She felt no fear. She was absolutely certain. The bargain her parents had forced her to make was broken. She would marry at no one's bidding but her own.

His hands came up, cradling her face. The gesture was unexpectedly gentle. He stared into her eyes as if straining to read her thoughts. "I want you," he said unevenly. "But I want you wholehearted. Don't come to me in anger, Cynthia. Don't wed me to spite your mother."

Another wave of joy broke over her. How dear he was. How unselfish. Was there another man on earth who would pause to warn her, to protect her from making a misstep, when blazing with the need she saw in his face? She gave him a smile so tender she felt it tremble on her lips. "Derek, I am yours. I've been yours since the night we met. You must know that as surely as I do."

The moonlight was behind him, but still she saw the emotions gathering in his face. "Yes," he whispered. "I suppose I do. You will stay here with me?"

"All night," she murmured. "If need be."

He lifted her hand to his lips and kissed her palm, almost reverently, then flattened her hand against his own warm, slightly rough cheek. "I shan't leave you untouched as Ellsworth would have done," he said huskily. "If you spend the night with me, Cynthia, you shall be well and truly compromised."

She curved her fingers against his jawline, loving the texture of his skin. "Oh, Derek," she murmured, reckless with happiness. "I hope so."

He gave a strangled laugh, then kissed her palm again. Fiercely, this time. His mouth felt hot and strong and exciting. The feel of his lips moving against the sensitive flesh of her palm seemed to shoot all the way up her arm, giving her gooseflesh.

"I love you, Cynthia."

She tilted up her chin and closed her eyes. "I know you do," she whispered, waiting. She did not have to wait long. He pulled her to him and kissed her. The kiss began softly, with infinite sweetness, but swiftly mounted in urgency. She slipped her arms around him and willingly gave whatever his lips demanded.

He took a step forward, backing her up, and her spine flattened against the door. He pressed the length of his body against her, slanted his mouth across hers, and kissed her again with a drunken abandon that made her head spin. This kiss was different from any-thing she had experienced before—hot and wet and intimate. The novelty of it, combined with the flood of sensations caused by his body pressing hers against the door, soon had her gasping for breath.

She had never felt a man's body against hers in quite this way. His heaviness—the sheer, masculine *bulk* of him—was dizzying. The sense that she was being overpowered should have frightened her, but it did not. It was not fear that was making her heart race. It was not fear that was turning her breath ragged. It was something else, something new. Something that blended seamlessly with her feelings for him and then, through some strange alchemy, ignited. The heat she had sensed smoldering in Derek's gaze had jumped from his mouth to hers. She was burning. Her very bones were melting. She molded herself to his form, mindlessly seeking to touch as much of him as possible.

The part of her mind that was still able to think was amazed. She thought she had known desire. She had desired Derek for years, longed for him, wept and mourned when she thought he was gone from her life forever. But the desire she had felt for him had been a desire of the heart, not of the body. She had longed for him with all her soul, but this . . . this was different. She had responded to his kisses before, but this, again, was different. Deeper. Wilder.

This was what the poets meant when they wrote of desire, likening it to madness. She had never felt desire's grip before, but she had read the poetry. This rush of insanity that caused her to tremble with need, to whimper like a wild thing, deep in her throat, to claw at the buttons of his waistcoat and then, abandoning them, run her greedy hands beneath it—this must be, could only be, passion.

His mouth left hers, and she felt his lips in her hair, then grazing her earlobe. She gasped and threw her head back. His lips left a trail of fire along her throat, making her head swim. She writhed against him, moaning his name.

"Come with me," he said hoarsely and eased his body away from hers. She followed him willingly.

He pulled her back toward the center of the room, retrieving his greatcoat and searching out a place to lay it down. The respite cooled Cynthia's blood sufficiently to allow her to notice her surroundings. He had led her to where a thick stand of potted trees clustered beside a window, waiting for dawn to catch the winter sun. Several were orange trees and the rest were lemons, their dense green foliage bearing globes of shiny, ripening fruit. The oranges and lemons glowed among the glossy leaves like baubles on a Christmas tree and smelled like sunlight in heaven. But the flowers—oh, the flowers! The white, waxy stars that dotted the trees exhaled the sweetest perfume imaginable. Cynthia drank the air deeply, smiling. The madness that had gripped her a few moments ago would soon return; the spark still burned, steady and bright. When Derek touched her again it would blaze up and consume her. And this, she thought dreamily, would be the perfect setting.

Above the little trees the window stretched tall, revealing the black expanse of night spangled with stars and washed with moonglow. And beneath this silver-lit window, sheltered by the flower-laden trees, on a cushion improvised from discarded sacks, Derek spread his coat. He then turned to Cynthia. His manner was so formal and respectful that his movements took on the rhythm of ceremony. It seemed fitting. The moment was oddly solemn; fraught with meaning, shimmering with significance. Neither of them knew what the night would hold, but Cynthia was at peace. Her commitment had been made. Her promise had been given. Whether he took her innocence tonight or on some future night, before or after their wedding, it was his to take. She had promised herself irrevocably to him. She was in his hands now, and content to be there.

Derek reached for the silken cord that tied her cloak at her neck. It fell away from her shoulders but he caught it, keeping it from puddling at her feet. "We can spread it over us," he told her softly. "If you like."

She felt herself blush, but she nodded. A tender smile played with the edges of his lips. He must have known, even in the faint light, that she was blushing. He reached to pull her close, then kissed the top of her head. "Trust me, love. If you want to hold back, we will. If you want to keep our true joining for the marriage bed, I shall honor your wishes. I'll do nothing tonight without your permission."

"I do trust you." She gave him a rather tremulous smile. "But it still relieves my mind to hear you say that."

His cheeky grin flashed down at her. "Once we're married, my pet, you'll ask *my* permission."

"Once we're married," she retorted, "I shan't need it."

He laughed and kissed her soundly. Then, before she knew what he was about, he scooped her off her feet and tumbled her down onto the makeshift couch. She gave a startled squeak, and he dropped down beside her, grinning. As he gazed down at her face, however, the mood shifted and his grin faded. Cynthia was lying on her back, gazing up at his face as it loomed above hers. His expression grew more serious than she had ever seen it.

"What's between us is sacred, Cynthia," he said gravely. "We did not choose each other. We were chosen *for* each other." His voice cracked with emotion. He lifted her hand once more to his lips, kissed it lightly, then held it between his own, gazing deeply into her eyes. "Do you understand me? Do you feel it, too?"

"Yes," she murmured. "And it doesn't matter how we came here, or why. We were meant to be in this place. Together."

He kissed the tips of her fingers. "I shall cherish and protect you always," he whispered. "Whatever happens tonight, my love, never doubt that."

"What *will* happen, Derek?" Her voice sounded small and worried. She hadn't meant to sound worried. "I mean—" She toyed with the edge of his cravat. "I've never experienced . . . I have never known a man. Intimately."

He propped himself up on one elbow. "How delightful it will be," he murmured, "to teach you." His smile flashed again. "Although some things are better learned through demonstration than description." He ran one finger lightly along her jaw and down her throat, making her shiver. "You see?" he murmured. His finger played briefly with the edge of her neckline, then skimmed down her bodice. Sensation leaped and burned beneath his fingertip, startling her. "It feels better than it would sound."

"Yes." It felt so wonderful that she could barely follow what he was saying.

"I will try not to rush you. I will rein myself in, for your sweet sake. But I warn you, Cynthia . . ." His mouth quirked humorously. "It won't be easy for me." He splayed his fingers along her waist. She could feel their warm strength heating the material of her gown, even through the light stays she wore. "I may get carried away," he murmured. "You must tell me if I go too far or too fast."

She nodded her acquiescence, although she wasn't entirely sure what he meant. "And what must *I* do?" she asked shyly.

Heat suddenly sparked in his eyes. In her ignorance, she had evidently said something tantalizing. "Do what you will," he said. His slow smile promised things she knew nothing of, things that were dark and exciting. The very sight of that smile made her tingle.

He leaned down and began leisurely tasting her lips again, his mouth moving slowly and softly against hers. Cynthia's eyes drifted shut, and she sighed, relaxing into his embrace. It differed amazingly from the bruising kisses he had given her at the door. Those had set her ablaze bright and fast, like a lightning strike. These kisses coaxed passion into flaring up, like a match held to paper. The fire licked along the edges of her being, warm and sweet. She hardly noticed when the fire caught; the moment was so subtle that it sneaked past her. One minute she was relaxed and drifting; the next, she was burning with need.

He seemed to sense it when she quickened in his arms. Cleverly, however, he did not increase the urgency of his kisses. He continued to coax her, kissing her with amazing softness even though she had turned from pliant to eager. But his hands began to move. Slowly, slowly. His fingers lightly traced her waist, then moved languidly up her rib cage. He must have felt, with his hand against her ribs, how rapid and shallow her breathing had become. He must *know* what he was doing to her. But he was giving her time . . . for what?

Through the confusion that swirled in her brain, drugged with his kisses, she realized what he was waiting for. He was waiting for her to acknowledge what she wanted. But what did she want? She didn't know. She only knew that she wanted. Wanted desperately.

"Touch me," she heard herself whisper. The words had risen from some deep, primitive part of her. This unacknowledged corner of her nature evidently knew, despite her inexperience, what she wanted. She wasn't even sure she had said the words aloud, but she must have. He instantly complied.

He broke their kiss when his hand covered her breast, as if he could not concentrate on two such overwhelming tasks at once. A tiny sound emitted from his throat, a soft groan of tortured excitement that magnified her own. He stared at his hand on her, watching his fingers stroke and outline and pet, finding the contours of her body beneath the clothes that confined her. The sight of his hand touching her so brazenly seemed to arouse him, and the look of arousal on Derek's face enhanced the sensation for Cynthia. She arched her back, wantonly inviting more.

His eyes lifted to hers, drowsy and heavy-lidded with the opiate of their intimacy. And then he lightly raked his nails across her bodice. A softer touch would not have penetrated her stays; this, however, sent a jolt of pure pleasure from the tips of her breasts all the way through her. Cynthia gasped, nearly crying out with startled delight.

"Do you like that, sweetheart?" he whispered.

"Yes," she replied, nearly sobbing with reaction. "Oh, yes."

He used his nails, then, to scratch rhythmically across the tips of her breasts while he kissed her. She was soon writhing mindlessly beneath his hands. It was the sharpest, keenest pleasure she had ever felt— it was almost unbearable, it was so intense—and yet it left her wanting more.

Amid the haze of sensation, she became aware that Derek was pulling her up to a sitting posture. She felt his mouth against her neck, kissing her throat, and then he whispered, close to her ear, "Let's get you out of these stays, my love."

An hour ago, such a suggestion would have embarrassed her. Now, however, it seemed such an excellent idea that she wondered why she hadn't thought of it herself. And another thought occurred to her, as excellent as that one. She plucked insistently at his coat. He complied with her wishes at once, letting her peel off the well-tailored coat, tug the cravat free, and unbutton his waistcoat even as he worked the buttons and ties at the back of her gown. There was a moment of breathless laughter when the coat pinned his elbows and hampered his movements, but somehow his outer garments came off and were tossed aside, together with her gown.

Shyness seized her when the cool air struck her skin. She was clad only in her stays, chemise, and stockings. Absent the cravat and waistcoat, Derek's shirt gaped open, exposing his chest from throat to waistband. He stood and, in one easy movement, pulled the shirt off. Cynthia felt the breath catch in her throat. His body was beautiful, with a clean, male beauty that filled her with awe even as it stirred her blood. He looked, in fact, like a statue of Apollo. Moonlight poured across his skin, bleaching it and adding to the impression that he had been carved from the purest marble. But the hand that reached down to her, and the smile that lit his eyes, were warm and living. She took his hand and let him pull her to her feet. He distracted her by nuzzling her neck while he unlaced the light stays she wore. It was strange to trust someone so completely, and that someone a man. Strange and wonderful and humbling.

She felt the stays loosen and part. He pulled the corset away from her body and dropped it. Her chemise, made of delicate lawn and almost transparent, clung to her form. His expression subtly altered as he peeled the sheer fabric away from her skin. His eyes darkened, and the muscles of his face seemed to slacken with desire.

"You are so beautiful," he muttered thickly, sounding dazed. "So beautiful."

A soft laugh of delight escaped her. She had heard those words before, but not from him. They had often struck her as insincere and meaningless, a crude attempt at flattery—but not this time. In Derek's beloved voice, in this place and time, being told she was beautiful filled her with joyous relief. *This,* she realized suddenly, *is what beauty is for.* For the first time, she perceived her allure as something other than a nuisance. For the first time, she *felt* beautiful. Her appearance gave Derek pleasure. And giving Derek pleasure gladdened her heart.

Smiling, her shyness vanished, she lifted the filmy shift over her head and tossed it on top of her discarded stays. Derek uttered the sound a famished hunter might make when catching the aroma of a feast, ready and roasted and round the next bend. She stepped back, away from him, and let the moonlight spill down her body. "Is it well?" she asked him softly, inviting his gaze. "Do I please you?"

Words seemed to fail him, but his face told her all she needed to know. He stared at her, dumbstruck, as she displayed herself for him, outlined in cool, bright silver. Then he shook his head slowly—not in answer to her question, but as if overcome by the sheer inadequacy of human speech.

She let her eyes roam over him as well, taking pleasure in the sight of sculpted muscle and tapering torso. *Derek.* A wave of hot possessiveness swept through her, and she went to him, splaying her hands against his chest. He did not move but stood rigid, holding himself in check while she ran her hands over his warm skin, marveling in the feel of his chest and arms, bared to her touch. A whiff of soap and the salty tang of clean, male flesh teased her nostrils, adding a welcome undercurrent to the overwhelming sweetness of the citrus trees. She felt her breathing become more shallow; a flush of heat that seemed to emanate from him, heady and drugging as steam off a witch's cauldron, enveloped her.

Her exploring fingers found the waistband of his trousers. She looked up at his face, her lips curving in a soft, provocative smile. "May I?"

But his hands came up to cover hers, stopping her progress. "Not yet," he said. His voice sounded hoarse and unsteady. "I might ravish you on the spot."

The words sent a surge of something hot and wicked through her. "I might like that," she whispered, tilting her face up to kiss his chin. The tips of her breasts grazed his chest. For an instant she felt her eyes widen at the shock of pure sensation, but for an instant only— Derek's control broke, and he pulled her against him. His arms closed around her.

Cynthia had pictured this moment in her most secret dreams, but the reality far surpassed her fantasy. Nothing had prepared her, nothing could prepare her, for how her bare body would feel when held against his. Even with his nether garments still between them, the sensation of his skin against hers was lovelier than rolling on satin sheets. Lovelier than sinking into a hot bath on a November evening. Lovelier than anything she had ever imagined. It took her breath away.

She slipped her arms around his back and clung to him, gasping. The strong muscles of his chest rippled beneath her cheek as he ran his hands hungrily over her body. It felt glorious. She wanted him everywhere, his hands, his mouth, as much of him as she could touch. She could feel the hard ridge of his desire pressing against her lower belly, awakening a need in her that answered his. She writhed against him, longing instinctively to run her hands over his body as he was doing to hers.

She felt his palms slip lower, down her thighs, and realized he was deliberately pulling her off balance. She gladly followed his lead and let him lower her back down onto their makeshift couch. He came with her, stretching out beside her. He immediately bent to nibble on her shoulder, while with one hand he deftly pulled the ties of her garters loose, letting the silk stockings slide down her calves. She pointed her toes and let them fall off her feet—the last stitch of clothing she was wearing. He raised up on one elbow then, drinking in the sight of her.

"Unbelievable," he whispered. His voice sounded rough with lust yet soft as prayer, filled with worship as well as desire. He hardly seemed aware that he was speaking.

But Cynthia could not contain herself. She did not want to be worshiped. She wanted to be . . . compromised. She ran her hand lightly, longingly, across the front flap of his trousers, letting her fingertips toy boldly with the buttons of his fly.

Derek inhaled sharply. His eyes locked with hers. "Cynthia," he croaked. "You mustn't do that. You don't know what it does to me."

She felt a slow smile lift the corners of her mouth. "But I want to know," she whispered, and reached to pull him down to where she lay.

Chapter Nineteen

Lady Ballymere slipped nervously out of bed and wrapped her dressing gown around her. She probably should lie abed and wait for Lucy to arrive with her morning tray—it was nearly her usual time to rise—but she could not bear the suspense another instant.

She had lain awake during most of the night, nerves stretched nearly to the breaking point, and was, therefore, almost certain that Cynthia had never come in. But almost was not certain enough. What if Cynthia had somehow returned without her hearing it? She had to know. She shoved her feet impatiently into the mules placed ready for her on the carpet and hastened to the door that connected her room to her daughter's.

The bed was empty. It was better than empty; it was untouched. A sigh of relief escaped her. The plan had worked! She had been so afraid during the night. A thousand things might have gone wrong, and in the wee hours of the morning she had been tortured by visions of disaster. But nothing had gone wrong.

The biggest gamble had been deceiving Cynthia. She had toyed with the notion of consulting her, but had decided against it in the end. Cynthia seemed to feel some silly scruples about attaching John Ellsworth, and heaven alone knew what game Cynthia was playing with Mr. Whittaker. So she had resolved that it was safer to deceive Cynthia as well as Mr. Ellsworth. Nevertheless, last night . . . after it was too late . . . she had suffered great anxiety regarding Cynthia's reaction to the deception. She had wondered whether Cynthia would play along once she realized what her mother was trying to accomplish, or whether she would be angry. She must have played along. It would have been a fairly simple matter to escape the trap. All they need do was break either the lock or one of the windows. Since they had evidently not done so, all must be well.

On the other hand, it would be a mistake to triumph too soon. There might be another reason why they had not broken out of the orangery; they might simply have felt squeamish about damaging His Grace's property. The young couple might have decided that it was better to stay where they were until they were discovered, claim innocence, and brazen it out. Matters could yet go awry; Cynthia might yet prove defiant. There was still work to do, to bring this marriage about.

At any moment, Cynthia and Mr. Ellsworth might be discovered and freed. The kitchen maid would go out at some point to gather the breakfast oranges. She might, even now, be at the orangery. Lady Ballymere must act immediately to ensure that her careful scheme did not dwindle into mere kitchen gossip. It would take more than kitchen gossip to seal this contract. The entire household must be set abuzz.

With a determined stride, Lady Ballymere went to the bell rope and tugged vigorously on it. Lucy was probably already on her way, but no matter. She must send a signal of agitation and uproar to everyone in the servants' wing. She tugged and tugged and tugged. And then, after a pause, she tugged again.

A grim little smile flitted across her features as she pictured the racket she must be causing belowstairs. The servants would doubtless begin by cursing her impatience. Then, as they recognized the urgency of her repeated summons, curiosity would stir. They would exclaim and wonder and speculate. And when the kitchen maid returned from the orangery, big with news, they would be primed to expect something scandalous. They would gather, eager to hear her tale. And then the gossip would spread like wildfire throughout the house.

When Lucy appeared, Lady Ballymere was pacing like a tigress, her dressing gown swirling about her dramatically. She pounced on the startled servant the instant she saw her.

"Lucy, thank heaven you've arrived! You will never believe it. Oh, I am distracted! I am *prostrate* with nerves! I hardly know what I am saying." She wrung her hands to emphasize how distraught she was and lowered her voice to a shocked whisper. "Lady Cynthia is not here. She did not sleep in her bed last night.

Oh! What could have happened to her? Where is my darling child?"

Lucy was a highly satisfactory audience. She nearly dropped the tray in her excitement, but managed, in the end, to deposit it without incident on Lady Ballymere's vanity. She then peeped through the connecting door into Cynthia's immaculate bedchamber and clasped her hands to her bosom, gasping with fright.

"Lawks!"

"Is it not terrible? Oh, what am I to do?" Lady Ballymere sank gracefully down upon the sofa, her hand to her head. "Where could she be? I am at my wits' end."

Lucy turned to her mistress, her eyes wide as saucers. "She's been kidnaped, my lady. Mark my words, she's bein' held to ransom."

Lady Ballymere quelled a stab of irritation. "I sincerely hope not," she exclaimed. "But she may have suffered some accident. We must send out a search party. Pray run out into the passage and find one of the footmen or housemaids. Cummings must be told at once. And then, for heaven's sake, child, come back and help me dress."

Lucy pelted out of the room as if pursued by hounds. It occurred to Lady Ballymere that she ought to be pale with fear. And, of course, she was not. While Lucy was away, rousing the staff, she carefully powdered her face with pure white talc. The effect was quite good, she thought.

Twenty minutes later, Lady Ballymere, suitably

pale, swept into the breakfast room. Breakfast was a fairly informal affair at Oldham Park, and one never knew how many members of the household would be present or at what time they would wander in. But Lady Ballymere's luck held; there was a sizable group in the room when she entered. The duke and duchess were present as well as Lord and Lady Grafton and their youngest daughters, Jane and Elizabeth.

Lord Grafton rose from the table, approached, and took her hand in both of his, an expression of deep concern on his face. "Lady Ballymere, we have heard the most alarming rumor this morning. I hope you will put our anxieties to rest."

She did her best to look pathetic. "Alas, my lord, I fear it is true. My daughter is missing. Her where-abouts are utterly unknown to me."

Above the low murmur of sympathetic exclamations that greeted her statement, Lady Elizabeth's young voice piped, "P'raps she's *eloped!*"

Lady Jane hissed, "Betsy, hush!" in a mortified whisper, but Lady Ballymere was secretly grateful for the girl's impertinence. It gave her an opportunity to clutch her throat, widen her eyes, and exclaim, "Surely not! Impossible! Lady Cynthia has been very strictly reared." She flung out her hand in a gesture of appeal. "You all know her. My daughter is a model of circumspect behavior, is she not? She would never do *anything* so lost to propriety." She shuddered and added darkly, "Not willingly."

The duchess gestured to her son, indicating that Lord Grafton should guide Lady Ballymere toward the table. "Lady Ballymere, pray sit down," said Her Grace courteously. Her calm demeanor threw cold water on the burgeoning sense of drama in the air. "I beg you will not distress yourself. Doubtless some innocent explanation for your daughter's absence will arise. These things happen, you know; people go for early walks and lose track of time. I hope she has not echoed my unfortunate granddaughter and taken a spill of some kind, but if she has, one of the servants will speedily rescue her. Two footmen, the groom, the stableboy, and my entire gardening staff are searching for her as we speak."

The gardening staff! Cynthia would, indeed, be speedily found. Lady Ballymere was running out of time to set the scene.

She murmured her thanks and sank onto the chair Lord Grafton held for her, her expression tragic. "I cannot eat until I know my Cynthia is safe. I have come here to beg your assistance," she announced. "I hope you will understand, Your Grace, that I mean no disparagement of your staff. But I do not care to leave this matter in the hands of servants. The explanation you have suggested is, alas, not possible. Lady Cynthia took no morning stroll. Her bed was not slept in."

This caused another minor sensation around the table. "Dear me," said Her Grace, her forehead puckering slightly. "How alarming."

Lady Grafton, usually self-effacing, leaned across the table to gave Lady Ballymere's hand a timid pat. Her eyes were dark with sympathetic worry. "I am the mother of daughters, myself," she said softly. "I can easily imagine the state you must be in. My heart goes out to you, Lady Ballymere."

"Thank you, Lady Grafton. You are most kind."

Her Grace touched her napkin lightly to each corner of her mouth, then bent a gaze of mild inquiry on her guest. "But—forgive me—how was it that you did not notice Lady Cynthia's absence, if she did not go to bed last night? Did she not go up to her room when you did?"

"Indeed she did, Your Grace," said Lady Ballymere quickly. "But I was feeling a bit down-pin last night, and took my headache drops before I retired." She gave a sad little shrug, looking helplessly around the table. "So unfortunate! When I take my drops, I'm afraid I sleep like a stone. *Anything* might have happened." She gave an eloquent shiver. "If my child has been harmed in any way, I shall never forgive myself."

The duke placed his fingertips together, as if he were pondering the mystery. "May I ask, Lady Ballymere, whether your daughter knew you were taking the drops?"

She opened her eyes in feigned surprise. "Certainly she did, Your Grace. I mentioned it to her before I— Oh!" She pressed her hand to her cheek. "What are you suggesting, Your Grace? Do you think—do you think she may have planned a *tryst* with someone? Indeed, indeed, I cannot think it possible!"

Lord Grafton glanced at Jane and Betsy. "We parents never think our daughters capable of bad behavior," he said wryly. "It has often astonished me, however, how much mischief girls will get into."

His wife looked distressed. "Arthur, dearest, really," she murmured, sotto voce. "We are speaking of Lady Cynthia."

"Quite right, my sweet." He glanced apologetically at Lady Ballymere. "I spoke without thinking. You are right, my lady, that your daughter's conduct has always seemed impeccable. I merely point out that—" He broke off, perplexed. "I almost said 'boys will be boys.' Is there an equivalent expression for girls? If not, there should be."

"My Cynthia has never given me a moment's worry," declared Lady Ballymere. "She has the keenest sensibilities—a precise attention to propriety unlike any I have known in a girl of her age. The idea that she would deliberately deceive her mother and— and *sneak about* is fantastical. She would do no such thing."

Lady Grafton spoke soothingly. "No one is suggesting anything of that nature, my lady. I am sure Lady Cynthia would do nothing clandestine."

"Certainly not." She blinked rapidly, as if trying to hold back tears, and put a catch in her voice. "But I fear for her safety, Lady Grafton. I fear she may have met with foul play. Such a beautiful girl, you know . . ." She let her voice trail off and was gratified to see the ripple of worry that went through the room.

Lord Grafton exchanged glances with his father. "I shall aid in the search directly after breakfast," he said grimly. "Malcolm is, naturally, otherwise engaged. But I daresay the Ellsworth men and Mr. Whittaker will join me."

The duchess clucked faintly. "But there has never been any crime of that kind in this neighborhood," she said. "Pray be calm, Lady Ballymere. I know of no dangerous persons in the vicinity who might have carried Lady Cynthia off. We must not let our imaginations run wild. She will doubtless return safe and sound. Why, she may walk in the door at any moment."

Lady Ballymere was still trying to frame an answer that would contradict the duchess without appearing rude when the door opened. Conversation ceased and all eyes lifted—but it was only Sir Peter and Lady Ellsworth who walked in.

Lady Ballymere was probably the only person in the room who was not disappointed. This was the audience she most desired to reach with her performance; these were the two persons whose opinion she must move. Her pulse fluttered with excitement. The prize was nearly in her grasp now. The days of cultivating Lady Ellsworth's friendship were about to pay off. She rose and flew to Lady Ellsworth's side. Lady Ellsworth seemed startled but did not pull away.

"My dear friend," uttered Lady Ballymere, actually sobbing with trumped-up emotion. Lady Ellsworth looked embarrassed at this display but not displeased. She patted Lady Ballymere in a vague sort of way.

Sir Peter coughed. "No point in pretending, I suppose, that we haven't heard the news," he said gruffly. "Servants always trumpet everything that goes on in a household, eh? Very sorry to hear it, though, very sorry to hear it. Thought Lady Cynthia might have turned up by now. She still missing?"

Lady Ballymere nodded silently, as if too overcome by emotion to speak. Lady Ellsworth led her back to the table. "You must not worry, Lady Ballymere," she said gently. "You accomplish nothing thereby. Did Lady Cynthia leave a note? No? Why, then, she must be somewhere on the premises. She would have left a note, did she intend to wander far."

Lady Ballymere gazed earnestly into Lady Ellsworth's eyes. "I had hoped to inquire of her particular friends—to ask them, you know, if she had said anything to them. She may have told your son, John, things she would not have said to her mother. You know how these young people are. Once they form intimate friendships, they confide in each other rather than a parent."

Lady Ellsworth looked surprised. "Why, you may speak with John if you wish, of course. If he can shed any light on Lady Cynthia's whereabouts, I am certain he will do so. But I can't imagine why she would confide in *him*."

Lady Ballymere laughed indulgently. "Oh, come now, Lady Ellsworth. You must have noticed, as I have, the friendship growing between your son and my daughter."

Lady Ellsworth appeared even more surprised—and not pleasantly. Her husband held her chair for her and she sat, looking as if she did not know what to say. "Thank you, Sir Peter," she murmured, then lifted troubled eyes to Lady Ballymere. "If you have noticed any sign of close friendship between Lady Cynthia and John, I confess it has escaped me. But I will admit that I have not looked for it, and often one must look closely to perceive such things."

Lady Ballymere gave another little trill of laughter. "I have not had to look closely, I promise you, to see the impression your John has made on my daughter. She has expressed to me repeatedly how much she esteems him. In fact, it crossed my mind that— Oh! No matter," she added hastily, pretending to discard what she was about to say.

Sir Peter was frowning. "What crossed your mind, pray?"

Lady Ballymere bit her lip in what she hoped was a pretty embarrassment. "Forgive me. I am distraught this morning, and my tongue is running away with me. I should think before I speak. I was about to say something so ridiculous! I was about to tell you that my first thought this morning, when I saw Cynthia's absence, was that she must be with Mr. Ellsworth. Is that not absurd?"

Lady Ellsworth's eyes flashed. "Perfectly absurd."

Lady Ballymere spread her hands apologetically. "Do not misunderstand me. I knew it was absurd the moment it occurred to me. For one thing, neither John nor Cynthia would do anything so improper. So *grossly* improper. And for another, why should they?" She shook her head, trying to look arch. "One does not steal what one might have for the asking."

Lady Ellsworth sat very straight in her chair. "My dear Lady Ballymere, what can you mean?" she exclaimed. "There has been no thought of marriage between Lady Cynthia and John."

"Certainly not," said Lady Ballymere, trying to look shocked. "I did not intend to imply it."

"John is far too young to contemplate such a step."

"Oh! Well, as to that, I have known many a young man greatly improved by marriage. And apart from his youth, I assure you, *I* would have no objection to the match. No serious objection, that is. Although"— she shook her head, trying to look firm—"it would be difficult to tolerate a match brought about by such sledgehammer tactics as these."

Sir Peter swelled like a toad. Lady Ellsworth looked ready to jump from her chair. The duke and duchess were stiff with disapproval. Lord Grafton turned to his wife. "My dear, may I suggest that this conversation does not concern us?" he said mildly. He rolled his eyes significantly toward their daughters. Jane and Betsy had stopped eating their breakfasts several minutes ago and were hanging on the unfolding drama, agog.

Lady Grafton bit her lip. "Of course, my dear. Girls! Come along." A brief silence fell while the marquess and marchioness shepherded their disappointed daughters out of the room.

Lord Grafton paused in the doorway. "Pray summon me if you require my assistance," he said dryly, "in searching for Lady Cynthia. Or, of course, for Mr. Ellsworth." The marquess bowed and departed.

Lady Ellsworth blanched at these fell words. "Good heavens," she exclaimed, her voice shaking. "Has everyone run mad this morning? Why look for John?

My son has not abducted Lady Cynthia!"

"Calm yourself, Eunice," said the duchess soothingly. "No one is suggesting such a thing. Lady Ballymere is overwrought."

Lady Ballymere decided to overlook this unflattering characterization of her behavior. It would avail her nothing to antagonize the Chases. "At any rate, this portion of the mystery will be quite easy to solve," she said brightly. "Where *is* your son, Lady Ellsworth? I would like to ask him a question or two. He may have some idea that has not occurred to the rest of us."

Lady Ellsworth played with the edge of her collar, looking uneasy. "I have not seen John this morning."

It was exactly the answer Lady Ballymere was expecting, but she pasted a look of astonishment and disquiet on her face. "My word! Can it be possible? Sir Peter, have you seen your son?"

Sir Peter was looking extremely disturbed. "No," he said bluntly. "But, my dear Lady Ballymere, we must not jump to conclusions."

She naturally ignored this piece of advice. Lady Ballymere flew out of her chair and paced the room, her voice rising to a pitch of near-hysteria. "We must find him! Send for his manservant—send for *someone!* Someone must know where he is. Oh, I shall go mad! *Both* of them missing— Sir Peter, I beg you!" She faced him, clasping her hands at her bosom. "For pity's sake, set my heart at rest! If anything has happened, if my daughter's honor has been compromised—"

"Preposterous!" cried Lady Ellsworth.

Sir Peter had risen when Lady Ballymere did. "Now, now," he said testily, "you are fretting yourself to flinders over nothing, Lady Ballymere. Whatever has happened here, whatever the answer to this mystery may be, I promise you that John has not compromised your daughter. My son absolutely, positively, would not do such a thing."

She flung out her hand toward the duke. "Your Grace," she said piteously. "I appeal to you!"

A formidable frown had gathered on the duke's features. "I find this entire scene highly distasteful," he said acidly. "But I assure you, Lady Ballymere, if anything untoward has occurred—which I sincerely doubt!—justice will be done. Loose behavior will not be tolerated under any roof of mine."

The duchess's mild voice interjected, "I cannot think you have anything at risk, Sir Peter, in making the promise Lady Ballymere desires to hear."

"Oh, yes, yes, of course," said Sir Peter hastily. "For heaven's sake, madam, sit you down. This will all come to nothing, mark my words. But if you must have my assurance, you have it. My son will do the right thing, never you fear."

Outwardly pathetic but inwardly rejoicing, Lady Ballymere sank back into her chair. "Thank you, Sir Peter," she said faintly. "I am sorry to be such a ninny. I should not have cast aspersions on your son's character. Of course he will do the right thing—should it be necessary."

Sir Peter snorted under his breath but sat back down.

"I make every allowance for your feelings, Lady Ballymere," he said grudgingly. "You are understandably overset by your daughter's disappearance. But I take leave to tell you, you have worked up a great lather with very little cause."

The duchess rang the little bell beside her plate. "I shall ask Cummings to ascertain Mr. Ellsworth's whereabouts," she said calmly. "We must put that portion of Lady Ballymere's anxieties to rest."

"An excellent idea," said Lady Ellsworth stiffly. "I shall be happy to relieve your mind, my lady, regarding my son's complicity in Lady Cynthia's little *adventure*. For I am quite certain he had nothing to do with it."

Lady Ballymere reminded herself that she had Sir Peter's promise, and the duke and duchess as witnesses to it. She could now afford to be charitable. She smiled weakly, therefore, and waved her hand in a gesture of apology. "I am so sorry, my dear Lady Ellsworth, to have offended you. Indeed, I hope you may be right. I even believe you *are* right. Your John is an excellent young man in every way. Forgive me. I am"—she placed her hand over her mouth and stifled a sob—"clutching at straws." She shook her head, as if refusing to cry. "I am hoping against hope," she said tragically, "that my poor Cynthia has fallen into such good hands. But I fear you are right, and she is not with your son."

It was impossible for her to weep real tears. With victory at hand, she was far too excited. But she covered her eyes with her handkerchief, uttering broken apologies, and then pretended to bravely master her emotions. The servants were duly dispatched to find Mr. Ellsworth, and the party fell silent as they waited. Lady Ballymere sipped nervously at a cup of tea. Lady Ellsworth poked listlessly at a plate of buttered eggs but did not consume anything. Sir Peter ate his way methodically through a slice of ham. The worry on his face seemed to indicate that he was not enjoying it. The duke and duchess were composed, as always, but the duke had a grim look about his mouth. Only the duchess seemed her normal, unruffled self.

Quick footsteps sounded in the hall. The door opened. Lady Ballymere glanced up, her sense of anticipation so keen she could hear the blood roaring in her ears. Whatever she was expecting, however, it was not this: Mr. Ellsworth entered, looking both flustered and harassed, and alone. Alone! Worse, *he was wearing morning dress*.

What could it mean? How was it possible? He had somehow found an opportunity to change his clothing. Where was Cynthia? Fear chilled Lady Ballymere's heart. She did not know what, or how, but something had gone terribly wrong.

All this she perceived in a flash. Mr. Ellsworth halted just inside the door, bowing in a perfunctory, distracted way to the assembled company. "Your Grace," he intoned. "My lord duke. Mother. Father. Lady Ballymere. You—you sent for me, Your Grace?" He looked apprehensive. "Is something amiss?"

"Come in, John," said the duke politely. "It seems that Lady Ballymere has a question or two to put to you."

"Lady Ballymere?" Mr. Ellsworth turned to her, astonishment writ large across his face. "I—I beg your pardon," he stammered and bowed again. "I'll answer anything you like, of course, my lady. Anything in my power."

He was plainly at a loss. Lady Ballymere, for her part, had been shocked into silence. She sat, stunned, and tried to think, while Sir Peter gave his son a terse outline of what had happened this morning. At the end of his brief recital, Mr. Ellsworth turned back to Lady Ballymere, horror and concern in every line of his honest, simple face.

"Missing, by Jove! Bless my soul, madam, you must be quite distraught. What can I do for you, if you please? Pray tell me at once. I daresay there's no time to be lost. We must find Lady Cynthia."

Lady Ballymere stared at him, amazed. What an actor! What a *consummate* actor! Who would have thought that John Ellsworth, of all men, would be able to pull off such a deception? Anyone would believe, looking at him, that his astonishment and concern were absolutely genuine! That he had no idea where Cynthia was or what had happened to her! The villain.

"Thank you, Mr. Ellsworth," she said coldly. "Perhaps you would be good enough to tell me where you were, just now."

"I was visiting Lady Hannah," he replied promptly. "She is in the morning room." He turned to the duchess. "You'll be glad to hear, Your Grace, that she is feeling much improved this morning. I urged her most strenuously to rest for a day or two, you know, and told her she should not come down to breakfast. She can easily have something sent up on a tray. In fact, I told her I would bring it to her with my own hands, just to ensure that all was done right. I think she will take my advice. She—"

"Mr. Ellsworth," snapped Lady Ballymere. "If you please! When did you last see my daughter?" She narrowed her eyes, looking very hard at him. "And where?" she added, daring him to lie.

"Well, let me see." He puffed his cheeks as if thinking hard. "Was it at dinner last night? Yes, I believe it was. I saw her at dinner."

Lady Ballymere almost gasped aloud at this piece of effrontery. Lies! Bald-faced lies! But Mr. Ellsworth was continuing, seeming oblivious to her gathering fury.

"And after dinner, you know, the ladies retired to the drawing room. I drank a glass of port and then, after a bit, I believe I went back to the library, to see Lady Hannah. And then I escorted Hannah up to—"

He broke off, a peculiar expression on his face. "By Jove. There she is," he said, pointing past Lady Ballymere's head.

What game was this? Lady Ballymere's back was to the French windows that opened onto the lawn. She turned, as did everyone in the room, and stared in disbelief through the glass-paned doors. She immediately saw what Mr. Ellsworth saw, but her mind rejected it as impossible. Shock immobilized her, while ice water seemed to rush in her veins. She could not make sense of the picture before her. She wondered, detachedly, whether she was about to faint.

Two figures were unhurriedly crossing the lawn, coming up from the gardens toward the breakfast room. One was Cynthia, clad in last night's dinner dress and looking decidedly disheveled. Her hair had lost most of its pins and tumbled untidily down her back in a shining river of gold. She was leaning, in a highly suggestive way, upon the arm of her companion.

Mr. Whittaker looked nearly as disheveled as she. His cravat was missing, which left his shirt—sadly crushed—open at the neck. As they ambled in a leisurely way across the lawn, Mr. Whittaker steadied Cynthia's steps with his right arm. He had a greatcoat, a muffler, a strip of creased linen that appeared to be his missing cravat, and Cynthia's cloak thrown over his left arm. Cynthia was speaking, smiling up at Mr. Whittaker in an adoring sort of way, and Mr. Whittaker, looking as besotted as she, was bending his head to catch her words.

The picture they presented was . . . loverlike. There was really no room for interpretation; no other gloss she could put on what she saw. This inescapable, unwelcome truth stared Lady Ballymere in the face.

Her hopes and dreams were crashing down before her eyes. Cynthia's marriage to John Ellsworth, an outcome that had seemed all but certain just minutes ago, was suddenly slipping into improbability. How had it happened? Bewilderment swelled within her, together with panic.

She discovered that, without realizing it, she had

risen to her feet. With her napkin still clutched in her suddenly bloodless fingers, she watched as the young couple approached. Her mind was in chaos, frantic with disbelief. There must be some way to salvage the situation. There *must* be.

When Cynthia and Mr. Whittaker stepped through the French windows and into the breakfast room and Cynthia saw her mother's face, at least she had the grace to blush. Still, she continued to cling to Mr. Whittaker in a manner that struck Lady Ballymere as nothing short of shameless.

"Good morning," said Mr. Whittaker with a breezy cheerfulness that grated on Lady Ballymere's ear. He bowed to the room. "Lovely weather we're having," he added.

The blackguard! He was *enjoying* the astonished stares, the surprise and disapproval, the rampant curiosity on every face! This, to Lady Ballymere's mind, was taking a sense of humor much, much too far.

She was too infuriated to speak. Luckily, the duke seemed to share her distaste for Mr. Whittaker's impudence. He had risen to his feet at the head of the table, and when he spoke, his voice dripped acid. "Do come in, Mr. Whittaker. Lady Cynthia, we have suffered a great deal of anxiety on your behalf this morning."

Cynthia's blush intensified. To her mother's annoyance, however, she clung even closer to Mr. Whittaker, as if seeking his protection. "I beg your pardon, Your Grace," she said humbly. "I did not intend to alarm anyone."

"Where have you been, child?" asked the duchess.

Cynthia lifted her chin. "I have been in the orangery," she replied composedly.

"The orangery? The deuce you say!" exclaimed Mr. Ellsworth. "Why, that's—" He seemed to catch the gimlet glare leveled at him by Mr. Whittaker, and broke off in confusion, clearing his throat.

Mr. Ellsworth was turning very red. Dastard! Why would he look so embarrassed, were he not guilty? He *was* guilty. She knew he was! Yet somehow, some way, he had managed to wriggle free of the trap she had so carefully set. Lady Ballymere felt her nails dig painfully into her palms as hot rage swept through her, sickening her. She rounded on him, livid.

"Pray finish your sentence," she hissed. "You were about to say, were you not, that the orangery is where *you* went to meet Lady Cynthia last night. Well?" Her voice rose to a challenging pitch. "Well, sir? What have you to say for yourself?"

Mr. Ellsworth's eyes looked ready to pop from his head. "I?" he gasped. "Meet Lady Cynthia? Good heavens, madam. No!" He shook his head so earnestly that his hair came dislodged and flopped across his brow. "Why, it never entered my head—bless me! Meet *Lady Cynthia?* Good God!"

"How dare you deny it?" she cried, nearly hysterical. "I *saw* you!"

The instant the words were out of her mouth, she realized she had given herself away. She had revealed, without thinking, that she had known all along where Cynthia was—and had believed Mr. Ellsworth to be with her.

An electric silence fell. All eyes were on her—accusing, condemning, horrified. Lady Ballymere sank abruptly back into her chair, pressing her napkin tightly to her mouth. For a moment, she was sure she was about to faint dead away. Then she *wished* she would faint. It would be a huge relief to faint. But apparently a swoon could not be had for the asking.

Derek Whittaker stepped forward, his arm around Cynthia. "It was I whom you saw, Lady Ballymere," he said quietly. "It was I who met your daughter in the orangery."

Confusion swirled in her brain, but she said nothing. She was afraid to speak, for fear she would say something dreadful again. What could she say? She could not ask how, or why, Mr. Whittaker had known Cynthia would be there. Had Mr. Ellsworth told him? It was impossible to understand, but she could not ask questions without exposing herself further. But Mr. Whittaker was speaking again.

"Lady Cynthia and I might have met for a few minutes only. It's hard to know, now, what *would* have happened. But when we tried the door, we discovered it was locked." He looked solemnly around the room. "Someone locked us in."

The eyes had all turned back to Lady Ballymere. She felt their gazes burning on her skin. She could barely speak under the weight of embarrassment she felt. "Perhaps," she croaked, then swallowed and began again. "Perhaps it was an accident."

"Perhaps," said Mr. Whittaker quietly. It was obvious he believed otherwise. "At any rate, Lady

Ballymere, the damage has been done. Your daughter and I spent the entire night there. Locked in the orangery. Alone."

Despair wracked her. Ruined! Cynthia had been compromised, but by the wrong man. Oh, what would she do? What *could* she do?

Her eyes lifted, pleadingly, to Mr. Ellsworth's face, mutely begging him to save the day. She longed to hear the words so much that they almost rang in her ears: *Allow me to intervene, Lady Ballymere,* she imagined him saying. *I would be honored to have Lady Cynthia as my wife.* But Mr. Ellsworth's expression as he looked at her was redolent of disgust. A wave of bitter shame washed over her as she remembered that he had seen the note. He knew nearly as much as Cynthia and Mr. Whittaker about what she had done. And, probably, he understood why she had done it.

Her gaze traveled, painfully, to Sir Peter and Lady Ellsworth. They were staring at her as if she had metamorphosed before their eyes into some sort of reptile. And they, unlike their son, did not know about the notes she had written. They did not know the trick she had pulled. What would they think of her, once they knew the whole? She could not flatter herself that her machinations would remain a secret. Mr. Ellsworth would, naturally, confide the details to his parents. How many others would learn of her shame? The story was too juicy to resist. It would, inevitably, be repeated.

Oh, this was ghastly. It was not Cynthia who had

been ruined. It was she, far more than her daughter, whose reputation lay in shreds.

The duke spoke again. His voice was stern and cold. "Mr. Whittaker, do I understand you aright? Have you compromised this blameless girl—a guest in my house?"

"I have, Your Grace," said Mr. Whittaker calmly. "Though I did not set out to do so."

The duke drew himself upright, glaring balefully. "Your intentions may go hang, sirrah," he snapped. "You will right this wrong you have done. You will offer marriage to Lady Cynthia."

"Yes, Your Grace." Mr. Whittaker let go of Cynthia long enough to bow very low. "With the greatest pleasure imaginable."

Panic stirred again in Lady Ballymere. "No," she said feebly. She was shaking so hard now that her teeth began to chatter. "Mr. Whittaker, th-that won't be ne-necessary," she rapped out, but got no further.

"Of course it is necessary," said the duke irascibly. "Good God, woman, look at them! I never saw a more guilty pair in my life. Mr. Whittaker knows the rules. He will abide by them, by thunder, or I shall personally show him the door—family member or no."

Mr. Whittaker placed one hand on his heart. "Sir, you terrify me," he said solemnly. "I hasten to obey." He placed his arm around Cynthia. To Lady Ballymere's pained astonishment, Cynthia nestled quite contentedly against the ruffian. "I shall offer marriage to Lady Cynthia immediately," promised Mr. Whittaker.

"And I shall accept," said Cynthia happily.

Lady Ballymere stretched her hand toward her daughter, moaning. "Cynthia. No. You are barely acquainted with Mr. Whittaker."

"I take leave to contradict you, Mama." Cynthia's voice was clear, her tone polite but distant, as if she were speaking to a stranger. "It is you, not I, who is barely acquainted with Mr. Whittaker. I know Mr. Whittaker very well indeed." She leaned adoringly on his arm, and as she looked up at him her face lit with happiness.

"I am glad, my dear," said the duke gruffly. "It seems you have no aversion to marrying this scape-grace of ours."

"None whatsoever, Your Grace."

The duke's keen gaze traveled to Mr. Whittaker. "And you, my boy? You seem content with your lot."

"I am more than content, Your Grace. I am ecstatic." His face broke into a grin. "I have wanted to marry Lady Cynthia for years."

Surprised exclamations greeted this pronouncement. Relief and congratulations filled the air. Lady Ballymere could only stare in confused amazement. "How can this be? What do you mean?" she asked, bewildered.

No one answered her. She seemed to have become invisible. The Ellsworths pushed past her to congratulate Cynthia and Mr. Whittaker. Mr. Ellsworth wrung Mr. Whittaker's hand and wished him happy. The duchess rose gracefully from her place and came to kiss Cynthia on the cheek, and even the duke visibly thawed. Lady Ballymere still sat, dazedly folding and refolding her napkin.

At last the duchess crossed to her husband and placed her hand on his sleeve. "Let us leave the young people to sort this matter out, my dear," she said placidly. "I hope no one will think me rude if I show less interest in these proceedings than I normally would. I simply cannot help it. I have more important things on my mind this morning."

The duke looked down at her in surprise. She gave him a demure little smile and patted his arm. "For heaven's sake, William, take me upstairs. I want to see the baby."

Chapter Twenty

It had been a happy but exhausting day. Derek thought they deserved a reward. He seized Cynthia's hand and ducked into the dark library, then pulled her toward the outside door. She hung back, laughing. "Derek, it's freezing out there."

She was wearing a paper-thin dinner dress of some clingy silk stuff. She looked breathtakingly beautiful in it, of course, but it provided no warmth. With a magician's flourish, he lifted her cloak from where he had hidden it behind the overstuffed sofa. Her eyes widened in delight. "Where did you get that?"

"Never you mind. I have my ways." He winked. "Come on. I've had enough congratulations for one day. I want to be alone with my bride-to-be."

She followed him through the door and out onto the marble terrace. The night was chilly, but the air was clear as crystal. The pale marble glowed beneath their feet as if the stone had turned to starlight. He placed the cloak around her shoulders and drew it gently across her arms.

"It's lovely to go off alone with you," she said dreamily. "Especially now, when I know that no one will disapprove."

"Your mother isn't exactly overjoyed," he reminded her. "I hope, for your sake, she will make peace with the idea eventually."

Cynthia's smile was serene. "I don't care," she said simply. "I can't tell you what a relief that is—not to care what she thinks. I know this is right. I know it in my heart. I don't need her permission to be happy." She sighed contentedly. "I am happy, with or without her approval."

He linked his hands behind her waist and looked searchingly into her eyes. He saw no shade of trouble there. Still, loving her, he wished he could have made it perfect for her. She saw his frown, and surprise moved across her features. "Derek, what is it? Are you not happy?"

He almost laughed at her. "What do you think?"

She smiled. "I think you are."

"Quite right." His own smile faded a little. "But, for your sake, sweet, I wish the circumstances of our betrothal had been different."

She shook her head. "No regrets," she said softly. "Had you courted me in the ordinary way, my mother would have somehow prevented this. We never would have been allowed to marry."

"I suppose you are right."

She gave him a saucy look. "I frequently am."

He grinned and pulled her closer. She came to him willingly, snuggling into the circle of his arms. "However it came about, I feel blessed," he told her, his voice thick with emotion. "Blessed beyond measure."

"So do I." She sighed again, then leaned back to look up at him, her eyes twinkling. "By the by, I think your giving up my dowry was a nice touch."

He laughed out loud. "Wasn't it? I'm a generous chap."

"I did not know until today that my grandmother had left me a dowry. Sir James never bothered to ask."

"I feared your mother was going to fall into a fit when I inquired about it."

She gave a little spurt of laughter. "Mama does not know you well enough to recognize that gleam in your eye. I knew you were only being sly."

"Still, I was as surprised as you when she admitted that there was one."

"It's only a thousand pounds."

"Only! Cynthia, you astonish me. A thousand pounds is a great deal of money to most people." He tried to look injured. "You do not appreciate the nobility of my sacrifice, in offering to sign it over to your parents when it arrives."

"Oh, *I* appreciate it, never fear." She looked mischievous. "It is my mother who seems to think it a paltry sum."

"If you were to ask me," said Derek grimly, "I would say that that is the crux of your parents' difficulties."

Cynthia nodded gravely. "I believe you are right. I was much struck by what you said this afternoon."

He cocked an eyebrow at her. "I said many things this afternoon. Which of my remarks impressed you?"

"Oh, all of them," she assured him demurely. "But I was referring to one in particular." Her face sobered again. "You said, I think, that there is no amount of money that can guarantee safety. That however much one has, it is always possible to spend it." A tiny crease appeared between her brows. "It immediately seemed, to me, that if my parents *had* received Sir James's thirty thousand pounds, it very likely would have done them little good. In fact, they might very well have run through it in the identical amount of time it took them to spend his ten thousand. They spend what they have, no matter what it is. So in chasing after a big marriage settlement for me, believing it would relieve them of their difficulties, they were chasing a mere phantom. Is that what you were saying?"

"Something like it," he agreed. "I couldn't use those words, of course, without offending your mother. Since she already seemed rather put out by our betrothal, I didn't like to antagonize her further."

She laughed up at him. "You are the soul of consideration."

"I try," he said modestly. "It is easiest, of course, when my own self-interest is at stake. I shall be unfailingly polite to your mother, at least until I place the ring on your finger. Since your twenty-first birthday is in May, and I am determined to wed you as soon as possible, your mother's goodwill is vital to me."

"She shan't refuse her consent. She wouldn't dare."

"For fear of the story leaking out? Yes. That is the one good thing about this havey-cavey situation we are in. Your mother seems completely cowed—for the time being. And another good thing," he added, adjusting her cloak across her arms, "is that you have already been at Oldham Park for three weeks."

She looked surprised. "How does that benefit us?"

He grinned. "Once you've resided here for four weeks, I can obtain a license and we can be married. In the duke's chapel, if you like."

"Oh!" Her eyes sparkled with eagerness. "I would like it of all things. We can really be married next week? I can hardly believe it! I had thought we must wait for banns."

He laughed, delighted by her response. "Cynthia, you amaze me! I was half-joking. Think, sweetheart! Don't you want parties and balls? Don't you want bride clothes? Don't you want to parade about like a queen and be the envy of all your acquaintance?"

"No!" He could not doubt her sincerity; she actually made a little moue of disgust at the picture he had painted. "I care for none of those things. I want to be your wife. I want"—her voice suddenly went a little breathless—"I want everything that comes with marriage." Her eyes darkened. "I want *you,*" she whispered.

Derek felt his throat tighten. He lifted her hand and kissed the tender spot of flesh above her glove on the inside of her wrist. "You shall have me," he promised. Her skin was so delicious, he could not leave it alone. He moved his lips farther up her arm, kissing and nibbling up to the inside of her elbow. Cynthia shivered and stretched her arm out to oblige him, inviting the caress. The cloak slipped off her shoulders and fell, unheeded, to the terrace floor.

"I wish I could come to your bed tonight," she whispered.

He groaned and caught her to him. "Don't say that," he growled. "You're torturing me."

"Is there a way?"

Derek felt the blood thundering in his veins. "If I think of one," he said hoarsely, "I'll let you know."

"Oh, Derek." Her face was full of longing. "Do you think we would get caught?"

"Almost certainly," he said reluctantly. "Your mother will watch you like a cat at the mouse hole. And servants always know what goes on in a house."

She sighed. "Well. If we've waited this long to share a bed, we can wait another week." She fitted her body against his, as if trying to touch as much of him as she could. "I suppose we were lucky to have last night."

"Lucky is the word for it," he agreed. He pressed his cheek against her hair. It was soft as duck down, and sweet as orange blossoms. Sweeter. And over their heads the firmament stretched, thick with stars. There were so many it seemed that all of heaven had crowded into the Lancashire sky to witness their happiness.

"Derek," she murmured.

"Yes, love."

"If I knew which star to thank, I would thank your lucky star."

He smiled. *So would I.* "Let's thank them all," he suggested. "A different one every night."

He felt her smile against his chest. "It would take forever."

He took her face in his hands and looked down at her. "Forever is what we have," he whispered. And he kissed her, then, for all the stars to see.

Center Point Publishing
600 Brooks Road • PO Box 1
Thorndike ME 04986-0001 USA

(207) 568-3717

US & Canada:
1 800 929-9108

Farr, Diane

Under a lucky
star

DATE		0705	28.95
OCT 2 6 2005